THE GRAVITY OF US

MASCOT BOOKS

www.mascotbooks.com

THE GRAVITY OF US

This is a work of fiction. Names, characters, businesses, places, events, and incidents are either the products of the author's imagination or used in a fictitious manner. Any resemblance to actual persons, living or dead, or actual events is purely coincidental.

For more information, please contact:
Mascot Books, an imprint of Amplify Publishing Group
620 Herndon Parkway, Suite 220
Herndon, VA 20170
info@amplifypublishing.com

Library of Congress Control Number: 2023924580
CPSIA Code: PRV0324A
ISBN-13: 978-1-63755-844-7

Printed in the United States

The Gravity of Us is for my fellow LGBTQIA+ family. We hope that one day we can be accepted for who we are without limitation and that children can freely be themselves and never know what it's like to hide in the shadows. Sometimes, it feels like that day will never come.

Our struggle is unseen. Our pain is real. Our love is genuine. This story is for us.

THE GRAVITY OF US

JAMIE AVERY KING

MASCOT BOOKS
an imprint of Amplify Publishing Group

AUTHOR'S NOTE & CONTENT DISCUSSION

The Gravity of Us is a gay romance featuring explicit sexual content, bullying, forced outing, bigotry, self-harm, suicide, and attempted suicide, which may activate challenging emotions for some readers.

If you don't want to possibly spoil yourself and these themes do not bother you, please feel free to skip the rest of this Author's Note and begin your reading journey.

The Gravity of Us is set in 2014, before the legalization of same-sex marriage in Virginia and before widespread acceptance of queerness and queer relationships. Some of the themes within *The Gravity of Us* may be upsetting given recent setbacks in LGBTQ+ rights.

The mention and discussion of suicide and self-harm may evoke powerful emotions in some readers. There is active self-harm by one of the main characters and discussion of his past suicide attempt.

I recommend caution if you continue to read *The Gravity*

of Us if the aforementioned themes may cause undue stress to your mental health and well-being.

If you or a loved one need support, please call or text the Suicide & Crisis Lifeline at 988 or visit 988lifeline.org. If you or someone you know needs immediate help, please call 911 (in the United States).

The Gravity of Us contains but is not limited to the following content: explicit sexual content, bigotry, bullying, self-harm, suicide, suicidal ideation, profanity, homophobia, biphobia, parental abandonment, mention of divorce, emotional abuse, disownment, familial estrangement, grief and loss, gray-area cheating, therapy, cyberbullying, forced outing, financial difficulties, and mild sexual sadomasochism.

Love is something none of us can control. Not who. Not when. It is irrational, aggravating, and euphoric. Neither of us thought our lives would cross as they did, but the space between us was ours. Our memories. Our journey.

Our love was real.

-NICK & TAKA

CHAPTER 1

NICK

The professor dismissed the class as my phone vibrated on the desk, but I didn't bother to look at the message and slipped the phone into my pocket. I had more important things to deal with. I grabbed my bag from the floor and leaped out of the chair, breezing past the other students.

"See you later," I said to Sky. He was talking with a girl, likely about our next project, and I didn't have time to wait for him.

Skylar Suarez, my best friend since high school. When he and his family moved to Virginia from California, we hit it off immediately, and the two of us had been inseparable, though we were opposites for the most part. His short dark hair was the same style as mine—an undercut with some length on the top—but he always cared how it looked. I didn't. He was always stylish in dress shirts and jeans, while I was the weird emo-turned-punk. To say black was my color of choice would be an understatement. His dark skin was smooth and blemish free. I was envious because he never had pimples, even at the height of puberty. Unlike me, he didn't have piercings or tattoos, but he liked to wear a simple gold cross that his grandmother had given him.

"Nick, hold up," Sky called as he hurried toward me, weaving through the group of students leaving the classroom. "Where ya headed?"

"I need to see my advisor," I said, my stomach twisting with nerves.

"Are we still on for dinner?" Sky asked, tugging my wrist to keep me from walking off.

"We're good for dinner."

A smile lit up his face as he released me. "Cool. And look, I know your laptop crapping out on you is stressful, but you'll figure it out."

"I appreciate your faith in me, but I'm not sure it'll work out this time," I said, leaving him behind as I headed down the cramped hallway before turning up the stairs to the advisors' offices.

I was lucky to have a good relationship with the advisors in the art department, but it was a long shot to expect them to help me this time. The door opened as I approached the office, and a girl passed me with a smile. I darted through the closing door into the cramped office space. A woman was at a desk to the right, typing away on her computer, and as I approached, she gave me a soft smile.

"How can I help you today?"

"I'd like to speak with Annabella. I have a question about my scholarship," I said, standing a few feet from her desk.

"Do you have an appointment?" the woman asked, checking her computer screen.

"No. I was hoping to pop in real quick. It'll be fast."

"She isn't with a student, so you could see if she has time to talk." She pursed her lips as she looked me over, and the familiar heat of judgment settled on my skin. "Next time, schedule ahead."

"Understood, ma'am." I passed down the short hallway and knocked on the last door on the right. Anna knew me well. She had worked with me on my scholarship since freshman year, but I wasn't looking forward to this discussion.

"Come in," Anna said, her voice clear and bright. She sounded cheerful.

I slipped inside the room and shut the door behind me. "Hi, Anna. Sorry to drop in unannounced. Do you have a few minutes?"

"Sure, Nick," Anna replied, gesturing for me to take a seat.

I dropped into the chair across from her as she set her glasses on the desk, tucking her graying hair behind her ear.

"What a pleasure to see you today." She smiled but tilted her head, likely realizing this wasn't a happy visit. "Did something happen?"

"I have a problem and hope you can help, or at least give me some good news."

She leaned forward, the creak of the chair loud in the silence, and laced her fingers together. "What is it?"

"My laptop broke last night. Do I have any money from my scholarship to pay for a new one?" The sight of her frown turned my stomach, but I continued. "I would need at least fifteen hundred for one that can handle the software. I could probably scrape together the rest if I pick up more hours at work."

"I'm sorry to hear that. Let me see." Her hands darted over the keyboard, and she scanned the computer monitor, her frown deepening. "It looks like you have spent the money for this semester. You paid for your meal plan and housing after tuition, which drained the scholarship funds completely."

Ice settled in my gut.

"Do we have any other options? Any programs that could help with even a small amount of money?"

"I'm sorry, Nick, but I have nothing for you this late in the semester. The soonest anything will be open for you is when fall classes start."

"That's, like, five months away. There isn't anything we can do?"

Her lips drew tight as she dropped her gaze to her hands, shaking her head. "I have nothing for you. I'm sorry."

I ran my hands over my thighs, catching a finger on a hole in my favorite black cargo pants. After years of abuse, they were finally developing signs of wear. "Thanks anyway. I'll see you next time."

When I stood, she lifted a hand in a quiet goodbye. "Good luck. I'm sorry I couldn't help."

The familiar weight of anxiety had settled in my chest like a brick. I left the office and made my way to the student art gallery on the first floor. I hesitated at the doors, debating whether to go in. It had been weeks since I'd looked at the print of my digital artwork—not since the day my professor begged me to hang it in the student gallery. I should've seen it as an honor, but it was a piece I had made for an assignment prompt on a whim. When I completed it and realized what I'd done, my first thought was to delete it. Now it was printed, half the size of a person, and displayed for all to see.

"Bring your deepest desire to life in a work of art," my professor said.

In my drunken stupidity, I did. Every scar and freckle. The dimple on his left cheek, visible only when he smiled. The soft tones of his pale skin. His dark hair, which covered his eyes in a curly mess. His thin jawline and high cheekbones. Scrawny teenage arms that, when wrapped around me, held me close with such love that my heart could've melted in his embrace.

I entered the gallery, unable to walk by without looking at him. The lights warmed my skin while I stood in front of the large print of a boy who held my heart in his beautiful hands, dripping the crimson contents of my soul over his pale skin as he smiled at the viewer.

A sharp pain gripped my heart like he was actually squeezing it. I rubbed my chest, chasing the tightness away. Sometimes I wished he had taken me with him and freed me from this existence.

In my short twenty years on this God-forsaken planet, I had learned one of life's harshest lessons: when someone genuinely loves you, and the world is brighter because that person exists alongside you, make sure you hold on to them and never let go. I made the mistake of letting go; regret was all I had to show for our time together. With a final glance, I spun on my heels and marched out of the gallery, leaving behind the demons who had lured me there.

I crossed the campus and soaked in the late afternoon sun. Chilled air brushed over my cheeks. This was my favorite time of year, when the earth woke from the dark slumber of winter, flowers bloomed, and plants sprouted. In this brief window of time, the campus filled with the beauty of life, reminding me that our time was fleeting.

The tall brick walls of the Ellis Center loomed ahead, blotting out the last bit of sunlight. It was the campus hub, constantly filled with people.

Silver Creek University was my top pick. Not only for the respected art department but also for the campus's location six hours away from home and painful memories. But I missed my family. Sometimes it was lonely, but I was glad I had Sky there with me.

The computer lab where I worked was on the third floor, away from most of the buzz. The main stairs of the building spiraled up six stories, leading up from the food court that, just then, was bright under the skylight that let in the last remnants of the day's sun.

At the top of the steps of the third floor, a group of students stood in my way, chatting and paying no mind to anyone attempting to get past. I pushed through them, slipping into the computer lab and ignoring their whispers of annoyance. Calm washed over my nerves as I entered the room lined with desks. The quiet hum of the computer fans and keyboard tapping were the loudest noises. It was comforting. My sanctuary.

River sat behind the reception desk, gnawing on the ID badge hanging from her neck—something she did when stressed.

"Riv, what's up?" I asked, resting my elbows on the wooden countertop.

Dropping the chewed ID, she said, "The university admins pulled me into a meeting today. Our budget won't increase until fall, which means I can't hire another person to help in the lab."

We were severely short-staffed. Everyone working in the lab was a student, and we made minimum wage with no benefits. In my eyes, not funding another position was the university being cheap.

"I can pick up some more shifts. My laptop finally gave up on me, and I'm gonna need to use the lab more anyway," I replied.

She ran her fingers through her strawberry-colored hair with a heavy sigh. "Damn, Nick. I'm sorry, but I'll take you up on those extra shifts."

"It is what it is. We can talk about the schedule later."

I stepped around the desk, pulling my ID from my bag and slipping the lanyard over my head. "I'll head into the back and set up."

"Your normal station is open. I reserved it for you." She returned the poor ID badge to her lips and waved me off. "You're the best."

I hurried to where the expensive workstations hid in a small side room within the computer lab, each machine was top of the line and able to run any software. Most visitors to this part of the lab were digital art and animation students.

The workstation closest to the door was my favorite. Riv always reserved it for me on days I was working. Seeing the workstation brought some light back into my heart. After a long day of stressing over my laptop, I could finally dive into my zone and let myself go. Before shoving my bag under the desk, I pulled out my flash drive from a side pocket. With a crappy laptop like mine, I always backed up my files. I tapped the power button on the workstation tower and watched the two monitors light up.

From early childhood, I knew the digital world was where I wanted to live and create, and I had set my sights on a freelance digital-art career. Bringing someone's dreams to life, watching their eyes light up to have a loved one captured in a beautiful moment, or a pet who spent their lives loving their human. I wanted to capture the moments that people cherished. Those moments were important; no one truly understood how important until it was too late. Until they were gone.

I connected the flash drive and opened my files. My throat tightened as the animation I had been working on moments before my laptop crashed displayed a simple error message.

The file was corrupted.

As I clicked through each file, more of my assignments appeared with the same error. A wave of heat spread through my veins, and my stomach sank into the depths of the earth.

Of course this would happen to me. It was my luck.

My phone vibrated in my pocket, grating on my already tense nerves. I fought the urge to throw it across the room and breathed in deeply, huffing out through my nose before answering. Seeing my mom's name, relief settled into my chest.

"Mom," I said.

"Hi, honey." Her warmth came through like an embrace, chasing away every ounce of stress. "Is this a bad time?"

"I'm at work, but I'm glad you called." I released a sigh, running my fingers through my hair and leaning back in the chair.

"Did something happen?"

I told her about the laptop problem but immediately regretted it. She didn't need the extra stress; she had her hands full already.

"Do you need it, or could you wait until fall? With Harper preparing for college applications, I don't have the spare cash for a new one right now."

"Don't worry about it. I'm working with River on adding hours to my schedule."

"Won't you be exhausted? I don't want it to impact your grades."

"I'll be coming into the lab to use the computer, anyway. Might as well make money while I'm here."

Her sigh was soft, like she was full of guilt. She had been this way since Dad disappeared and sent someone to serve her the divorce papers. She became a single parent, raising three kids.

"Did you call for something?"

"I wanted to chat. But if you're at work, I won't keep you."

"I'm glad you called. I miss you."

"I miss you too. Give Sky a hug for me."

I could sense her smile through the phone. I wanted to see that warmth, wrap my arms around her, and let everything fade away.

"I love you, buddy," she added.

"You too."

Silence descended on the room, and the error message on the computer monitor stared back at me. Redoing that work would cost me days that I didn't have.

"Excuse me," a deep voice said, startling me. "Can I use this workstation?" The guy pointed to a desk near mine.

"Sure. Do you need any help?"

"Actually, I do."

I rolled my chair over to him and did what I would with

anyone: I asked questions. I lived for this kind of interaction. I loved that job because it gave me practice for interviewing clients once I was a freelance artist. Each student who walked into the lab was a client. The sense of accomplishment that filled my heart when I was helping others was one I could rarely find elsewhere.

CHAPTER 2

TAKA

Laughter poured into the mudroom as I locked the door to the garage and kicked off my shoes. My routine every morning was simple: wake up before sunrise, workout to music so loud that it quieted my thoughts, and return home for breakfast with my family. Mom and Tamiko would giggle away as they prepared breakfast, and Dad would be getting ready for the day before we all gathered in the kitchen. My initial reaction coming through the door was always to quickly disappear to my room, but as usual, I made my way across the small mudroom and entered the kitchen, donning the usual cheerful smile I presented to everyone. The mask that I wore. A smile. A laugh. Pleasant conversation laced with a cold air of loneliness.

"Good morning," I said. I dropped my gym bag, then slid into a chair at the table.

Tami had her long black hair down, cascading over her

shoulders, and wore an apron with a cupcake in the middle of her chest—a gift from me for her birthday last year. Tami and Mom loved to cook together, and I enjoyed seeing them happy. But though the connection between them was deep and loving, I always felt disconnected. I was envious of their relationship. My whole life, I had longed for something like that. Instead, I was distant. No matter what face I put on, I could never feel it. No connection. It was as if a barrier existed at all times between me and everyone else.

Mom nudged her hip against a drawer, pushing it shut. Then she carried broken eggshells in her hands to the trash. Her hair was arranged neatly and tucked behind her ears. She was turning fifty this year; I couldn't believe it.

Mom and Dad had picked up their whole lives to move to America when I was five. They left everyone and everything they knew behind while Mom was pregnant with Tami. Every memory I owned was from the perspective of living in the United States, making it hard to connect to my Japanese heritage in the same way my parents did. As their oldest child and only son, I had felt this pressure to be someone, something. To uphold the standards of our heritage while also blending into American society. It was a weird place to exist, and I was always split in two, caught between worlds. Yet, Americans only ever saw me as generically Asian—not specifically Japanese. That was all I was, no matter how American I was. It didn't matter that I had a slight Southern Virginia accent. It didn't matter that I was a naturalized citizen and raised here; I was always simply Asian. And when we visited Japan every summer, I was American. I didn't fit in there either. It was laughable that I could be seen as neither American nor Japanese. Never entirely accepted by either. College had made it more bearable. I had a group of friends who made me one of them.

I had seen my parents deal with Americans who treated them like trash, as if they didn't belong, but they brushed it off every time. I didn't understand how they did it. I felt like an outcast, existing in the shadows, unable to find my place.

The eggshells fell from Mom's fingers, landing in the trash bin. "Good morning, Taka. How was your workout?" she asked.

"It was great, but now I'm starved."

Tami sat beside me with a smile—a smile that always tugged at my heart strings and turned me to putty in her hands. "Will you be home after classes to help me with my project for my science class? This chemistry stuff isn't clicking in my brain."

I gave her an apologetic look. "I'm stopping by the fraternity house to help Casey with the event that is coming up in a few weeks, and then Izzie and I have a date." I gave her nose a gentle poke, then tousled her hair. "I can help you tomorrow. Is that okay?"

She wrapped her arm around my shoulders, giving me a little squeeze. "Thank you," she whispered.

Mom looked up from the pan she had been focusing on. "What do you need to do today? I thought you boys had planned everything already."

"I'm helping Casey with the budget," I said.

"Let your father know if you need help. This is a great opportunity for him to teach you some bookkeeping techniques."

"Sure, if I need help, I'll ask."

"If you're seeing Izzie, I need to find that book she lent me. I've been meaning to give it back," she said.

Tami went over to Mom and took a serving dish from

her, then sat across from me at the table, placing the plate in the center.

"Hopefully, I remember to give it back to her," I said, spooning scrambled eggs onto my plate while waiting for the other dishes to be set.

Moments later, my father's voice boomed, "Morning."

He sat beside me, adjusting his tie like he had put it on moments before entering the kitchen.

"Hi, Daddy," Tami said with a huge grin.

Dad offered her a slight smile before pulling out his phone to look at emails.

My father owned Akiyama International Imports, a business he started in Japan in his twenties. He was dedicated to his work, more than anyone I had ever met. He wanted me to start working with him right after graduation so he could prepare me to take over the company. I couldn't say it would be a terrible deal. The problem was, I wasn't sure I wanted to run the business. It never felt like I had a choice. It was expected of me since birth, and my entire purpose was to learn the trade from my father.

"Morning, Dad," I said, shrinking back as Tami put a mound of eggs on his plate. "I'll be home late tonight."

He slipped a fork under his eggs and took a bite before acknowledging me. "As long as it doesn't interfere with your assignments." He took another bite, then glanced at me. "How are things at your fraternity?"

"We're planning for that fundraiser still."

Dad nodded as he went back to his food. "Which fundraiser?"

"A children's charity. They help kids in foster care."

"Let me know when the fundraiser starts, and I'll donate."

"Of course."

All conversation swiftly centered on my father, leaving me to fade into the background, insignificant in his shadow.

• • •

Greek Row was desolate as I ascended the brick steps of the fraternity house for Delta Gamma Zeta. The neat, clean exterior matched the rest of the university style: red brick and white accents. Even new buildings would conform to the design aesthetic. Not a hair out of place. Exactly like everything else in my life.

SCU wasn't on my radar until the out-of-state schools rejected me. When my father suggested SCU, I was hesitant, partly because it was so close to home. I wanted to be on my own, away from the suffocation of being prim and proper and the heavy expectations of my family to be the perfect son. My father would not allow me to move out, since I was only fifteen minutes from campus, so I could never experience the college life of living in a dorm room. Yet, with one of the best business degrees in the entire state, SCU was not a bad option, so I settled for it and suffered through the rest.

I entered the four-digit passcode at the door of the building and entered the fraternity house. It was a typical dorm with a living room, study area, and bedrooms, but it had the added benefit of a full-size private kitchen. The smell of beer and sweat assaulted my nose as I walked through the wrecked living room. It was everything I would have expected from a frat house—full of rowdy guys and furniture that had seen better days. Beer bottles, plastic cups, and sundry items littered the floor.

"Yo," one guy said as he came out of the kitchen. His hair was standing up in all directions, and his shirt was torn and hanging from his body.

If there was ever a time for me to be grateful I didn't live on campus, it was now.

"Did I miss a party?" I asked.

Another guy came up behind the first, rubbing his eye. "Man, we got completely trashed last night. You shoulda been there."

"Maybe next time. Have you seen Casey?"

The guys pointed to the ceiling, and I took that to mean he was in his room. "Thanks," I said, taking the stairs two at a time.

I stopped in the dark hallway. Casey's door was shut, so I tapped my knuckle lightly on the wood. It was quiet, with no sounds of life, so I knocked again.

A moment later the door flew open, and Casey Grant stared back at me, dirty-blond hair falling into his hazel eyes, chest bare, standing in only his boxers, looking every inch the stereotypical frat guy with the physique of an American football player—which he was. Most of the frat members were on sports teams, and, as people, they were reliable as long as you were a brother.

"My bad," he said, spinning around, looking for pants. "I forgot to set an alarm."

I walked in behind him and closed the door. "No problem. Seems you all had a big party last night. I would have needed a nap too."

"It got way out of control. I think over a hundred people were here at some point." Casey slipped into sweatpants and sank onto his bed. It was a small twin-size with navy blue sheets.

It made me glad I never had to give up my king-size mattress and live in a place where a hundred people got drunk pretty much every night.

"So, the event. Can you help me with these numbers?" Casey asked as he pulled his laptop from under his blanket. "We need to figure out how much food we need from the caterers and how many shirts to order."

I pulled a chair out from his desk, rolling it beside the bed. "What's our budget?"

"I was told our max is six thousand for both. I think it'll cut it close."

I leaned in, looking at the spreadsheet for line items we could trim to free up more money for the food and printing costs. Casey handed me the laptop, pointing to some negotiable budget areas highlighted in yellow. Since it was a fundraiser, the budget was tight. I scrolled through the sheet and pulled up the fraternity budget, working through potential solutions.

Hours passed, and the room grew dark as the sun fell behind the horizon. We were getting nowhere with the budget, and I was late for my date with Izzie.

When there was a rough knock on the door, Casey rose from the bed, frustration from the past few hours fizzing off him. Casey yanked the door open. "What the fuck are you hitting the door for?" he demanded.

"T's girl is here," said the messenger.

"Thanks, man. He won't be long." Casey puffed a breath through his cheeks as he closed the door in the guy's face. "You and Iz got a hot date?"

I shrugged as I calculated a quick budget change. "Dinner. Nothing special." I pulled up the browser and searched for new caterers. There had to be a cheaper option.

"Should I bring her up here?"

"Leave her be. I'll be done soon."

Izzie was probably angry about the delay, but what was I supposed to do? Leave Casey in a tough spot? Dinner could wait.

I found what I was looking for, entered their number into my phone, and then pressed the call icon. Casey dropped onto the bed as I waited for the company to answer, and when they did, I went into full business mode. My negotiation skills were a gift from my father. He had raised me to be a businessman from the moment I was born.

When I hung up the phone, Casey chuckled from his bed. "How do you do that?"

"It doesn't matter. We got what we needed." I handed him the laptop and rolled his chair back to his desk. "Let me know if we need more money, but that freed up about five hundred dollars."

"You're amazing," Casey said as he folded his laptop, placed it on the bed, and followed me out of his room.

Izzie's sky-blue eyes glared at me as I walked down the stairs, Casey close behind. Her dark hair was pulled back into a French braid, and she had dressed up in a black dress and red shoes. I used to get butterflies when I saw her, but it was becoming harder to even smile at her. Was this normal for a long relationship, to feel nothing? It wasn't always this way. I used to think she was God's greatest creation: strong, independent, beautiful. Her sour pout stung in a way that made me want to run away.

"You made me wait, again," she began.

"I apologize. Casey and I had to handle something."

My excuse did nothing to lessen her annoyance.

"Iz," Casey greeted her. "You look ravishing. Where are you two lovebirds headed?"

"Taka is supposed to take me to that new restaurant that opened up last week. But we've missed our reservation now."

I slid my hands into the pockets of my slacks and stared at a button on my dress shirt. Thankfully, I didn't need to change for dinner. Since Dad drilled the idea into me that I should always be dressed as if ready for a business interview, I already looked as smart as my date.

"T, you could've left me to handle the budget, or it could've waited," Casey said, glancing at the furious Izzie.

"We can go another time, Iz," I said. I could hear the exhaustion in my voice. I didn't have the energy to argue. The day seemed to have dragged on forever, and all I wanted was for it to be over. Besides, the restaurant was not a place I had wanted to go.

"I got all dressed up for nothing. Are we even having dinner now?" she snapped.

I wanted to go home and sleep. I was so exhausted that I felt like my body was worn thin, my mind a cloud, straining to form thoughts. But I said, "We can go to one of our usual places."

"I'm tired of the same old things," she said. Then a thought seemed to pop into her head. "I heard the gallery in the art building is hosting a showcase of student art, and there'll be food there. I wanted to go see the artwork anyway."

"Sure. If that's what you want."

Her anger dissipated in an instant. "Good. Come on, before

all the food goes. You know what starving artists are like." She grabbed my hand and pulled me out of the fraternity house. Her hot, clammy fingers were like a vice on mine as she dragged me across campus to the art building. I was surprised she wanted to go. She was into marketing, not art. If something wasn't commercial, she wasn't interested.

It was rare to find myself on this side of campus. The art department seemed to be secluded from the rest of the university, like they had been shoved off to the side where no one could see them. Maybe they liked it that way, but I couldn't imagine being this far from the center of everything.

The doors were propped open, and students mingled with professors and parents. It was dark inside, lit by area lights that pointed at paintings, drawings, and prints on the walls. Curious eyes and smirks circled sculptures that stood on the gallery floor. I had always appreciated art and once took a life-drawing class, but my skills were worse than even my parents expected. All my figures had impossible proportions and never looked pleasing.

Izzie pulled me to the food table, where only a few morsels remained, and then grabbed us both a glass of fruit juice. Leading me like a pet, she guided us back to the gallery to stare at paintings we knew nothing about.

"Iz!" a girl I didn't recognize exclaimed as she ran up to Izzie, pulling her into a hug. Immediately they began chatting intensely.

Great, I thought. *They'll be gabbing for an hour.*

I sidestepped them and roamed the gallery alone, taking my time examining and admiring sculptures and paintings. They were all well done. Skilled artists created these works.

I was envious. They could capture an essence and evoke emotion. They had passion. A calling.

Something in the center of the gallery had drawn interest from four people I assumed to be professors from their manner and nature of their discussion. I moved closer to hear them more clearly.

"His skill is phenomenal. He understands color and how it translates to print," a woman said, rubbing her chin as she squinted at the wall.

One of the men beside her nodded and took a sip from the champagne glass clutched in his hand. "He's going places, and I'm honored to be one of his mentors."

I slipped in behind them, curious about the artwork they praised so highly. Soon, I was absorbed in the picture that filled my vision. It was like someone had reached in and gripped my heart. Appropriate, since the young man depicted was holding a bleeding heart in his hand. It was dark. Gritty. Blood poured over his bare chest. Droplets of blood fell from his face like crimson tears. His pants were stained red. His hair fell into his eyes, but the gaze that peered through the strands was full of profound sadness, yet he seemed to invite me to join him. Join him in what? I didn't know. Something in that stare spoke to me on a primal level. He looked into my eyes as if he knew my pain. Like he knew me—the real me, the me hidden from the world, tucked in the deepest recess of my mind.

When I ripped my eyes away, I found the small square note from the artist at the bottom right, next to the corner of the print.

"Adam's Apple" by Nicholas Dawson

I wouldn't pretend to understand the title, but it seemed

to mean something. When I looked at the painting again, there was a need to know more, but the image scared me. Something about that boy hit a nerve deep in my gut, sending a chill down my spine. What had the artist experienced to create something so hauntingly beautiful?

CHAPTER 3

NICK

The student gallery was packed with people. It was opening night, and I was required to attend. I'd been to events like this before, but this was the first time I didn't want my art on display. Professor Doyle was ecstatic to exhibit my work, and I couldn't say no to him, not after all the support he'd given me. It was too late to take down the image now.

I slid through the doors like a shadow, hoping to go unnoticed. Someone had turned a classroom into a makeshift cafeteria, where tables draped with cream-colored cloth were surrounded by folding chairs. I grabbed a soda from one of the tables, minded by a bored-looking student volunteer, then slunk into the gallery.

A hand smacked my shoulder, sending my heart leaping from my chest.

"You look cool," Sky said as he stepped in front of me,

thumbing my tie between his fingers, grinning.

The tie was ironic, plain black, a nod to the formal art world. It was the only thing formal about my attire. I wore a sleeveless tank, which showed off the feathers of my tattoo, and black cargo pants adorned with chains and various political and protest buttons.

"Thanks," I said. "I thought you weren't coming tonight."

He crossed his arms and squinted his eyes as he examined the gallery. "I didn't plan to, but I heard there was free food."

"Whatever, man," I said, leaning against a nearby square pillar as a group of people marched up to my print. "I hope they don't make me speak."

Sky chuckled and leaned against the pillar with me. "I would pay good money to see that."

I grumbled, "You're too tight to part with hard cash."

Students, professors, parents, and members of the public swarmed the place. They eyed the student artwork like judges at a contest. Our work served as unpaid promotion for the university, drawing in prospective art students and donors for the department.

"Nick," a deep, gravelly voice said from a short distance to my right. Professor Doyle hurried toward me with a wide grin on his round, full face. "Here you are." He moved close to me, gently gripping my arm. His head barely came up to my collarbone, and it was almost laughable how he looked up at me with bright eyes wide from excitement. "I thought I would have to chase you down."

"I wouldn't miss it, Professor."

My tone gave away my lie. Thanks to those corrupted files, I had too many assignments to redo, and this event cut into my precious time.

"Well, I'm glad you made it," he said, squeezing my arm before releasing me. "I have a few people who want to meet you. Come with me." He guided me toward my artwork, where three people stood around talking to one another. They were dressed as if they were attending a premier at a major art institution, not a student show. As we approached, they turned to us, expectant looks in their eyes as they inspected me like an animal up for auction.

"This is the young man I was telling you about," said Professor Doyle, nudging me forward. I wanted to resist. Crawl back into the shadows and disappear.

One of the women, wearing a plum-colored dress, extended a slender arm and gave me her hand. I shook it firmly. "Hilary McCarly," she said with a deep Southern drawl. "I hear you're one of the top students in your department."

"I don't know about that," I said, shoving my hands in my pockets. I hated when people praised me. I was my own worst critic and never saw myself as good enough. I could never unsee my own flaws, especially in my art.

Professor Doyle placed a hand on my back in a comforting gesture. "Don't be fooled by the modesty. Nick won a prestigious art scholarship. He's a talented artist."

The trio seemed impressed as they nodded and looked me over. Standing beside Hilary was a woman with cropped hair, her dark skin contrasting with the pale man next to her of average height and features.

"If you don't see your value, young man, it's okay. Continue to improve your craft." She smiled and aimed a slender finger at the woman beside her. "This is my business partner, Beth Asendae, and her husband, Frank Woods."

"Nice to meet you," I said with a nod.

"What are your plans after graduation?" Beth asked.

Wherever this was leading, I assumed Professor Doyle knew them well enough that I could trust them. "I haven't decided yet. I was thinking of finding a job around DC to start my career."

"Would you like to stay in Fernworth?" Hilary asked.

"Possibly."

"My company specializes in marketing and design. We could always use someone with your skills on our team."

Beth reached into her tiny handbag and pulled out a business card. "If you want to stay in the area, call us after you graduate."

I took the card with a smile. "Thank you. I'll keep you in mind."

"Clark," Beth said, tugging Professor Doyle close and kissing him on the cheek, "a pleasure to see you again."

"The pleasure is all mine."

Professor Doyle released a deep sigh as they left the gallery. He turned to me, saying, "Nick, keep them in mind. They might be your ticket to success in the future."

"Yes, sir."

I shoved the business card in my wallet and let Professor Doyle lead me around, mingling with other professors and anyone he felt I needed to know.

It was exhausting.

• • •

A text notification popped up on my phone screen, and I ignored it—again. Logan had texted me four days in a row, and he wasn't letting up. No matter how many times I denied him, he kept asking.

Sky lounged on the sofa in his boxers, a bag of chips resting on his stomach as he channel surfed.

"Coffee?" I asked.

"Sure," he said, and I grabbed another mug from the cabinet.

The campus dorm we'd snagged at the start of the year was the closest to living in an actual apartment. It was the last one in the building and one of the few dorms with a full-size kitchen. Because only the end units next to the emergency escape stairwell had two rooms instead of four, we didn't have to share with anyone else—the icing on the cake. It meant a smaller living space but more privacy. Perfect for the two of us.

My phone buzzed on the counter again. This time a call.

Again, I ignored it, pouring the coffee into the mugs.

"Who's being annoying this early in the morning?" Sky grumbled.

"Logan. Who else?"

Logan was cool for a hook-up, but outside of that, I didn't like the guy. He and I met by chance and agreed to keep our relationship casual. We didn't speak to each other except to schedule a meetup; I didn't even know his last name.

"He must really want to see you," Sky said from the sofa as he shoveled a handful of chips into his mouth.

I grabbed the mugs filled to the brim with steaming coffee, walked over to Sky, and handed him his cup. "I'm not in the mood. I might stop seeing him, actually."

"Bored of him already?"

I sat in the armchair across from him. We had found it at a local thrift store. After a few days of cleaning it up, it turned out to be my favorite seat.

"He's getting a little clingy," I explained.

Sky sat up, finally shifting his attention from the TV. "But, if Logan isn't around, who will warm your bed on those cold, lonely nights?" Sky winked and then sipped his coffee.

His teasing wasn't lost on me, but the truth in his words still hurt.

"Sometimes it's better to be alone," I replied.

The phone buzzed from the kitchen again. That was why I silenced my phone all the time. I hated hearing the notifications.

"He might have real feelings for you."

"Too bad I don't have any for him." I laughed as I sunk further into the chair. I didn't have the energy to worry about Logan when I still had to figure out how I would afford a new laptop. It would be rough if I had to use the lab the whole time.

"I'm serious, Nick. When was the last time you felt more than physical attraction to someone?"

"Oh, shut up. Have you met yourself?" I tried to play it off, hoping he would let me off answering. His question hit too hard.

"What kind of question is that?" Sky set his mug on the coffee table between us and preened himself. "I always answer my booty calls."

"Speaking of . . ." I eyed him, wondering if it would be too touchy a subject. "Never mind." I dismissed the idea with a wave and got to my feet, chugging the rest of my coffee. "Come on, we have to get to class."

"No," Sky said, drawing out the word as he chased after me through the apartment. "Speaking of what?" He grabbed the back of my shirt, tugging me back. "Speaking of what, Nick?"

Damn it. I shouldn't have said anything. But I couldn't leave it hanging. "Have you spoken to Will lately?" I asked.

Sky's scowl darkened, then he turned and went to his room. I wished I had kept my mouth shut.

• • •

My phone rang for the millionth time as Sky and I entered the art building twenty minutes later. Sky had forgiven me before leaving the dorm and was already back to his cheerful self.

The gallery was empty, a stark difference from the night before, even though the exhibition would continue all week.

"Nick," a voice called from behind, and I immediately wanted to hide.

"Shit," I whispered.

Sky sucked a breath through his teeth beside me.

I turned to face my assailant.

"Why the fuck have you been ignoring me?" Logan asked as he marched toward me wearing a stern expression.

I could never deny my attraction to him. Shorter than me, but only by about two inches, he wore his soft, wavy blond hair shoulder-length, and I loved to run my fingers through it. I especially liked it done up in a messy bun. On his chin and cheeks was the permanent stubble of reddish hair that I would run my nose over. Logan was hot, but that was all he was.

My lips twitched as I tried to smile. "Logan, good to see you."

"Don't pull that shit with me. Why are you ignoring me?"

"Can we not do this here?"

"I can't get you to speak to me anywhere else, so no."

"This is too much drama for me. I'll be over there," Sky said before disappearing across the hallway and slipping inside the art gallery, leaving me alone to deal with my mess.

"I have a lot going on right now," I said.

"And it made you so busy you couldn't answer my texts or calls?"

I stared, unsure how to handle him. This was the first time he had gotten like this with me. He was acting like he was my boyfriend.

"What's going on with you?"

Me? This felt more than clingy. Sky was probably right about him having feelings for me.

"Are you going to say anything?" His lips curled into an annoyed snarl, like he was losing his composure the longer I was silent.

This entire encounter told me everything I needed to know, solidifying my decision. "Logan, I think it's time to end this thing we've been doing."

His jaw fell half open, like he was searching for the words to respond to me.

Before he could say anything, I continued, "I don't have feelings for you, but it seems that isn't true for you. You've been up my ass for days, and now you show up like this."

Crossing his arms, he blew out a breath. "Yes. Obviously I have some feelings for you. I thought after all the time we'd spent..."

I stepped in closer, softening my approach. I was used to this. How many times had I broken the hearts of guys like him? More than I cared to count. "Look, man, I'm sorry. You're a fun time and cool to hang out with, but I don't have any feelings for you. Not the way you want me to."

Logan looked me in the eyes, defiant. "I get it. Good enough to fuck, but not good enough to love."

What could I say to such a statement? That's the kind of thing only a therapist can address, and I hadn't seen mine since graduating high school. All I could do was shrug.

He stepped back, wounded. "Whatever, dude. I hope you find what you're looking for."

Doubtful, I thought. "I'm sorry, Logan."

"Sure," he huffed, looking disgusted.

His retreat was a familiar sight. For years, all I did was this. Meet someone, fall into bed, then keep them at arm's length until one day it was over. They always walked away from me, and I never chased after them.

There had only ever been one person I had loved. But he took every ounce of love from me, and I had none left to give. Maybe one day I would meet someone who could bring that spark back to my life, but Logan was not that person.

I noticed that people had stopped what they were doing to eavesdrop and gawk, like I was some kind of sideshow. When my eyes landed on them, they quickly returned to their business or started walking away.

"Did he take it badly?" Sky asked as he appeared at my side.

"You're a rat."

Sky gasped as he stepped away from me. "Why do you say that?"

"How did he know where I would be?"

Sky raised his eyebrows as he took a wide step back, slinking away from me. "Don't be angry with me. I just wanted you to deal with it. He deserved some honesty."

Before I could berate him, we were interrupted by River.

"Nick, are you okay?"

I turned my head, the warmth of a smile spreading across my face, replacing my frown. "Riv, my love," I said, opening my arms for a welcome hug.

She wrapped her arms around my waist. Her giant portfolio bag slipped off her shoulder, landing against my thigh. She was so tiny, her head only reaching halfway up my chest. But I knew better than to think of her as delicate. Being raised by a single mother and older sister taught me to never underestimate women. Despite River's petiteness, she was a spitfire.

"I could hear what happened." The corners of her mouth turned down, tugging those cute lips into a pout. "Are you okay?"

"I'm fine," I said, then kissed the top of her head as I gave her one last squeeze.

"Well, if you want to talk, I'm always here for you." She swung the strap of her portfolio bag back over her shoulder. "Sky, how are you this morning?"

"Filled with sunshine as always," he said, taking his turn to pull her into a bear hug.

When she was released, I said, "By the way, if you come across any used laptops for cheap, can you let me know?"

"I can ask around for you," she said. "See you tonight."

She waved as she turned down the hallway and disappeared through a door.

"Let's go to class," I grumbled. I bumped into Sky as I turned, pushing him back a step, although he deserved a punch for telling Logan where I would be.

"You would have let it fester until he came to find you himself."

"Doesn't give you the right."

"I live with you. I have to deal with it." Sky hopped up the stairs ahead of me and turned to face me, stopping me in my tracks. "I was tired of your phone ringing off the hook and you not making any decision. You'll thank me later." He spun around and bounded up the stairs, clearly proud of himself.

"Asshole," I mumbled, but he was right. I would've ignored Logan for as long as possible.

My classroom was packed. I was five minutes early, and my chest was tight as I dropped into the chair at the desk and shook the computer mouse, bringing the screen to life. Sky had let me borrow his laptop when he wasn't using it, but I still hadn't had enough time to redo my assignment.

The professor was always late, which only intensified my nerves. At five past, he waltzed in, coffee in hand, his cheeks red from rushing to the classroom.

I leaped from my chair. "Professor Brown, may I speak with you?"

His cheek twitched. I had pissed him off by interrupting him as he was about to start class, but I didn't care; I needed the extension.

"Can this wait until after class?"

"It can't."

He took a swig from the paper cup and beckoned me through the threshold of the classroom into the corridor.

"What is it, Mr. Dawson?" he asked in his usual formal way.

"I had an incident with my laptop while I was working on my assignment a few days ago. It caused my file to corrupt, and

I had to restart my project." He stared at me with an empty gaze, like my disaster had no bearing on his life. "I started my project over again, but I haven't finished yet."

"Nick, I understand things like this happen, but if you're hoping for an extension, I can't give it to you."

It was a punch to the gut that knocked the breath out of me.

"If I gave an extension to every student who came to me with a similar excuse, then I would have to make exceptions all the time. On principle, I can't do that."

"I'm telling you the truth. My laptop died and corrupted my files on my flash drive."

"It doesn't matter if it is true or not. I cannot make an exception, or I would have to grant everyone an extension." He released a sigh, telling me I was an annoyance interrupting his day, as if keeping my grades up wasn't a condition of my scholarship.

"Professor, this is the first time I've ever been late. Why can't–"

"I will accept it late for a deduction in points. Have it to me by the end of the week." Without another glance, he disappeared into the classroom.

It was unfair. How could he treat me like a liar? As if I was playing the system? Not even bothering to ask me questions?

With my eyes closed, I sucked in a long, deep breath, trying to get a handle on my emotions. I could only hope the lab wouldn't be busy tonight so that I could get a lot of work done.

CHAPTER 4

TAKA

Casey hovered beside me as we found ourselves face-to-face with Izzie and a few of her friends. She looked cute that day, wearing oversized sweatpants and a loose hoodie. Her smile was wide as she skipped toward me. Latching onto my arm, she fell in line at my side.

"Baby, want to have lunch together?" She looked up at me with her big, bright eyes.

My throat tightened as I pushed down the need to pull away from her. "Casey and I are having lunch."

She pouted and glared at Casey. "You don't mind if my ladies and I join you, right?"

Casey and I exchanged glances. He seemed hesitant but aimed a wink at her. "Anything for you, Iz."

A part of me had hoped he would tell her off, push back, save me from this existence, but how could I expect that when everyone thought I was happy?

"Lunch it is," I said.

I let her pull me through the food court, then sat like a statue as she chatted away with her friends, taking over every conversation and pushing me into the background. I should have been used to it. I spent my entire existence overshadowed by other people's prominent personalities. I couldn't quite explain why, but it had begun affecting me lately. Each time I was shoved into the background, a deep sting shot through my heart, telling me I was nothing. I was a shadow. No one saw me. No one wanted to hear me.

Casey leaned over, dipping his face near my shoulder. "You okay?" he asked, then pulled away, monitoring my face.

I nodded, too tired to respond with words. What was I doing? What was the point of remaining in this relationship?

The woman I once loved was beside me, laughing with her friends. I should have been happy. I expect most people in my position would laugh with her, insert themselves into her conversation, become friends with her friends, find joy in moments like this. Instead, I was left feeling hollow. Lonely.

It scared me.

• • •

Students stood as the professor dismissed the class, grabbing their bags and notebooks. They poured from the room while I sat wondering how I would make a poster and brochure for this marketing class. I had never used photo editing software before, and I didn't think the basic one on my laptop would suffice.

As I stared blankly at the front of the empty classroom,

a hand waved past my face a few times before I pulled myself from my thoughts.

"You look so down. Everything okay today?" Casey asked. He slid into the seat beside me and set his bag on the desk, waiting for my answer.

"I don't know what to do about this project. I've never used photo editing software. I don't even know where to begin."

"Chill, T. I had an assignment like this last semester, and I got help from this guy in the computer lab."

"Lucky you," I said.

"No, what I'm saying is there's someone there whose job it is to help you with stuff like this, doofus," Casey said.

"Someone is there all the time? Like now?" I said, a rush of relief clearing away some of the anxiety.

Casey nodded, picking up his bag. "Let's go, and I'll help you get what you need."

"Thanks, I appreciate it." I stood and followed him into the hallway. "Where is the lab? The library?"

"Nope, the one in Ellis Center, where the art students hide away. There're a lot of geeks who know what they're doing with computers, so even if the lab doesn't have their guy on hand, there should be someone with more clue than you."

"I'll take any help I can get at this point."

I imagined a lab full of crazy-colored hair, piercings, and paint-splattered clothes. In high school, I was friends with enough art students that this was the image stuck in my head. In college, I hadn't had much chance to make friends outside my department or the fraternity. I was always busy with assignments or the DGZ, and when not in class, I was home with my family.

Casey seemed on edge as we walked across campus. I chewed the inside of my cheek and debated whether to open the floor to whatever was bothering him. I settled on leaving it alone, but then he spoke and removed the option.

"Are you and Iz okay?" he asked.

Here we go, I thought.

I wasn't even sure yet. How long had I been unhappy? A year? I had noticed that I was distancing myself from her about six months ago. I attributed it to my stress between home and school and the frat. I was tired. I barely had the energy to pay attention to myself, let alone a relationship, so I had let it go until we reached this point.

"We're fine."

"You didn't seem fine today. And the other day, you missed your dinner plans over finances, and that isn't like you."

Was it not like me? I almost laughed. What was I like? Who was I? I was the boy that followed all the rules, ensured I was likable to everyone, kept on my poker face so no one could ever think I disliked them. I was perfect–on the outside.

"I appreciate your concern, but we're fine," I repeated.

I was met with silence, and I was sure Casey didn't believe a word, but at least he ended his prying.

Casey finally stopped in front of a glass door, and I stood dumbfounded beside him. After nearly two years at this school, I'd never been to this room. I hadn't felt out of place on campus before, but standing in front of the computer lab about to ask a bunch of nerds for help made me feel very much out of place.

"Don't just stand there," Casey said, ushering me inside the lab.

When the door snapped shut behind us, the sounds of the

busy building were silenced.

A desk clerk broke the silence. “Welcome. May I help you?”

I approached the reception desk and could only see the crown of pink hair above her monitor.

“My friend needs some help with photo editing,” Casey said as he gripped my shoulder and propelled me closer to the counter.

I put on my most confident smile, battling the impulse to turn around and give up on this idea. “I have an assignment to make a poster and brochure, but I don’t know what I’m doing.”

She nodded, twirling a pen between her fingers. “Sounds like you’ll need a workstation. Nicholas is in there right now; he can help you. He’s in the Digital Arts Program and has extensive knowledge of the software you would need to use.” She tilted her head to the side and shoved a clipboard at me. “Sign here, and then head to the back right corner. Tell Nicholas what you need, and he’ll help you as long as he’s on duty.”

“Looks like you’re all set. I’ll see you later,” Casey said.

“Thanks, Casey,” I said.

When he opened the door, the sounds of campus flooded the room briefly, begging me to return to the comforting noise. It was gone as soon as the door snapped shut again.

“You all have some amazing soundproofing in here,” I said, signing the paper and handing the clipboard back to the girl.

Black eyeliner emphasized her deep-green eyes, but the rest of her makeup was reasonably light. No lipstick or dark eyeshadow. But her eyes gave her a bold, striking look.

She giggled as she took the clipboard back. “I wouldn’t survive here if we could hear everything.”

I thanked her with a smile before I headed to the back of

the computer lab. A small sign was mounted on the wall near an open door, with the words *Lab2* written in bold black lettering.

The sound of a belly laugh pulled my attention inside the room. A man with undercut black hair was curled in on himself, turning red with laughter. He had a striking presence with his sharp, angular features and strong jawline. He wore a black hoodie, cargo pants, and a pair of all-black high-top chucks. His hoodie cuffs were pushed up his arms, exposing a black leather bracelet on his left wrist. He cupped his face as he sucked in a breath and released another deep laugh that ripped through his core. The movement drew my attention to the piercings in his ear: a double lobe piercing with black hoops and two more earrings higher in the cartilage. His style was very much art student meets punk rocker, and for some reason, I liked it.

The guy next to him was in a similar state of mirth. His darker skin was bright red, and tears ran down his cheeks. His face was square and strong, with full lips accented by his short undercut, styled to perfection, and he had on a crisp, white button-up shirt tucked loosely into his jeans. If I had seen them outside this room, I would never have imagined them to be friends.

"Damn, Sky," the one in black said to the other. His voice was deep and raspy as he caught his breath between laughs. "I'm still working. Turn around and shut up before you get me in trouble with River." He turned his gaze to me with a huge grin, his cheeks red and deep brown eyes glistening. "Hey, man, can I help you with anything?" he asked as he breathed through the remainder of his laugh.

It took a moment before I realized he was talking to me. "I was told to speak with Nicholas." I stepped into the room, closing the distance between us.

"I am he," he announced with mock gravitas. He pulled a chair from another desk, rolled it beside him, then motioned for me to sit. "And call me Nick."

"I'm Taka," I said.

"Pleased to meet you, Taka. What do you need today?"

I explained my assignment, and he listened intently to my questions and concerns and asked me questions in return. It was a comfortable discussion; he seemed to care about my needs, and the questions he asked were relevant to my assignment. He didn't bother with pleasantries or fluff. It was a breath of fresh air.

Nick leaned back in his chair with a smile, running his fingers over his chin. "I can definitely help you with that. A brochure is fairly simple. There's a template for it, which will make it easier for you. The poster will also be pretty easy, but I recommend making the brochure first."

"Why is that?"

"You'll do all your idea planning for the brochure to get your theme down and will need to create fake details about what you're marketing. That's the hardest part. The content and layout of a poster will come much easier when you have a better understanding of what you're advertising."

"Makes sense," I said. "What would the next step be?"

"We can get you set up at this station." Rising, he moved to the desk that he had taken the chair from and powered up the computer tower. "I'll get you set up here and then take my break. I can help you more when I get back from dinner."

"Great, thank you."

I hadn't expected to start on this now, but since this guy

was here to help me, I needed to take advantage of his knowledge. I rolled my chair over to the desk, and he expertly opened the editing software, changed settings, and then navigated to a webpage full of pictures.

"These are all free stock photos, so you can use them and not worry about spending money on your project." His thumb tapped the side of the mouse, clicking a silver ring against the plastic as he set up the file for me. After a few moments, he leaned his hip against the desk as he faced me. "Do you have any more questions?"

"How long do you work tonight?"

"I'm closing with River, our manager, so until ten. If you need help while I'm on break, River can help you. She's a BFA student, but she uses these tools enough to be useful."

"Thank you, I appreciate it."

"No problem. It's what I'm here for." He turned and grabbed his bag from the floor. "Sky, let's grab some food."

"Finally," Sky said. He jumped up from the chair to follow Nick from the room.

CHAPTER 5

NICK

“Don’t tell me you didn’t notice how much of a hottie that guy was?” Sky asked as he bit into his burger.

“I noticed. I promise you, I noticed.” I’d have to be blind not to see how hot the guy who came into the computer lab was.

Sky was the one who encouraged me to come out in high school. I’m glad he did; it was a turning point in my life. But he knew how careful I was about who I asked out.

“Sky, he seems straight.”

“You never know,” he said, before taking another bite of his burger.

“I’m not bugging some random guy and possibly creeping him out. I want to survive the rest of my program and graduate, not create problems with people. That thing with Logan this morning was bad enough.”

He raised an eyebrow as he shoved his burger into his

mouth. With a disgusting mouthful, he asked, "Is asking someone out a problem? Besides, the situation with Logan was different."

I watched a chunk of food fly from his mouth and land on the table.

"Don't pretend not to know how it goes, Sky. He seems like the athletic type. You know how those sporty guys can be. I don't wanna be the butt of their jokes if I ask him out and he freaks. I had enough of that in high school."

Sky swallowed his food. "Well, it will be your loss, dude." A crooked smile appeared on his face. "Maybe I'll ask him out. I wonder what he'd say."

I rolled my eyes at him. I knew he wouldn't make a move on Taka.

"By the way," he said, popping a fry into his mouth, "I found a laptop for you, but the guy sold it already."

"Thanks for trying. I picked up more shifts at the lab to get a new one, so it's okay."

"Sorry, I know you were hopeful. I'll keep my feelers out just in case."

"Not your fault." I stood, slinging my bag over my shoulder. "My break's over. See you later."

"Enjoy your time with the hottie. I can't wait to hear all about it."

I groaned, flashing him a smile as I rounded the stairs and headed back to the computer lab.

He wasn't exaggerating. The guy was my type, but there was no way I'd risk it. My campus life was quiet. I wanted to keep it that way.

"Hey, Riv," I said, returning to my sanctuary. I leaned over the reception desk, glancing down at her sprawled-out papers surrounding the keyboard, then picked up the sign-in sheet, reading through the names of students using the lab until one name caught my eye. "Takahiro Akiyama, BS," the entry read.

"Welcome back." She smiled. "That guy from earlier is still in there. But he's the only one. Should be a quiet session tonight."

"Good. Maybe I can get some work done." I tapped the top of the counter before pushing off, trying to hide that I was pleased Taka was still there. "I'll get back there and see if he still needs help."

"Sure," she said, returning her attention to the computer screen. "Oh, Nick, you're closing with me tonight, right?"

"Yeah, why?"

"I've got to pick up my sister from ballet practice. Would you be okay closing if I left here at eight?"

"Yeah, no problem. Do what you need to," I said, heading toward the lab.

Taka appeared to have settled into the groove of planning. He had a notebook open with writing scrawled on it, and his laptop was flipped open to a document. His headphones were in, and he was clearly in the zone.

I set my bag down near the desk across from Taka, which I had been using before my break, and began working on my own project. But my eyes kept wandering back to Taka of their own accord. His black hair was parted down the middle, and his bangs hung around his face, brushing against his cheeks. His cloud-gray dress shirt was unbuttoned at the collar, displaying the divot between his collarbones, leading my gaze up his slender neck to his strong jawline. The cuffs of his shirt rested halfway up his forearms, and a silver watch that encircled his left wrist looked expensive. Nobody I knew even owned a watch these days.

I sucked in a breath and counted to ten. It was impossible to deny he was handsome. I needed to keep myself in check around this guy.

I waved at Taka to get his attention. He looked up and took his earbud out. “Hey. You’re back already?” he said, looking at his watch. “Wow. I lost track of time.” He laid his headphones on the desk beside his laptop.

“I wanted to check in on you. Do you need any help?” I said, hoping he’d say yes.

He smiled, showing his straight white teeth, and my heart picked up speed.

He angled his whole body toward me. “I think I have everything I need to start the brochure.” He pointed to the double monitor screens. “I found pictures I want to use, and I placed those text boxes you showed me in the areas I think it would fit, but I need a second opinion. And maybe even some help to remove the background of this picture.”

I went over to look at his work. “That was fast. I was only gone, what, fifty minutes?” I said.

He tilted his head with a slight smile. I swallowed and schooled my expression; this guy was dangerous.

“I wanted to make sure I got it ready so you could help me with this stuff.”

I laughed. “You know, you don’t have to do your whole project tonight. I’m here every day, even some weekends.”

He pulled his lips together like he hadn’t thought about it. “You’re here that often?”

"I essentially live here. My laptop wasn't strong enough for rendering animation. It barely made it through the modeling program without blowing up, but it at least ran." I leaned back in my chair with a heavy sigh. "Sadly, it can't even do that anymore."

"Why not?"

"It died. The poor thing was going on seven years old and was already on its last legs, but I was hoping to make it through the rest of the semester with it."

"Seven?" He leaned forward with a laugh, resting his arm on the desk. "Don't laptops last like three?"

I chuckled. "Something like that, but it doesn't matter because I have this lab, so I'm not completely screwed." I moved closer to him and reached over for the mouse. "Let's get you set up with what you need."

Hours passed as I bounced between my artwork, assisting other people, and working with Taka on his brochure. He finally got the hang of everything and could make an initial draft of his poster. As we worked, we chatted casually, but mostly we sat in companionable silence. I enjoyed his presence. He was there but not begging for my attention, and he didn't talk my ear off to the point of annoyance.

It felt safe. Comfortable.

I knew I needed to keep clear of him.

CHAPTER 6

TAKA

A yawn escaped me, and I rubbed the sleep from my eyes before looking down at the bottom right of the computer screen: eleven-thirty. That couldn't be the right time. I took a moment to stretch my stiff muscles and check my watch, but it told me the same.

"Nick," I said, spinning my chair toward him.

He pulled the headphones away, and his music faded out as he blinked at me like I had yanked him away from a far-off world. "What's up?"

"Have you looked at the time? It's after eleven."

"What?" He quickly glanced at his phone and then jumped out of his chair. "Shit." He rushed into the main lab, leaving a rush of air behind.

I could hear him ushering people out, apologizing for not realizing the time. I packed up my own things, shut down my workstation, then entered the main lab. Nick stood in the center of the room, his face flushed, watching people leave. Clearly flustered, he lifted his hoodie over his head, catching the hem of his shirt and briefly exposing his waist and a dark line of intricate feathers. The black ink of the tattoo contrasted with his pale skin. I wanted to know what those feathers represented and how far around his waist they went. The moment stunned me and made me blush.

Nick had caught me looking and held my gaze with an intensity that had me squirming out of my skin. My stomach sank as I realized how far I had dropped my guard. When was the last time I looked at a man like that? It had been ages. I cleared my throat and shut off those curious thoughts racing through my mind, returning to the man I was expected to be. A momentary slip-up meant nothing.

"I'm sorry, Takahiro," he said. "I totally lost track of time. That happens when I'm in the zone." He began inspecting the lab, quickly checking everything was in order.

"You're fine. Nothing to worry about," I said. "By the way, everyone calls me Taka or T. Takahiro is a very formal way to address me. And Taka is less strange."

"I don't think it's strange," he said. "Is it Japanese?"

I nodded. "I'm named after my grandfather. My parents moved us here from Japan when I was five."

Kids would make endless jokes about my name, so I asked everyone to call me T. Even Taka felt too foreign. I would go to every teacher before class started on the first day of school to make sure they called me T and never by my name. I was lucky that they were always willing to accommodate my request. The teachers were kind and understanding, at least. Being bullied for my name made me hate it until a good friend, Rylee, helped me get past it. She helped me embrace Taka as a name to be proud of. The scars were still there, though.

"That's cool. Do you ever get to visit Japan?" he asked, leaning against the doorframe.

"Every year. I have family in Chiba."

"That's really neat. I've never been out of the country." He laughed as he ran his fingers through his hair.

"Never?"

"Not a single time," he said, dipping his head like it was something shameful to admit. "I've barely even left the state. I don't count going to DC and Maryland as going out of state. They're basically extensions of where I live."

"Where do you live?"

"Northern Virginia, a tiny little town that no one has ever heard of." He laughed as he rubbed his hand over the back of his neck. "Even people from the area have no idea it exists."

"Nobody has ever heard of Chiba either," I said. Americans had only heard of Tokyo and Osaka. And, because of history, Hiroshima or Nagasaki.

He smiled. "We have obscure origins in common, then."

The lab was empty, finally. He walked over to the desk he'd been using, tossed his things in his bag, and then slung it over his shoulder. "Man, I'm starved. Dinner was hours ago."

"Me too," I said. I had skipped dinner since I had come directly from class.

"Are you getting food on your way home?" he asked.

"If there's anywhere still open."

"Do you want to grab a bite together? There's this after-hours place near my dorm. They have some pretty good food for being a restaurant on campus."

Mom probably had food waiting for me, so I didn't need to eat out. But I really enjoyed Nick's company, and my stomach was rumbling now that my focus wasn't on the computer. "Okay."

"Awesome," he said, his face lighting up. "It's a small hike across campus."

I followed him through the computer lab and into the main hallway of the Ellis Center. It was a ghost town.

"This is the most peaceful I've ever seen this building," I said as we descended the stairs toward the basement level.

"This is my favorite time to come through here. A small escape from the insanity of the day."

"Do you like the quiet?"

"You have no idea," he replied. "I have an older sister and younger brother. Lori would have her friends over all the time, and they were so loud that I would end up blasting music in my ears to drown them out. Harper, my brother, would scream and run around the house because he was a little kid, and that's what they do." He laughed, flicking his wrist as if waving the thought away. "Anyway, it doesn't matter."

"I only have a younger sister and she's fairly quiet, so I can't say I know what that feels like."

We walked across campus in silence. The cool spring air rushed over me, passing through my shirt and sending a wave of chills over my skin.

The area surrounding the restaurant was crowded. It was like all campus activity had moved from the Ellis Center to this little restaurant. A lit sign on the slanted roof read "Jay's" in white letters. The outdoor courtyard was packed with tables, and students filled every space.

"I didn't know this place existed," I said.

"Unless you live on campus, no one knows about it. It opens at nine and closes at five."

"Is it like this every night?"

"Pretty much."

Nick opened the door, and the aroma of food and the sound of people talking washed over me.

"Do you live on campus, Taka?"

I shook my head. "My parents' house is fifteen minutes away, so I didn't see a reason to live on campus."

"What year are you?"

"Sophomore," I said, taking in the insanity of Jay's. People were crammed into small booths, happily munching on an assortment of food, from burgers to pancakes to ice cream.

"Aw, pity you missed out on that experience. I wouldn't say I enjoyed sharing a bedroom, but after freshman year, you're allowed to apply for shared dorms with private bedrooms, and that's where college life gets better. You have privacy and can hang out with friends all night." Nick laughed. "I talk like I'm some socialite."

A wave of giddiness bubbled inside me as we stood in the long line. The lamps nestled in the ceiling made the yellow walls almost orange. It was like walking into a nineteen-eighties diner, but not one of those tacky diners with neon lights and crazy colors. This was toned down. No gimmicks. Just good food, good company, and a great time.

"So, if you don't live on campus, do you do activities or sports?"

"I'm a member of Delta Gamma Zeta. I mostly hang out on

Greek Row and participate in their events."

"Oh no, a frat guy." Nick laughed and covered his face with his hands.

I laughed. "Oh, come on. We aren't that bad."

He dragged his hands down his face in mock horror. "You have to admit there are a lot of assholes in frats."

I nodded, thinking of some people I had met who wanted to pledge or ended up pledging. "Some are not so great."

After a few minutes talking about my fraternity, we ordered our food and found a couple of spare seats in a back corner booth. A group of people piled in when we sat at the table, adding to the already deafening volume.

"Maybe Jay's wasn't such a good idea tonight," Nick said, biting into a sandwich.

I shook my head. "I'm glad we came. It's fun to see it and experience campus life."

Nick tilted his head. "What else have you not experienced?"

"A lot of things. I mostly focus on studying and reading."

Outside of events for DGZ or classes and required department events, I didn't go out with friends. I didn't party. Even with Izzie and my past girlfriends, I never did much. We would have dinner dates, but nothing out of the ordinary.

"Taka, are you serious? You don't do anything social?" His eyes raked over me, as if looking for the lie in my words.

There was something I liked to do—car meets—but he didn't seem like someone who would be into cars.

"I swear it. I'm very boring as a person."

"I doubt that," he said, returning to his meal.

My phone buzzed in my pocket, startling me. I pulled my phone out; sure enough, it was Mom calling. She was probably worried sick, thinking something had happened. I let it ring off but started to eat more quickly. My time was running out with Nick.

Of course, the phone rang again. I couldn't ignore it again.

"Sorry, Nick. I need to get this." I stood, grabbed my half-eaten plate of food, and tossed it in the trash on my way outside. The seating area near the building was as busy as inside, so I walked further away to pick up the call. "Mom?"

"Taka? Are you okay?" Mom sounded worried, and her voice was rough, like she'd woken up and realized I wasn't home.

"I'm fine. I'm still on campus."

"Was there an event today that I forgot about?"

"No, this was my fault. I lost track of time getting help on an assignment, and my friend and I got some food before heading home."

"What friend?"

"No one you know, Mom. I met him today. He was helping me with a new assignment for my marketing class."

"Will you be home soon?"

"I'm on my way in a few minutes. Okay?"

My father's voice could be heard in the background as he asked if everything was all right. "Okay, but be careful."

"I will. I love you," I said, hanging up the phone.

"Sorry, man," Nick said. He hovered nearby with his hands shoved in his pockets. "Were they worried about you?"

"Yeah, I forgot to let them know I would be late."

"Do you want company back to your car?" he asked.

My heart thundered at his tempting offer. A part of me wanted to accept. Uncertainty washed over me as I stared at him, trying to make sense of my feelings. "I'm okay, thank you,"

I said and opened my phone, navigating to my contact list. "Uh, do you mind if I get your number?" My heartbeat quickened. "You know, for school-related stuff." It was the only excuse I could think of.

"Ah, cool. Yeah." He grabbed my phone, entered his information, and handed it back to me. "Text me whenever. And it doesn't have to be about school." He chuckled. "I apologize in advance if I don't respond quickly. I forget to answer texts a lot."

"Should I call you then?"

"No way." He rubbed the back of his neck. "Calling is even worse. My phone's always on silent. I hate hearing the notifications when I'm concentrating. Text is definitely the better option."

"Um, okay. Also, thank you for your help today. I hope I can return the favor in the future."

"It was no problem, man. It was real nice to meet you."

He reversed away, the ghost of a smile on his lips. "Oh, and maybe I can get you out for some fun before your college life is over." He turned before I could reply and left me wondering what he meant by that.

When I reached my car, I unlocked my phone. What greeted me was the new contact profile: Nick Dawson.

CHAPTER 7

NICK

I'm in trouble.

Taka was easy to talk to. He drew me in right away and his manner had me questioning if he was straight, if he felt the same connection I did. Usually, I could tell right away, but this guy gave me mixed signals. He either wore an impenetrable mask or he honestly wasn't interested. It was hard to say. I groaned, tugging my keys from my pocket. It all built up inside me, like a dam ready to overflow after a heavy rainstorm. The inescapable fact was that I was interested in him. Not only physically, but we clicked. There was something between us. I wanted to explore it.

The lamp in the living room was on, and Sky was stretched out over the sofa, his face lit up by his phone. I was thankful for his night-owl tendencies as I collapsed onto the floor next to his head and propped myself up against the cushions, gazing at my feet. I needed to talk before getting lost in my thoughts more than I already had.

"Sky."

He groaned a reply.

"I like him."

"Like who?"

"Who else, dude! Taka!"

Sky was still absorbed by his phone, and I needed his attention.

I knocked his phone gently, and it dropped to the floor. Sky flipped onto his side and stared at me. "What the fuck, man!"

I confiscated his phone. "Listen a moment, will you?"

He huffed and sat up. "I'm all ears."

"Taka. The guy you said was hot. I like him."

Sky grinned and nodded. "I called it! So? Spill, my friend."

"Man, I lost track of time and forgot to close the lab at ten, and we didn't get out of there until after eleven. Then I asked him to eat with me at Jay's, and so we did and–"

"Nick!" Sky burst out laughing. "You're speaking faster than lightning. Relax." His chuckles died down as he patted my head affectionately. "I'm not going anywhere."

I took a deep breath, attempting to calm the rush.

"Did you find out if he's gay?"

A sigh rolled out of me as I rubbed my temples. "I didn't ask, and I don't know."

"Nick." Sky drew out the word like a warning. "You know better than this."

I paused, thinking about how Taka's eyes had focused on my tattoo. It was different from general curiosity. I'd seen that look plenty of times, and it always led to something more than looking. But before I knew it, Taka had pulled back, and it was gone. "It's nothing. Maybe some wishful thinking."

"Nick, please avoid this guy. I don't want to see you fall in love with someone you can't have."

"I know, but I had fun with him."

"No, none of that. You clearly cannot be friends with this guy. Look at you right now. In a matter of hours he has you like this!"

"I gave him my number."

"Fucking hell," Sky groaned. "Nicholas!"

"I know."

"What am I going to do with you?"

My phone vibrated against my thigh, and my heart soared with hope. The phone was in hand, and I stared at the screen faster than I'd ever cared to look at a message. The notification showed an unknown number, and I clicked on it immediately.

Hey, Nick, this is Taka. Had a great time today. Maybe we could hang out once my assignment is over.

Oh, no.

Damn, this text was confusing as hell. Was he being friendly? Was he flirting?

"Fuck," Sky breathed as he dropped his chin on my shoulder.

• • •

I marched into the computer lab with purpose. I was prepared for anything River had to throw at me. Any punishment she wanted to dish out. But she was relaxed, sitting at the front desk, her strawberry-red hair in a bun and a scowl aimed at the computer. "Riv," I said as I came up to the desk. "I have to apologize to you."

"For what?" She turned her big eyes on me with a frown.

"You left me to close up last night, but I lost track of time and didn't close until after eleven."

River blinked at me. "You're always on top of the time. So why were you distracted?"

"I got in the groove of my artwork after helping Taka."

"Oh, the one with the marketing assignment?" She tapped the pen she was holding on the notepad in front of her. She wiggled her eyebrows suggestively. "You two seemed to hit it off."

I felt myself blushing. "Shut up, Riv. We hit it off as friends, that's all."

"Friends," she whispered before pursing her lips.

"Don't you start, too. Sky already gave me crap. It isn't like that."

"Okay, if you say so," she said, raising her hands in surrender.

I shrugged her off, making my way into the workstation room to settle in my usual spot.

I pulled my drawing tablet and pen from my bag, then connected them to the computer. This short animation was due in a week, and now that my laptop was out of commission, I had to use every moment I could in this lab before closing. I was sure River would let me stay after hours, but I didn't want to abuse our friendship or my position as an employee.

I fell into the deep focus I always did, listening to music and gliding the electronic pen across the tablet. It wasn't the same as having a real pencil and paper in hand; it was a different type of art. Still soothing and beautiful, with more forgiveness than traditional art. I used to think I would be a fine-arts student and get my art into a gallery or sell my paintings for hundreds of dollars, but that was a pipe dream. I realized all too quickly that if I wanted to make a living with art, it would need to be something I could market, and digital art was one of the best options.

My dream was to freelance. People would pay me a ton of money to have a custom painting printed and framed. I had been planning the freelance avenue since the previous year. As a junior, I still had enough time to complete a portfolio and build the website before I got deep into graduation preparations. I pushed the thoughts of my future to the side and dove back into my project. School needed to be my focus for now.

CHAPTER 8

TAKA

Nick never responded to my text, but he said he would forget to reply a lot. And yet, I couldn't help the twinge of unease that crept into my chest because he didn't answer.

For the first time since high school, I had dreamed about another man. I thought I had pushed those types of thoughts away. Suppressed them to where they no longer plagued me. I had done so well at ignoring this side of me, I almost forgot what I was. Who I was.

"Taka, did you get the help you needed in the computer lab yesterday?" Casey asked as he dropped into the chair beside me.

"I did. Thank you for telling me about them. They helped me a lot."

"Good." He smiled and pulled his laptop from his bag. "They're a bunch of weirdos, though, didn't you think?"

"What do you mean?"

"Y'know, those art students. They're a little weird."

I shrugged and chewed the inside of my cheek. "I don't know. I only met two people, and they were very nice."

"Oh, maybe the weird guy wasn't there yesterday. You'll know him when you see him." He leaned back and scrolled through his phone.

I didn't really use social media and didn't understand the appeal. I had a Facebook account but barely touched it; I don't think I even knew my password anymore.

"Good afternoon, class," the professor said as he strode into the room.

In an instant, he had jumped into his lecture. I fought to pay attention as my mind wandered back to Nick again and again, and I hated myself for it. It had been years since someone consumed my thoughts this way. Despite wanting it to stop, a small part of me resisted. That tiny part of me wanted to let it happen.

• • •

I hovered at the door to the computer lab. My mind was filled with Nick. How nice it was to talk to him. How it would feel to run my fingers over his skin. How he would react if I asked to see his whole tattoo.

I pushed through the door into the silence of the computer lab, shaking the thoughts from my mind.

"You're back," the pink-haired girl said from behind the counter. "Do you need a workstation again?"

"Yes," I said, taking the sign-in sheet from her.

She was looking intently at me, and I tried to ignore her. It was rude to stare that way. When I handed back the sign-in sheet, she said simply, "Nick's in there." But the way she said it—with a hint of smirk—told me I had been the topic of discussion. I was torn between thrill and horror at the idea.

"Thanks," I replied with an awkward smile.

Though my stomach fluttered with joy on hearing he was there, I reprimanded myself for the feeling. I walked past her toward the lab and lingered in the doorway for a moment. Nick's attention was on the screen. Headphones covered his ears and a tablet lay on the desk before him. He wore another hoodie, a dark gray one with white lettering running along the arms, and worn jeans that hugged his thighs.

Two others were in the room, sitting with their backs to me, chatting and working with software similar to the one I used yesterday. I moved closer, hesitating, before tapping Nick's shoulder. "Hi," I said as he looked up at me.

"Hi, Taka," he said, pulling the headphone from his ear. "I didn't expect you back so soon," he added.

"I like to complete my assignments as early as possible." I chewed the inside of my cheek, mulling over my excuse. My assignment wasn't due for a week. I didn't have to be here today, but I wanted to see him.

"Did you need some help today, or are you good with where we left off last night?"

"I think I'm okay, but I'll let you know if I need more help."

I sank into the chair at the same workstation I used the day before and switched the power on. The fans whirred. My heart thumped, and my hands shook as I plugged in my USB drive. It was odd for me to be this nervous around someone, but I couldn't control it. No matter how often I told myself to relax, my nerves were in overdrive.

Time passed in silence, and before I knew it, my project was complete. My reason for seeing him was over. I should have been slower. I should have made it last longer, but the faster I finished, the quicker I could get out of his presence. It was a good thing to take temptation away. And he most surely was a temptation.

Nick appeared behind me as I was about to close the program. "You finished it?" he asked.

I nodded. I didn't trust myself to speak.

"Here, let me," he said.

Then, to my surprise, he laid his hand over mine, which was cupping the mouse. His hand was hot as it guided my hand and the mouse. His chest pressed softly against my shoulder, and I could smell the scent of his sweet, woodsy cologne. His presence lingered on my back, sending a wave of warmth over me. "You did a great job on the project. You have a natural eye for composition and design," he said.

I did? I always thought creativity was beyond me.

"It's nothing special," I said.

He turned his face toward mine. "Seriously. I don't say that to everyone. Credit where credit's due."

My heart raced as I tilted my head, making eye contact. When our eyes met, my breath caught. His eyes were ablaze with excitement, as if seeing my assignment gave him joy. My stomach somersaulted, and I swallowed my nerves as too many emotions to comprehend swept over me. "Thank you," I whispered. I so rarely received praise, but I took the gift from Nick with gratitude.

His smile faltered as he stepped back, leaving a cold emptiness in his wake. "I was coming over to ask if you wanted to grab dinner with me, but it looks like you're done. Would you be interested in dinner still?"

"Yes," I said without thinking, but it was too late to take it back. "Give me a few minutes."

He nodded and wandered around the lab as I sat, staring at the dark monitor before packing away my things. A few minutes later, he was waiting for me in the doorway, chatting and laughing with someone on the other side of the wall. A twinge of fear forced its way in as I watched him. Did he treat everyone the way he treated me? Had I misread him?

I approached him. "Ready," I said, my voice small and shaky.

"You okay?" He glanced at me, drawing his eyebrows together.

I plastered on a smile, hoping to hide my inner turmoil. "I'm fine."

Why did it have to be this person who made me feel this way? Poking holes in my carefully constructed walls; walls I worked so hard to build. I tried so hard to bury these kinds of thoughts. Why was it so challenging to do the same with him? He would hate me if he knew the truth. Anyone would. Who could blame them?

I was unnatural. Abnormal.

Disgusting.

I learned at a very young age how the world views men in romantic relationships with each other. I used to think I was confused, that I only liked them as friends, nothing more. In sixth grade, I proved it wasn't confusion. While on the school camping trip, I kissed Owen in the bathroom under the cover of night. I liked him. Truly liked him. Then, in ninth grade, I secretly dated Juan for a year. Breaking up with him was a cruel experience, but I was too scared of getting caught. The thought of being found out terrified me. I knew my father's opinion on it, so I shut off those feelings. I buried them deep down. Locked them away, hidden from the world. I was grateful that I also liked women and could shield myself from detection in their company. After Juan, I had small crushes on guys but, thankfully, never felt the need to act on them. This situation was no different: I would not act on my feelings.

"Is the food court okay with you?" Nick asked as we left the computer lab behind. "I only have thirty minutes and can't go too far."

"Food court is fine with me."

Nick glanced back at me again, a look of doubt in his eyes.

Was I acting weird?

It was taking all of my strength to contain my unraveling emotions. I had put my mask back on and would return to being the respectable young man my parents expected—needed—me to be. The man they raised me to be. Nick was only, and would only ever be, a friend. Period.

CHAPTER 9

NICK

We grabbed food from a vendor in the food court. I didn't care what I got and ordered at random. Taka led the way to a small table at the corner of the seating area, which was mostly empty. His face was flushed, and I couldn't read his expression. Fear? Worry? Regret? Had I made him uncomfortable by touching him? Perhaps he was here to tell me to back off.

His final product surprised me, and I meant what I said. His understanding of composition and design was phenomenal for someone who'd never done anything like it before. I didn't think about my actions until I was already bent over him, immediately high on the scent of his hair—a delicate floral aroma. And the softness of his fingers pressed against my palm was intoxicating. I should never do it again. This should be the last time I see him.

"Hey," a deep voice called from a few feet away. "Taka." A guy, clearly a frat boy, jogged toward us. His sandy blond hair was unkempt, but in a way that was somehow attractive. In an instant, the odd expression was wiped from Taka's face, replaced by the most insincere smile I'd ever seen. The transition made me squirm.

"Hi, Casey. Good to see you." Taka shifted toward the guy, resting his arm over the back of his chair.

"What are you doing here? Aren't you usually home by now?" Casey asked, glancing at me.

Taka nodded in my direction. "I was in the computer lab wrapping up my assignment with Nick's help."

I nodded with a half-smile. My mother raised me to be polite in any situation, and I couldn't shake the training.

Then a girl appeared. Her makeup was light, and her long black hair was tied back in a French braid with fly-away strands falling into her face. Her saucer-like, sky-blue eyes peered at Taka, and her face filled with joy.

"Izzie," Taka said, his voice strained, like someone had punched him in the gut.

"Baby," she said as she leaned over him, planting a kiss on his lips. "I've been looking all over for you. Why aren't you answering your phone?"

"I have been working on an important project," Taka said, red in the face. He looked like he wanted to run.

I wanted to run, too. My gut instinct about him had been right after all. I had no chance with him. The disappointment I'd been avoiding finally caught me, sucking all of my hope away. I couldn't believe I had actually thought . . . I felt like an idiot. I knew I had been imagining it all. He was simply a nice guy being friendly to me.

When the girl pulled away, Taka looked defeated.

The boorish blond guy aimed his gaze at me. "Yo, Nick, what's your last name?"

I tilted my head to the side. "Me?"

"Yes, obviously."

"I fail to see why you need that information."

He glanced down at Taka, then back at me. "Weren't you the guy who got into a fight with my frat brothers a couple years ago?"

Taka's head shot up, eyes wide as he stared at me over his half-eaten food.

I groaned, leaning back in my chair and crossing my arms over my chest. Just what I needed.

"People still remember that?" I said.

"Get this, Taka," said Casey. "This guy attacked Charlie and Jax a couple years ago, and they were all almost kicked out of school over it. Your new friend nearly ruined a lot of people's futures. I told you the guys in the computer lab were a bunch of weirdos." He flashed a smug grin as he gripped the back of Taka's chair.

"I didn't attack them. It was a fight. I was defending myself and my friends," I said, glancing at Taka.

"A bunch of gays," Casey added, a sneer on his lips.

It took every ounce of self-control not to reach over and smash his face in, but I couldn't get into more trouble on university grounds. Not for some worthless scum like this. After the brawl freshman year, the university administration warned that if anything like that ever happened again, my scholarship would be revoked, and they would remove me from my program. Nothing was worth risking that.

The girl's cold gaze slithered over me like I was a parasite.

"Why are you hanging out with him, baby? Your father wouldn't approve of you hanging out with a violent troublemaker, especially one who's . . . you know."

Damn, this was why I didn't make new friends. It always came down to my sexuality. I shifted under Taka's gaze. Was it shock? Disgust?

I stood, pushing the chair out hard enough that it fell. The clatter drew attention from around the food court. I let them gape open-mouthed at me. What did I care? "I'll see ya," I said to Taka and walked away. I didn't have the guts to look back.

• • •

A knock stirred me from my self-deprecating thoughts.

Standing at my bedroom door was a fuming Sky and his friend William Greene. Will's dark hair was kept short, and he had a mole above his lip. Next to Sky, Will was a giant, though he was an inch shorter than me and packed with muscle. Even beneath his black long-sleeved shirt, his muscles were well defined. Probably a part of why Sky liked him so much, other than he was absolutely infatuated with Sky and would do anything for him. The pair had been dating off and on since freshman year, but Sky always ended things when he thought Will was getting too serious. I had a feeling Sky's flightiness was wearing on him.

"Join us in the living room," Sky said.

"Come on, guys. I just want to be left alone."

"You should talk about this," Will said.

I sighed like a bored teenager. "Why?"

Sky folded his arms. "Do I need to spell it out?"

I knew what he was referring to. He knew my history and that I could spiral. It wasn't fair of me to deny him his need to be there for me, to look out for me.

I headed to the kitchen and grabbed a bottle of vodka from the cabinet, courtesy of River, who was twenty-one. "I don't really want to talk about it." I popped open the top and poured it into a shot glass.

"Well, I want to talk about it," Sky said. "I told you it was a bad idea to get involved with that guy." He turned to Will. "He ignores all of my warnings."

"You told me to ask him out five minutes after meeting him!" I said.

"But that's before I knew he was straight. He is, right? That's why you're upset?" Sky said.

I downed the vodka and poured another. "Partly."

Sky leaned back on the sofa, watching me as I downed another shot. "What else, then?"

I sighed. "He looked so, so—shocked."

"What do you mean?" Will asked.

"Shocked you're gay?" said Sky.

I shook my head. "I think he knew that."

"Then what?" Sky demanded.

"That fight, remember? The one with the frat guys in freshman year."

"That was three years ago."

"Right? How did that guy, Casey, even remember me? Was I that memorable to this asshole that, after nearly three years, he picks me out like my face is burned into his memory?"

"Dude, come sit down and bring me a glass, too." Sky rubbed his face and dropped his head back on the sofa. "I barely remember that night. I couldn't tell you who was there."

I handed them both shot glasses and sat in the armchair across from them, pouring another shot for myself before setting the bottle on the coffee table. "Taka looked shocked. I wasn't able to give him a proper explanation. But from what his girlfriend said, I don't think he'd be sympathetic to my side."

Sky downed his shot, then set the glass on the table. "Sorry, dude. Both straight and anti-gay. That's a double blow."

We all drank a shot, mourning the state of the world. After a respectful pause, Sky said, "So, I brought Will here tonight for a reason."

"A threesome?" I asked, wryly, trying to lighten the moment.

"No, smartass. Apparently, Will and Taka run in the same social circles."

A wave of dizziness hit me as I turned my attention to Will. *Damn, I drank too fast*, I thought. "How do you know him?" I asked.

"Our moms know each other. Taka and I never hung out before college, though. My mom, she's Thai, was always looking for non-American friends when she moved to the States, so she joined a community group when I was a kid, and that's where they met." He paused a moment, rubbing his chin like he was debating if he should continue. "You can't tell anyone what I'm going to tell you, okay?"

"Who would I tell?"

Will nodded before continuing. "When I was in high school, I heard a rumor about Taka and a guy hooking up. Taka never came out and never spoke of anything, so I thought it was a rumor and left it at that. His parents are rigid, and his dad puts a lot of pressure on him."

I blew out a breath. "Do you think the rumor could've been true?" Hope flooded through me, but that girl's face flashed in my mind and twisted my stomach into knots.

"It wasn't anything concrete. It was only a rumor. I've only ever seen him date women. But he could be bi. Or he could be gay but hiding it."

"I hope the women weren't all like the one I met today."

"What was she like?" Sky asked, a little too interested.

I glared at the floor. "Shoulda heard the way she spoke to him."

"It's obviously complicated for him," Will warned. "Might be best if you steer clear."

"Will's right. You barely know him. It's better to go through the grief and disappointment now," Sky said.

"Yeah, yeah." I sighed and puffed out a soft laugh. "Let's drink some more. Help me get over this grief and disappointment faster."

"Sure, buddy. I'll take one for the team." Sky chuckled as he poured us all another round, then raised his glass. "Cheers."

"Cheers," I said, tapping my glass to theirs. The alcohol went down smoothly; a sign of how much I'd already had. "Cheers to being gay in America."

CHAPTER 10

TAKA

Nick marched away without a second glance. He must have been furious. The whole food court was watching us, waiting for something to happen.

Casey had smirked at me as if I were a conspirator. Assuming I was disgusted by what I'd heard. Instead, I was terrified that Casey's disgust would be turned on me if he saw that I was excited, relieved even.

Casey hovered beside me, whispering his hateful words to Iz and me as we watched Nick walk away. If he knew the real me, would he say the same things? Would he hate me because I'm not normal?

Casey picked up the chair that Nick had knocked over and sat. "Did you know, T?"

I didn't reply, only continued to stare at the table like it had all the answers.

"Shut up, Casey. T isn't like that, so it wouldn't matter if he knew or not," Izzie said, her words grating on my nerves. She didn't speak for me, but she often did, assuming what I felt, what I believed.

"I'll bet he's interested in you," Casey said. "I've never seen him hang out with anyone but those weirdoes from the art department."

My stomach turned sour, and I tasted bile. If I said something, would Casey treat me the same as Nick? Would he call me names and belittle me too? Would Izzie join in? She appeared closer to neutral, but the way she spoke to Nick made me think she was no better than Casey.

"You should stay away from him, T," Casey said.

Who was he to give me an order? Scorching heat shot through my veins, as if I had finally reached the end of the thin line that I had been walking my whole life. I picked up my bag and stood in a smooth, quick motion. I was standing at the edge of a cliff, about to jump. Where was I heading? I couldn't see the bottom, but I knew I couldn't ignore how much their words hurt. "I didn't know you were such assholes," I declared.

Without looking at either of them, I quickly retreated. My heart pounded as I raced out of the cafeteria and across campus to the parking garage. The intense rays of the setting sun bounced off the windshield as I pressed the button, unlocking the doors of my car. The sleek black paint called to me, inviting me to escape from the world, protected within its strong form.

Hold it together. Another second, and I'll be safe.

I gripped the handle, swung the door open, and slid into the seat of my S2000. She had been my project for the past three years. I put my heart and soul into building the car, and she gave me the escape I needed. I gripped the lime-green gear shift, checking it was in neutral. My foot hit the clutch as I slid the key in and turned her on. The rumble of the engine caused vibrations to run through me. Pure physical pleasure. One thing had always helped me relax: the feeling of a car under my command. I needed it. Especially when I was speeding along quiet roads. Euphoric was the only word for it.

Gauges flashed their stats, indicating she was ready. I gripped the steering wheel and dropped the e-break before sliding the gear into first. The first tap of my foot on the gas ignited my soul.

I didn't want to go home yet. I crawled out of the parking garage so that I could listen to the growl bouncing off the concrete walls. The feeling of a slow crawl must be the same feeling jockeys get as they ride their horse up to the gates before a race: the feeling that you're about to enter a realm of freedom like no other.

I turned out of the garage and onto the quiet road that circled around the university and headed toward the back roads. The sun was falling behind the trees as I turned down the road that led to a hidden straightaway I knew. The section of road was near warehouses and junkyards, in the middle of nowhere, far enough outside city limits that no one would hear me; the only sign of my being there would be the tire tracks inevitably left behind.

I stopped at the end of the road, my rearview reflecting the bright red of my taillights cast over the chain-link gates to the junkyard. I gripped the steering wheel, scanning the dark road ahead. My heart was racing. My hands were shaking. An uncontrollable smirk formed on my lips, and I launched.

Tires squealed as they fought for traction. Pops erupted from the exhaust, and I was flying. I didn't let up. I reveled in the sound of the turbo spool before I shifted up again. Then again. When I reached the flagpole near the end of the straightaway, I finally let off the gas, and the engine roared as it angrily decelerated at my command. I came to a stop and laughed. All the tension had vanished from my body; my mind was clear.

Calm enough now for regular roads, I pulled away and left the area, heading down the back roads toward my house. My chest was light, and nothing in the world existed outside of me and my car.

The engine was silenced when I pulled the key from the ignition inside the garage of my family home. My spot was the furthest on the right of the three-car garage. The other two spots were my parents'. Tamiko was still too young to drive, but by the time she was old enough to have her own car, I would be living on my own and she could take my place.

The house was warm and bright. Laughter came from the living room. I kicked off my shoes and headed in; my fingers tightened around my bag like it was my life buoy. Reality was sinking in again. The adrenaline of my drive and the subsequent euphoria was wearing off.

Mom and Tami were curled up together on the sofa. They were glued to some TV show while my father sat in his armchair reading a book with his glasses resting low on his small nose.

I loved them, but I didn't feel like they knew me. They didn't see me. I had always been the son and brother they expected me to be. But it was wearing on me. I felt fragile, like I was teetering on the edge of something. One wrong move and I would fall.

"Taka, you're late," my father said as he looked up from his book.

"Sorry, Dad, I was at school and then went for a drive."

He released a grumble, showing his unhappiness, but it was only for show. He didn't mind that I went for drives. Rather, the grumble was for my mother, who freaked out whenever I got home late.

"There's dinner in the fridge if you're hungry," Mom called from the sofa.

"Thanks, I'll grab some."

I warmed up the plate of food Mom left me and gulped it down at the kitchen table. I watched the TV show from the corner of my eye. It was the latest crime drama they were obsessed with. Dad and I didn't understand the appeal, but Mom and Tami seemed to love it.

It was hard to be the person they wanted after today. I knew I needed to return to him. The perfect son. Perfect brother. Yet, a part of me begged not to. A growing part of me wanted to be seen.

• • •

The dormitory was peaceful as I marched through the wing of the large U-shaped building. Izzie lived on the second floor on the west side, furthest from the entrance.

Last night's events helped me come to a decision after months of debating with myself. Izzie didn't explicitly say the same things that Casey did, but she was still complicit, and she didn't understand why I was angry with her. She had texted me all night asking me to forgive her, but she couldn't understand why she needed to be forgiven. Our relationship had been sitting on my mind with the weight of a planet. It was nothing like it used to be because I didn't love her anymore. After two years together, I admitted I was lying to myself and everyone—again—leaving me with an overwhelming sense of emptiness. I felt like a lifeless shell, devoid of emotion.

With every breath, my body tensed, and a heaviness settled in my chest. She would be like all of my exes and tell me how this had come out of nowhere, that we were happy only yesterday.

But it was me. The problem was me.

I probably stayed with her for too long. I tried to fix it. I did, but…

I knocked on the door, and Izzie's roommate, Maddison, greeted me in a towel. Her blonde hair was still soaked, dripping water down her shoulders.

"Oh, Taka," she said, tugging the towel tighter as she stepped back to let me in.

"Hey, Maddison. Sorry to bother you this early in the morning," I said, sidestepping her and turning away so she wouldn't be uncomfortable.

"It's fine. I'll get Izzie." She swiveled and disappeared down the hallway toward their shared bathroom.

A few moments later, Izzie was walking down the hallway. Her long black hair was wet and tied back in a bun. She wore her usual gray sports bra and black sweatpants. Seeing her now, as beautiful as she was, confirmed that love was gone, at least in the romantic sense.

"Taka? What are you doing here so early?"

"Can we talk in your room?"

I hated this part. It always left me feeling like an asshole.

Her eyebrows dipped, and a thin frown tugged on her lips. "Everything okay?"

I cleared my throat and followed her into her bedroom. I stood as stiff as a log, staring at her as I mustered the courage to break her heart.

But there was no other way; I had to dive into this hell.

"Izzie, you know I care for you, right?" She nodded, but kept her eyes trained on me, almost as if she sensed what was coming. "But I want to break up."

Silence.

Then, her voice low and steady, she asked, "Is this about what happened yesterday?"

I shook my head. "I've been thinking a lot about my feelings, Izzie. I love you, but it's not the love a romantic relationship should have as a foundation."

Her hands balled into fists, but her face remained calm. "What does that mean?"

"I'm no longer in love with you." I rubbed my hand over my mouth as we stared each other down. "I no longer feel that way about you."

She looked at me, her fists still clenched.

I took a deep breath. It was time for me to be truly honest. "I don't mean to sound harsh, Iz, but I don't think my feelings are even platonic at this point. And that is because of what happened yesterday."

"Are you for real?" Her eyes shimmered with the threat of tears.

"I'm sorry," I said.

"How long?"

"How long what?"

Her voice raised as her shoulders tensed. "How long have you been lying to me? How long have you been pretending?"

I ran my hand over the back of my neck, rubbing the tight muscles. When was I not pretending? My whole life was built on pretending. "I don't know," I replied. "I realized yesterday. Before that, I didn't know I was pretending."

Her face grew red as she looked expectantly at me. "I gave up my dreams of going to a school in California for you."

"I never asked you to do that."

She sucked in a tight breath and rolled her eyes. "You didn't have to ask me. I did it because we had talked about marriage!"

"You can't blame me for that, Iz. I never once asked you to come to this school. I never once asked you to stay for me."

She snorted loudly as she crossed her arms. "Are you fucking joking?"

"Why would I joke about this?" I ran my fingers through my hair, hating this entire situation. "I can't see our future together. I can't picture us getting married and having kids. That image I used to have in my head is gone."

"Answer me, Takahiro, what's changed?" She stepped toward me, cheeks burning red and tears streaming down her face.

"I saw a different side of you yesterday, and it made me see everything in a new light." Even if it hadn't been for the way she treated Nick, I would have made the decision, eventually. Yesterday was merely my excuse to do what I knew needed to be done.

"Why do you care about that guy? He beat on Casey's friends. You're ending it because I'm on Casey's side?"

She wouldn't understand. It was beyond my ability to explain and hers to comprehend. I needed to bring this conversation to a conclusion before I said something I would regret.

“The fact you cannot see why I was upset about what happened proves my point. We are not on the same page, Iz. It’s time to go our separate ways.”

She stared at me, anger boiling in her eyes.

“I can’t believe you right now,” she said through the quiver in her lips.

The shaking in her voice ripped apart my heart. I didn’t much like her in that moment, but I am not a cruel person. Besides, we were friends before we started dating. Now she was a part of my family. My mother adored her. Tami looked up to her. They were all close. After bringing her so close to my family, I was ripping her out of our lives. I had not done it deliberately; I truly had thought I would love her forever.

“I’m sorry, Iz. I didn’t want to hurt you.”

“Get out.”

“I’m sorry. I hope you can forgive me one day.”

“Get out!”

The sob that rolled out of her chilled my bones, and I left her dorm in a fog. Every single time, I was the asshole, despite the fact that I always worked hard to keep them happy and feeling loved, even when I wasn’t happy. So why was it that no one ever bothered to worry about me? No one ever asked how I felt. No one cared to know.

• • •

Unable to concentrate on my assignments, I pushed my notebooks to the side and leaned back against the headboard.

It had been days since the incident. Days since my breakup. My mind had been in a clouded haze ever since. I barely cared that my marketing assignment received an A. Casey had given me an apology, which I had no choice but to accept, and was his usual self, but I couldn't look at him the same and kept my distance as much as possible. It wasn't me he needed to apologize to. I didn't think our friendship could be the same anymore. I had even stopped speaking to my fraternity, too afraid to hear their opinions on the matter.

Every pledge in the fraternity was assigned a mentor, our big brother. We called them our Big. They provided guidance and support to their little brother, their mentee. Next year I would receive my own brother to mentor. I trusted Jax, my Big, but I felt conflicted knowing Jax had been involved in the fight with Nick in their freshman year. When I didn't attend fraternity meetings after a couple days, Jax called me, warning me I could get into a lot of trouble if I didn't attend meetings and events, but I couldn't bring myself to face them. It was inevitable that they would stand by Casey's side.

Dad was furious because I missed the fundraiser. He still donated money, but he lectured me on my unprofessional behavior.

"A minor argument with a brother is no reason to skip out on your duties," he said when he found out.

I couldn't tell him what the fight was about. I couldn't tell him why I broke up with Izzie. Everyone was confused and angry with me. Tami cried for two days when she realized Iz would no longer be her big sister. And Mom was beside herself.

She had accepted Izzie with open arms, welcoming her into our home and our lives. No one could understand how I could end it without warning. All of this drove home the fact that none of them knew me, like a sharp knife cutting into my heart. It was an incredibly lonely feeling. While surrounded by people claiming to love me, I was invisible.

A wave of guilt engulfed me as I contemplated the pain that someone else had endured due to this situation. I hadn't seen Nick since that evening. I couldn't decide if that was a good or bad thing. If we continued to get to know each other, would I give in to myself? The distance was probably best. I wanted to go back to normal. Back to the version of me that pretended everything was fine. But something was changing in me, and Nick was on my mind. I couldn't shake him from my thoughts. My carefully crafted mask was slipping, and I didn't know how to put it back on.

I mulled over a plan for hours, my impatience finally got the best of me. I wanted to see him.

The clock on the bedside table read six-fifteen. Changing into jeans and sneakers, I tugged on a sweatshirt and grabbed my keys off the dresser. I *needed* to see him. But first, I needed to visit the electronics store.

While standing in the store, I googled the best laptop for digital art. I didn't know what I was doing or trying to accomplish, but I found one and bought it. I placed it in the passenger seat, inside a black bag, and drove to campus. For the first time in years, I allowed my emotions to take control and didn't try to rein them in.

The hallway leading to the computer lab was empty. The only sound came from my footsteps and the swaying bag I held.

"Hi, Taka," said a soft voice from beside me. The pink-haired girl pushed the door to the lab open and held it for me.

"I'm looking for Nick," I said, boldly.

"He left a few minutes ago. Sorry."

"I thought he was here all the time."

She nodded as she made her way around the reception desk. "Yeah, but it's nearly ten. We're closing for the day."

"Oh," I breathed. How did I not realize the time? "Do you know where I can find him? It's important."

She pursed her lips, giving me a once-over. "Don't you have his number?"

I chewed the inside of my cheek as I thought through excuses, but I couldn't find one. "Something happened, and now Nick is ignoring me."

"What happened?"

"It's complicated."

She kept her gaze on me for a minute, like she was trying to decipher my intentions. Once she made her choice, she jotted something down on a sticky note. "You didn't get it from me. As his manager, I'm not allowed to do this, but as his friend, I hope you find what you're looking for." She handed me the note and turned her attention to the computer.

"Thank you," I said, turning around and marching out of the lab.

She'd given me his address.

CHAPTER 11

NICK

I sighed heavily and sank onto the hard metal bench. I closed my eyes and breathed in the cool air, debating why I hadn't listened to my gut. From the first moment I saw him, I knew Taka was trouble. Knew it was a bad idea to have hope. So, why was I drawn to him, knowing it would hurt me in the end?

Normally, I wouldn't be so upset about someone throwing hate my way. That kind of behavior hadn't bothered me in a long time. This time, though, felt different.

Someone nearby cleared their throat.

I didn't want to look, but it felt like I was being stared at, so I cracked my eyes open. Taka was looking at me from a few feet away, a black bag clutched in his hand.

If God was real, he was cruel.

"What's up?" I asked.

His face lit up for a moment, sending warmth into my heart.

He said, "I wanted to talk. Do you mind?"

"Sure." I motioned for him to sit beside me.

He landed beside me, the bag rustling as he sat it between his feet. "I'm sorry about what happened."

"I'm used to it. It's been a long time since I let people's words get to me."

Taka chewed the inside of his lip. I wanted to grab his face and stop the behavior before he chewed a hole through his cheek.

"Used to it? How can anyone be used to it?" he asked.

A heavy sigh escaped me. "Taka, I've been open and out since high school. That guy said the same shit I've heard for years. At this point, it's just stupid and not worth my time."

"It bothered me."

"Why?"

"Because I thought of you as a friend. Or I want to be friends with you. But people I thought were good showed me a side of them I didn't like, and I don't think I can accept."

"Was that the first time you've seen them behave that way?"

Taka nodded, leaning forward and resting his elbows on his knees. "I didn't know what to say when it happened."

Silence hovered between us.

Taka stared at his shoes, moving his feet on the concrete. "I broke up with my girlfriend. Not exactly because of what happened to you, but it was the final nail in the coffin." He released a breath, rubbing his hands together. His shoulders were tense, and he looked as if he hadn't slept in days. "She was complacent about Casey's behavior. I would say she contributed to it with what she said about you." He released a choked sound, like he wasn't sure if he should laugh or cry. "I was the worst of it. I couldn't say anything until after you left, and even then, I only called them assholes." He picked up the bag and handed it to me. "Take this as an apology gift. Don't open it until you're home, please."

Curiosity had me reeling as I looped my fingers through the handle, brushing against his chilled skin as I did so. I put it on the bench beside me. He seemed nervous, as if deciding whether to run away now that he'd handed off the gift. "You didn't need to get me anything."

"I wanted to," he said as he stood. "I have to go, but is it okay if we hang out sometime?"

Should I allow this to keep going?

"I enjoy our time together. I know we just met, but I would like to get to know you more." He swallowed and chewed his lip. "Also, I got an A on that assignment you helped me with. The gift is also a thank you for your help."

"Sure." I nodded, unsure of what else to say. I knew I couldn't be friends with Taka, yet I wanted to see him more. Talk to him more. I knew I was breaking my own rules, the boundaries I set in place for people like him, but when he stood in front of me like this, asking to be in my life, I couldn't deny him. I couldn't restrain myself. I didn't want to.

"Good. I'll see you later." Taka stepped back a few feet before turning around and disappearing down the path.

• • •

The keys jangled against one another and felt heavy in my hand as I unlocked my apartment door. I lingered in the doorway, encased in darkness, before laying the bag on the kitchen counter.

Taka and I didn't know much about each other, so why was he buying me an apology gift?

Turning on the electric kettle, I eyed the bag. I wanted to open it but also wanted the anticipation to last. The little voice at the back of my mind kept telling me not to think too deeply about it. He probably felt bad, as he'd said, and the gift would be nothing more than a token of regret. Not that I felt he had much to apologize for. I had suspected that Taka had friends like Casey. How could he not, being in a fraternity? People like them flocked to those kinds of social clubs. But the way Taka had looked earlier, it felt like more than an apology gift.

The kettle flicked off. I grabbed a mug from the cabinet and a teabag, then poured in the boiling water. While the tea steeped, I changed into sweatpants before returning to the kitchen. The black bag still sat on the countertop—untouched, full of possibility.

My phone buzzed in my pocket, and I quickly picked it up. Sky's name lit up the phone screen. How did he always catch me at times like this? It was like he received alerts to his brain every time I was in a tough situation.

I touched the answer icon and leaned my hip against the counter.

"Yo, Nick," he yelled through the phone. "I'm on my way home right now. Are you there?"

"I am. Got here a few minutes ago."

"We'll talk when I get there, then. I'll see you in five."

He hung up before I could say anything more.

A few minutes later, Sky kicked off his shoes before he bounded to the sofa, and I poured another round of hot water into my mug before joining him.

“What’s up?” I asked, sitting beside him, resting my arm on the back of the sofa. “Come on. You called me out of nowhere to make sure I was home.”

“Will asked me to be his boyfriend.”

Whenever Will wanted to get serious, Sky always ran away. It had been like this for nearly three years. Poor Will was probably on the verge of giving up, but he loved Sky more than anything. “And how did that go?” He was on our sofa, so I assumed he had run away again.

“Not well,” he said, releasing a puff of air as he leaned against the cushions. “You know how I am. The whole ‘slap a label on it and magically we’re different,’ isn’t for me.”

“Sky,” I scolded. “I know you love him. Why keep stringing him along?”

He drew his lips together and groaned.

“Nick, I’m not like you. I don’t like the idea of being tied down to another person, but I can’t seem to let this one go.”

“But you’re basically an item right now.”

“It isn’t the same. We aren’t exclusive.”

“No way, Sky! Are you with other people too?”

“Sometimes.”

“Does he know that?”

He dropped his gaze to the side. “I think so.”

I dropped my head back and ran my palm down my face. “I can’t believe you right now.”

“I like him a lot, Nick,” he said and sank deeper into the sofa. “But I don’t know about proper relationships.”

“I know you don’t, but there is going to come a time when he will realize that you’re never coming around, and then it will be too late for you.” I paused a moment, letting Sky mull over my words while I sipped my tea. "I'm not telling you to change for him, but I think it's time you decided: shit or get off the pot."

His cheek twitched, and his eyes softened. "Charming choice of words, bro." He looked at me with a frown.

Conversations like this usually ran for hours. Sky would review his relationship history with me before he avoided Will for days. Then the cycle started again. But I had other things on my mind. I got up and found my way to the kitchen, passing by the black bag that I still refused to open, and dropped my mug in the sink. I went into my room and dipped into my closet to grab a shirt.

When I returned to the living room, Sky was asleep, looking like a corpse that had been tossed onto the sofa. His feet were on the floor, his torso twisted awkwardly, and his head rested on his shoulder. I adjusted him, making sure he was comfortable, before draping a soft blanket over him.

Overcome with tiredness, I decided to leave the bag unopened so that I would have something to look forward to in the morning and went to bed.

• • •

My alarm went off at seven, and I begrudgingly rolled out of bed, dragging myself into the kitchen where that black bag was waiting for me. Begging me to look inside.

I grabbed the French press and coffee grounds, then hit the power button on the kettle. I swiftly poured the steaming water into the French press. The warm notes of coffee hit me and immediately sent a wave of calm through my body.

That black bag kept drawing my attention, and I finally

gave in. When the bag slipped off the box, I was stunned. I snatched my hand away from it as if it had burned me. It was a new laptop. Not any old laptop but a top-of-the-line laptop that was as close as one could get to having a portable workstation. Even if I saved up for three years straight, I couldn't afford it.

I couldn't accept it. What did I do to deserve this type of gift? Was he so rich that this purchase was no big deal to him? A simple apology was worth thousands of dollars in his mind?

No way would I keep it.

As I sipped my coffee, I eyeballed the box like it was going to sprout legs and walk into my bedroom.

"Nick?" Sky drew out my name in a long question. "What the hell is that?"

He was pointing at the box I was transfixed by.

I set my coffee down. "That is an apology gift from Taka."

He hummed as he lifted the box, turning it over in awe. "Apology gift?"

I nodded. "So he said."

"You can't keep this."

"I know." I poured coffee into another mug and slid it toward him. "I'm giving it back."

"When did he even give this to you?"

"Last night. He caught me on my way home from the lab."

"Why didn't you give it back right away?"

"I didn't open it until this morning. He told me not to open it until I got home. I debated opening it last night, but I didn't think it would be a big deal. Curiosity got the best of me this morning."

"Text him right now and tell him to take it back."

I tapped my fingers on the counter. “I don’t think it will be that simple.”

“The hell it’s not!”

“Don’t worry, I won’t keep this,” I said as I slid the box back into the bag. “Let’s get ready for class.

CHAPTER 12

TAKA

A mile from campus, I parked in the tiny parking lot of Riki's café and cut off the engine. I was on edge. Another text had come in from Nick during my morning workout, and I wasn't looking forward to reading it. Finally, I opened the message. He wanted to meet up so he could give me back the laptop.

I ignored him. I wasn't taking it back.

"T!" I heard a soft voice say.

I spun around and was pleased to see my friend, Rylee. I hadn't seen her in a long time, and it was a relief to see a friendly face. I lifted her into a bear hug. We had been friends since elementary school. She knew when I kissed a boy for the first time. And she also knew why I'd never been with a man after Juan. Rylee was the only person in this world that knew the real me. No barriers. No lies. The exact reason I asked her to meet me that morning.

"Rylee. I'm so glad to see you," I said, releasing her from my grip. "You look stunning, as always."

She spun toward me with an adorable smirk. Her way of thanking me for the compliment. She wore a yellow blouse and light jeans that perfectly showed her figure, and her long black hair swayed with new braids that ended at her waistline.

Her huge bright eyes sparkled as she wrapped her arm around mine and guided me into the café. "How are you?"

"Could be worse," I said, opening the door for her. As we joined the line, I said, "Ry, it's my treat, so order whatever you want."

"Aw, you don't have to, but I will." She shot me a wink. "So, T," she said, leaning closer to me, her voice low, "what has your panties in a twist?"

"Wait until we sit."

"Fine." She pouted.

The wait for our coffee was short, and the moment my butt hit the chair, she was on me again.

"Okay, we're seated, spill."

I sipped on my coffee to prolong the inevitable. "Ry, I think I like someone."

Her thin eyebrow raised higher than I thought physically possible. "Did you not break up with Izzie, like, a week ago?"

"You don't have to remind me." I aimed a scowl at her playfully. "You know I was done with the relationship well before I even considered breaking up with her." Guilt crept into my chest again, drawing me toward the darkness.

She eyed me over the rim of her coffee cup, her deep brown eyes seeing parts of me no one else did. "Go on."

"He is..." I trailed off, knowing that those two words would need to sink in with Ry. She knew my situation. She knew the problem with my statement. "He's an art student. He's openly gay. He's easy going, good company. Everything I'm not," I said.

Ry looked at me sternly. "You know you're good company. But, yes, on the other factors, you seem like total opposites. Is he worth the risk?" she asked.

I knew the risk that she referred to was the effect on my family. I replied, "I don't know, but I can't stop thinking about him." My hands shook, so I put my mug down. The last time I admitted feelings for a guy was during my freshman year of high school. I was terrified at the time, but looking at myself now, I was no different now—no better than a high schooler.

Her tiny hand reached across the table for mine. "You know I'm here for you and always want you to be happy. I know you've likely thought about this already, but I feel I need to say it." She stared at me with such intensity that I felt like her eyes were boring holes into me. "This is big. Have you thought about your family?"

"Of course I have."

"Okay." She nodded and scooted her chair closer. "Tell me all about him."

I told Rylee everything I knew about Nicholas Dawson. Even the minuscule pieces of information I had found on the internet. He was a star art student in his high school. He had been in a youth community art group that placed the top ten artworks on display in a DC art gallery for a month each summer. They had picked Nick's work three years in a row. He won a full-ride scholarship that was only handed out to three art students at a time. SCU school officials praised him as a rising star among digital artists. I had a feeling he was great at what he did, but I never expected him to be famous, even if his fame was limited to the local area.

"I want to get to know him more. I'm not sure he is interested in me; it's just a hunch. But it's been a long time since..."

"T, let's be real here. You're very straight-passing." Rylee pursed her lips as she gave me a once-over. "You've been very careful. He might think you wouldn't be into him."

I dropped my face into my palm. "You're right."

"Why don't you make it obvious for him? Tell him."

"I don't know," I groaned, running my fingers through my hair, getting loose strands away from my eyes. "I'm nervous."

"Of course. Nobody likes offering their heart on a platter."

"It's more than that. There's my family, as you know, but I find myself drawn to him in a way I have never experienced before. If I embrace these feelings, I know I will fall for him quickly and it scares me."

Ry blew out a breath. "That's a big deal."

I hummed my agreement as I finished my coffee. "I should tread carefully."

Was I getting ahead of myself? If I was, I couldn't help it. Nick had taken over my dreams and waking thoughts. The desire to be near him outweighed all rational thought. I knew intellectually that pursuing these feelings was a bad idea, but every fiber of my being screamed for me to try. I needed Ry's blessing.

"Look, T, no one ever said you had to rush into a relationship. Why not try to be friends? Get to know him, see how things go, then decide."

"I could. But he's always working. I would need to hang out in the computer lab to see him."

"Then do it and then invite him somewhere. Show him who you are, T. Once he gets to know you, he'll love you as much as I do."

As soon as her words registered in my mind, I knew exactly what I wanted to do. I took her hand and squeezed it, saying, "I knew talking to you would be helpful."

• • •

I slipped into the computer lab around nine-thirty in the evening. It was mostly empty, only a few people here and there. Familiar pink hair poked up from behind the counter.

"Hey, Taka," River said as I approached. "Did you meet up with Nick last night?"

I nodded. "Thank you for your help."

"My pleasure." She handed me the sign-in sheet before waving me on my way. "But we're closing soon, Taka."

I felt guilty being here when I didn't need to use the workstation. My heart pounded as I stepped closer to the secluded room, and I nearly lost my nerve.

"See ya later," a deep voice called, then the guy I had seen with Nick the first night I was there came rushing out of the lab and nearly collided with me.

"Shit, sorry," he said as he hit the brakes, skirting around me. A flash of recognition crossed his features for a split second before a smirk overtook it. "Oh, the rich guy," he whispered, leaning close to my ear. "I recommend you stop leading my friend on. Even if you didn't do it on purpose, it's not cool." He patted my shoulder and walked off as quickly as he appeared.

My stomach dropped at his accusation. Had I been leading

Nick on? Did he like me but think I wasn't interested? Of course, he would think I wasn't interested; I was careful to make sure no one would.

Before stepping into the secluded lab, I pushed the thoughts away and summoned my courage. Nick was alone, scribbling away on a drawing tablet. I pulled a chair from another workstation and positioned it beside him. I could sense his displeasure as I sat. The air grew heavy with tension.

He was working on a digital painting of a woman in the center of a field of long grass. She clutched a flower to her chest with tears streaming down her cheeks. It was a gut-wrenching sight, inviting me to search for hidden meanings. I didn't know much about art, but how could such a beautiful painting be so heartbreaking? It sucked me in. The bright colors that hinted at happiness collided with the pain-stricken face of the woman.

"Why is she sad?" I asked softly.

"Her husband died," Nick said, his tone flat and emotionless. It was like he couldn't even bring himself to be courteous toward me.

Had I offended him that much with that laptop? I didn't think it would be such a huge mistake.

A tap came from the doorway. "Closing time," River said.

Nick hit the save icon and started packing his things. "You can leave now, Riv. I can close up alone."

"Sure. I already sent everyone on their way. It's just the three of us here." She offered a wave and a goodbye before leaving.

Nick made a sweep of the lab while I sat in the chair. He never glanced in my direction or sparked a conversation. The silence was agonizing.

"Can we talk a minute?" I implored, still rooted to the chair.

He moved toward me and grabbed the black bag from under the desk he'd been working at. "I'm giving this back." He shoved the bag at me.

"I don't want it back. That's yours now."

"I refuse to keep it."

"Why?"

"This isn't the kind of gift a random acquaintance gives."

He towered over me, but I refused to take the bag. "I want you to have it," I said, hoping he understood that I meant it.

"I don't want it."

"Please, Nick. Take the laptop."

"No." He dropped the bag in my lap and turned toward the doorway.

"Why are you being like this?" I grumbled as I grabbed the bag so it wouldn't slide off my lap and hit the floor.

He whirled around, cheeks flushed a deep pink, and lips curled in a snarl that sent chills down my spine. I wasn't sure of myself anymore. What was I most upset about? That he had called me a "random acquaintance?" That he didn't want the laptop, even though he desperately needed one? Or was it that he wouldn't accept it from me specifically? What gave me the right to be upset? He was right; I was an acquaintance. We were complete strangers to one another. I had no right to have expectations of him.

He gave me a long, hard look, the tension between us hanging in the air. "I'm being 'like this' because I'm confused, Taka. About you. About us."

My breath caught in my throat. As I looked into his eyes, the world seemed to melt away as if I was suspended in time.

"Happy now?" he asked, leaning against the doorframe.

I struggled to find words suitable for this situation.

Nick's expression softened as he crossed his arms. "Also, I don't like when people give me expensive gifts."

I sprang up hastily, holding onto the bag, unsure what to do.

"I did not mean to insult you, Nick. And I didn't mean to confuse you. I . . ."

I faltered. If I allowed myself to become friends with Nick, would I fall in love with him? If we became more than friends, what would my future look like?

The other side of me immediately raced to suppress those thoughts. There was no way I could do this. And my father would lose his mind. Why had I let the momentum of my conversation with Rylee bring me to this point? She would give me an ear full if I gave up now, though.

All this time, Nick was watching this internal debate playing out across my face. He stood watching, giving me space, his face showing less anger than before.

Butterflies danced in my gut. I clung to the bag, hugging it against my chest. But not a sound left my body. I couldn't even remember the last time I took a breath.

"I'll take it back. I understand."

"Good." His shoulders dropped like a mass of tension had released from him. Then a wry smile appeared. "Who the hell does that, anyway?"

I coughed out an awkward chuckle. "I'm sorry. I don't know much about computers, so I listened to the person's recommendation."

"Why were you buying me a computer?"

"I felt terrible about Casey and honestly wanted to thank you for your help."

He rolled his eyes, tilting his head back. "You're crazy if you think throwing money at people is a way to apologize. And it's my job to help you, doofus. Store-bought cookies would've been an acceptable gesture."

My only thought was to do something useful. Something that would help him. I never thought it would backfire like this. "I wanted to help you."

He ran a hand over his face. "You're such an asshole and you don't even know it." As he sat on the desk, he released a soft laugh. "I don't want handouts. I'm on a full scholarship, and having to earn and buy the things I need is a fact of life. I don't need some rich kid rushing in to be my savior."

My gaze dropped to the floor as a rush of warmth spread over my cheeks. "I'm sorry. I didn't mean anything by it. I honestly wanted to help you. It never crossed my mind that there was a boundary I would be crossing."

Nick's features softened before releasing a soft breath, like he was uncomfortable with the confrontation.

"You're forgiven. Just don't do anything like that again."

I nodded, letting the quiet of the moment pass between us. Was this the right time to invite him to hang out? I gathered my courage, looking at him a moment before asking, "Do you think we could still be friends?"

He looked at me, a little puzzled, and I was afraid he would deny me.

"Nothing wrong with that," he said.

"Thank you." Relief settled in my tense muscles. "This may be too soon or out of nowhere, but I was wondering if you like cars."

"Cars?"

"Like racing and stuff."

"I enjoy racing games. Does that count?" he asked, smirking. "Why do you ask?"

"Well, remember when you asked me about my hobbies?"

He nodded. "You said you had none and that you're boring."

I hadn't mentioned my car hobby at the time. I wasn't used to sharing with others, and it was rare for anyone to truly hold an interest in what I liked to do.

"Well, I do have something I like to do. I like cars a lot. I've done a ton of work on my car. She's my baby, and I usually go to car meets with Casey. So, I don't have anyone to join me anymore."

"Are you asking if I want to go to a car meet with you?"

My pulse pounded through my veins so hard that I could feel my heart beating everywhere, even my toes. "There's a car meet this Saturday morning before we all head to the raceway. It's an all-day affair. Usually, I leave for the meet by six, and I get home around ten that night. Sometimes people grab dinner after the meet."

"Six in the morning. You're serious?"

I dipped my head, a little disappointed. I had a feeling he wouldn't be interested. "If you don't want to come, it's fine."

He paused, considering.

"Sure, I'll go. It sounds fun."

"Seriously?"

"Yes." He laughed. "Text me what I need to know. Do you want me to meet you somewhere? I have a car, it's run down. A complete beater, but it drives."

"No, I'll pick you up. I can pick you up near your dorm, and we can head to the meet from there."

"Sounds fun," Nick said. "Let's get out of here, though. I don't need River thinking that I've forgotten what closing time means."

I laughed and followed him through the lab, clutching the laptop to my chest. I knew Rylee would praise me for taking this leap, but I was terrified of what it meant.

CHAPTER 13

NICK

The alarm on my phone blasted in my ears, jolting me from my dreamless sleep. Whatever kind of person voluntarily woke up this early on a Saturday must be out of their minds. Burying my face in the pillow, I groaned with pure regret. I fumbled in the dark for my phone, which should have been on the nightstand. It wasn't. It was precisely where I'd left it the night before—across the room.

The alarm gave up after a few minutes, but then the notifications started. A notification chimed on my phone. And then another.

"Fucking hell," I muttered.

Another chime sounded.

"Jesus," I grumbled as I raised myself from the bed. My feet touched the floor, and I took a moment, staring into the dark, contemplating my life choices with absolute dread before I finally shuffled to the dresser where my phone was charging.

With a single swipe of my finger across the screen, the phone unlocked; each ding had been a text from Taka, of course. I read the messages through the blur of my sleepy eyes.

Taka: *Hey, I hope you're awake.*

Taka: *I'll be there around 5:20.*

Taka: *Are you awake? It's close to 5.*

Was he worried I would bail? I couldn't help the grin that tugged at my lips as I typed my reply.

Me: *You're crazy for waking up this early. I feel like death warmed over.*

Seconds later, another text came in.

Taka: *I usually wake up around this time for the gym, lol. We'll have coffee at the meet. Breakfast too.*

Me: *I'm gonna need a gallon of coffee to get me started today. I'm jumping in the shower. Text me when you're here. Park in the lot behind my building.*

The small lot was meant for university staff and maintenance trucks, but this early on a Saturday, no one would notice or care if he parked there for a few minutes. I set the phone back on the dresser and got myself ready for the day. At five-ten, my phone chimed again. I was deep in my closet, trying to decide on clothing. I groaned and checked my phone. Sure enough, Taka was here ten minutes too soon.

I texted him back, telling him to come up to the apartment. I marched to the door, unlocking it so he could come in before I turned my attention back to the closet.

The weather would be sunny in the low sixties, but I debated on a T-shirt and hoodie or a long-sleeve shirt and no hoodie. Before returning to the shirt debate, I slid into my black skinny jeans and tugged on my all-black high-top Chucks. The Chucks were worn, but I loved them anyway. I finally settled on a long-sleeve gray shirt. I heard the front door close.

"One sec'," I called, slipping on my leather bracelet, my thumb brushing over the raised scars, a brief reminder of the past. With a rapid click of the clasp, I grabbed a hoodie from the shelf and emerged from the closet to be greeted with the purest form of eye candy I could ever ask for.

Every time I saw Taka, he was wearing the same style outfit: work slacks, dress shoes, and a dress shirt. Only once had I seen him in jeans and a sweater, and he managed to make that outfit look formal. But, looking at him now in black sneakers, dark jeans, a white button-up, and a sleek leather jacket, it was as if God had placed my ideal man directly in front of me.

"I like the jacket," I said, attempting to pull my jaw off the floor.

"Thanks," he said, shoving his hands in the front pockets of his jeans. The movement lowered his waistband slightly, exposing a band of smooth skin, and I about crumbled. *What I would give to . . . no, no. None of that. We're here as friends.*

"Ready?" he asked.

I drew in a breath and gathered myself. "As I'll ever be this early in the morning." I admit I was excited to spend the day with Taka, but in the same breath, I was terrified.

"Cool, we should get going. I want to get a good parking spot." He tugged his keys from his jacket pocket and led me out of the apartment, a lime-green lanyard bouncing against his thigh.

A shiver rolled down my spine as we exited the building. The streetlamps cast a soft light over the path, reflecting off the fine layer of frost. The early morning silence made it feel as if we existed in the world alone. Only the two of us.

"So, how often do you join these events?" I asked as we rounded the corner that led to the parking lot.

"Maybe monthly." He stepped off the edge of the curb and crossed the parking lot toward a tiny black car with lime green accents.

My steps faltered as I came up to it. It was like a car transported right out of a racing game. "Dude," I said.

"What?" he asked as he opened the driver's side door.

"This is your car?"

Taka scoffed, smirking as he slid into the driver's seat.

When I opened the passenger door, I was met with black racing seats with lime-green trim, a lime-green shift knob, and a black steering wheel with lime-green accents. If I ever wondered what this man's favorite color was, I needed to look no further. The car was a tiny two-seater, and I hesitated at the door, wondering if I would fit.

"Well?" Taka looked at me, leaning over. "Getting in?"

I cleared my throat and slid into the seat. Thankfully, my knees were close to the dash, but not crammed, and my head was a decent distance from the roof. The seats, it seemed, were basically on the ground, so there was more room for me than I had guessed.

"What kind of car is this?"

"Honda S2K." He chuckled as he moved the shift knob and pressed the clutch before turning the key.

I was not prepared for the menace that awoke when the engine turned over. The car roared to life, shaking my entire body. "Jesus," I muttered, fearing that the entire dorm block had woken up wondering if an earthquake had hit.

"She's heavily modified." Taka dropped his chin to his shoulder as he glanced at me with a grin.

"Show off," I grumbled, grabbing the seatbelt and fastening myself in.

• • •

The streetlights lit the road as Taka pulled into a parking lot at a local mom-and-pop diner. Sports cars were backed into every available parking space. Hoods were propped open. People stood around cars with coffee mugs in their hands, laughing and talking over engines. As we crawled past them, their gazes lifted to look at us. Well, not us, but Taka's car. They probably cared nothing about the people in the car.

Taka rolled the windows down, and a rush of cool air whipped my face. He found a parking space and expertly backed in. Before he even turned the car off, people swarmed him.

"'Sup, T?" A burly guy in his thirties, I guessed, approached the driver's side window and rested his palm above the door. His beard reached down his chest, and his head was clean-shaven. His worn jeans rode low on his waist, and his plain red hoodie had a coffee stain on the chest.

"Glad you came today. You gonna join us at the circuit?" he asked.

"Of course," Taka said and bumped fists with the guy before turning the car off. "This is my friend Nick. It's his first time at a meet, so go easy on him."

The man bent to get a look at me. "Yo, Nick. Nice to meet you. Name's Dave."

I waved, realizing how out of place I felt. I wanted to run back to the comfort of my dorm.

Dave patted the top of the car and sipped his coffee. "Let's get you caffeinated and fed so we can get our asses to the raceway." Dave stepped away from the car and headed toward the entrance of the small diner.

Taka turned to me with a smile. "Welcome to my secret passion."

"I never would've guessed this. Not in a million years."

I climbed out of the car and pulled on my hoodie. It was too cold to stand around in my thin shirt. I thanked myself for being prepared and followed Taka to the front of the building.

People surrounded us as we joined a larger group, and Taka introduced me to a bunch of fellow enthusiasts. It was a gathering of people from all walks of life. There were a surprising number of women; some were with their partners, but most were there for the cars and to join in the day's events. It was insane to see, right out of a movie.

Taka was open and laughing. He looked relaxed as he chatted with people and checked out their cars. I sipped my coffee and stuffed a doughnut in my mouth, following Taka around like his shadow.

This was not my scene: way too much human interaction for me. But, damn, Taka was brilliant as he spoke with people. His passion for cars radiated from every pore of his body.

An hour of mingling passed, and the sun grew brighter by the minute. Finally, Dave stepped up next to an orange muscle car with two black stripes down the hood and silenced the crowd. "All right, everyone, let's roll out to the raceway. We have a full day of drag racing, and a few of you signed up for the circuit. Let's head out!"

The parking lot roared to life as everyone started up their engines. More than fifty cars rumbled around me.

"Holy fuck," I breathed. "This is insane."

Taka leaned close, shouting over the noise. "We should go too. Don't want to be left behind." He gave me a bright grin as he got into his car. The engine rumbled to life, joining the rest of them. I folded myself into the passenger seat and watched him play with the radio, his other hand resting on the steering wheel. Somehow, it was the sexiest thing I'd seen in my whole life.

When satisfied with the radio station, he ran his fingers through his silky black hair; the sunlight caught the strands as they dropped back into his face. In that moment, I realized two things: I could love this man as easily as breathing, and I regretted coming.

His gaze rested on me as he slid on black sunglasses. "You good?"

My heart was racing. My body was on fire. And all I wanted was to kiss him. God, did I want to kiss him. I should've listened to Sky, but I honestly thought I could be his friend. What a moron I was.

CHAPTER 14

TAKA

As Nick buckled in beside me, his eyes went cold and his shoulders tensed. I eyed him, hoping I had read the situation wrong, but something appeared to have changed in a matter of moments.

"Everything okay?"

Nick nodded and pointed his gaze through the window, sending my stomach sinking as I ran through every moment of the morning. I was at a loss as to why the atmosphere had shifted and hoped I wasn't the reason.

Dave honked, telling the pack to leave for the raceway, and cars began filing through the exit of the small parking lot. Then, one by one, we turned onto the main road toward the raceway. Virginia had a few different raceway locations. This one was about an hour from SCU and the biggest in the state, with two drag strips and a large circuit.

Dave led the pack down the highway, the sun glinting off the chrome of his 1970 Camaro Z28. Dave ran the meets in this area and had founded the Fernworth Alliance with a couple of other members. They wanted to find people to share their hobby with. A lot of the guys were like a second family to me. They understood my passion for cars and were a mix of people willing to help one another in any situation.

Last year, one member lost his job and his family lost their home. Dave appealed to the Fernworth Alliance, and we donated food and money to help the family get back on their feet. One guy in the Alliance even gave the guy a job at his company. Some of the kindest people I knew were part of this group.

Nick and I had fallen into conversation to pass the hour. It was about minor things—school, hopes, and life—but it was nice. I typically dislike small talk, but it was fun to get to know Nick. Gradually, the original change in his mood vanished as we spoke, but there was still a tension that I couldn't ignore.

The raceway building came into view, and I trailed the cars before me into the large parking lot. I backed into a space and pulled up the e-brake, letting my engine run a moment after the long drive.

"You aren't getting cold feet on me, are you?" I asked, unable to shake the feeling that something was wrong.

He smiled, but it didn't reach his eyes. "I'm fine. Let's go."

I didn't believe him, but what could I say? I didn't want to press the issue and start an argument or make him think poorly of me, so I left it alone.

"We need to register my car for the event today. We're driving the circuit," I announced. I cut the engine and hopped out of the car. "The registration process for the entire group typically takes an hour before the event can start." That day, we had over sixty people at the raceway. One of the biggest turnouts of the season so far.

"Cool, I'll just follow you."

Nick kept close while I registered and mingled. He kept to himself, speaking only when others initiated conversation. His shift in behavior filled me with unease, but I tried to pretend I didn't notice.

Dave moved to the edge of the group and raised his hands into the air, motioning for everyone to quiet down. When his hand motions went unnoticed, he yelled, "Quiet, everyone!" He waited for the group to simmer down before he continued. "Circuit is first in line today. Anyone not taking part in the circuit can follow me. The rest of you, mount up!"

A loud roar of enthusiasm echoed from the group, and the majority followed Dave into the building.

"We're up," I said, patting Nick on the shoulder.

When we reached my car, I opened the trunk and pulled out my gear. "Nick, here, put these on." I pulled a helmet, gloves, neck brace, and a racing suit out of the trunk.

"Why do I need to wear this?" he asked, looking at the gear dubiously.

"In case I crash. The suit is fireproof."

His eyes wide, he pulled the hoodie over his head, tossed it into the trunk, and quickly slipped the suit over his clothes. The all-black racing suit only just fit him. Short in the arms and legs but it zipped up.

"That's a relief," I said. "I didn't want the hassle of renting you one. Here, these too." I handed him gloves and helped him put them on, then I popped the helmet on his head and fastened the neck brace before gearing up myself.

"Do you always drive the circuit?" Nick asked as I positioned the car behind the group waiting at the starting line for the circuit.

"Not always. Sometimes I race on the strip."

"The drag strip?"

I nodded. "I like the circuit more, though. It's relaxing."

His hands fisted on his knees, and he said, "Don't kill us, okay?"

"You don't trust me?"

He shook his head. "Not yet. My life is in your hands."

A chuckle erupted through me. "I promise I'm a skillful driver. To drive the circuit you need training, plus I've driven it so much that I know every corner and bump."

"I may trust you if I come out of this with all my limbs."

A horn sounded, signaling drivers to ready their cars.

"Here we go. Remember to breathe," I said.

The red light ahead turned yellow for a few seconds before it began flashing. When the light turned green, a horn blared, and the pack took off as one. We soared over the pavement in line with the Fernworth Alliance members. I passed other drivers, cut corners, and floored it over the straightaways. This was my freedom.

I didn't have much time to focus on Nick, but as we drove the circuit, he slowly relaxed. The tension fell from his body, and I could tell he was finally putting his trust in me. As we completed our third lap around the circuit, I stayed with the pack and followed them to the exit. I parked and turned to Nick.

"How did you like it?" I asked, lifting off my helmet.

"It was really fun," Nick said, muffled.

I reached for him, helping him take the helmet off.

"I didn't expect it to be like that," he added.

"It's definitely not street racing, but it's fun in its own way."

"Have you ever done that?"

"No. I wouldn't risk it."

"Is it dangerous?"

"I mean, kind of, but the worst part is getting caught by the cops. At least here it's all legal, and there is no risk to random strangers who didn't sign up for it, you know? The scenery isn't as nice here, but it's the safest option."

We packed our gear into the trunk, then quickly entered the building that led to the drag strips. We stopped at the food stand before finding seats high on the metal bleachers overlooking the drag strip, and I handed Nick a hotdog and a bottle of water as we sat.

"Thanks," he said, taking it from me. "How long will this last?"

I glanced at my watch. It was after one, and the first pair of cars hadn't started yet. "Probably four or five hours."

"Good Lord."

I smiled. "Many people sign up for the drag strip, and some go more than once. We're in for a long one since this is a big turnout. We also have random people here, adding to the time. But it goes fast . . . for fans, anyway."

The first pair of cars pulled up to their respective space, although I didn't pay much attention to them. As they spun their tires and revved their engines, my attention was on the man beside me. His eyes lit up as he watched them take off down the quarter-mile black top. The roar reverberated through the stands, vibrating over my skin, but what had my heart fluttering was the smile on his face. I saw something I wanted to treasure for a lifetime.

When the cars crossed the line, he yelled, "That was fucking awesome!"

The look in his eyes was reminiscent of a child's glee, and it pulled at those high walls of mine, threatening to tear them down. With a restrained smile, I offered a nod. "I saw."

"Taka, wanna take some pictures? This is so much cooler than I thought it would be." Nick whipped out his phone and scooted closer to me before snapping photos of us on the bleachers. "When the next cars are about to take off, can you take a picture of me? I want a shot of them behind me."

When the next pair of cars pulled up, I did as Nick asked. I snapped photo after photo—selfies and whatever request he had. I indulged him and, in turn, indulged myself. Seeing him like this had me wanting to see his reaction to other things, other places. How would he be at a concert? Would he jump for joy and light up like the sun as his favorite band walked on stage? What if we visited an art museum together or took a trip to the beach? Would he have reactions like this? I wanted to see more of this.

• • •

The sun sank lower by the minute as the FW Alliance members funneled out of the raceway. Nick was flying high after hours of watching drag racing. He was chatting with Alliance members, getting phone numbers, following people on social media, and talking about coming out to the next event. Dave was eating it up.

“Taka, Nick, you want to join a few of us for dinner before heading home?” Dave asked as we made our way to the parking lot.

“Up to Nick,” I said, hoping Nick would want to. I wasn’t ready for our time to end. He didn’t disappoint me.

“Fuck, yeah. Where we goin’?” Nick hooked his arm around my shoulder and tugged me close. “I’m starved,” he said, his breath tickling my neck. “Do you have a place you like to eat at?”

I shrugged. “I usually go wherever the group wants to go. I’m not picky.”

“Awesome. Dave, you leading the way?”

“Sounds good. Taka, you know the steakhouse off highway forty-three?”

“A steakhouse? I would love a steak right now,” Nick said so close to my ear that goose bumps spread down my side.

“Let’s go then.” Dave spun around and motioned for the crowd to close in. “FW Alliance, thank you all for another amazing day. As always, it was a pleasure. If anyone wants to continue the fun with food and beer, come join us at Buck’s Steakhouse. If you need the address, let me know.” Dave turned around and tugged open the door to his car. “Oh, damn, almost forgot. Does anyone need gas before we leave?”

Nearly the entire group responded, so we stopped at two gas stations on our way out. Those going to Buck’s went to one, and those going home to the other. About twenty people agreed to join us at Buck’s, so Dave called ahead to get us a table. Although the building was not particularly large, it was not a small shack either. Still, twenty people rolling up probably had the staff losing their minds as we piled through the double doors of the cramped entrance. Nick hovered behind me. As more people joined us, they forced us closer until the heat of his chest pressed against my back. I tried to take my mind off it, but we squeezed together to let others inside, forcing us closer. I wanted to lean into his warmth and wondered what it would be like to be skin on skin.

"Sorry, man," Nick said, his lips close to my ear as he spoke, sending a wave of chills down my right side. "These guys are crazy." He chuckled, and little puffs of air brushed over my neck. My pulse picked up as I looked around, hoping some space would free up, allowing me to escape my personal hell.

When the host finally motioned for Dave to follow, it was as if the floodgates had opened, and we marched en masse to our table. The host had us sit at three long tables shoved together at the back of the restaurant. Nick and I sat near the end, across from Dave. The crowd grew louder when they got their hands on menus. It was chaotic, but Nick still looked like he was having the time of his life.

We scarfed our food down amid boisterous conversation. Dave was prying into Nick's life and, before I knew it, they were on the subject of me.

"When T was new to the scene, he didn't know anything. He had his cute stock S2K and no idea what to do with it." Dave laughed as he swallowed some beer. "You wouldn't believe that scrawny kid would've turned out to be this fine fellow three years ago."

Nick glanced over at me with a smirk. "Scrawny? This guy was?"

"Oh yeah, he was skin and bone. Like he never ate a day in his life." Dave pointed to Greg, whom I had known well for three years. "Greg over there took T under his wing and trained him at the gym."

"I don't believe it." Nick laughed. "So, who taught Taka about building cars?"

Dave ran his hand over his beard. "That would be me." He grinned and flashed me a wink. "I'm a mechanic and have been around cars my whole life. T is like a little brother to a lot of us, and like a good brother, I showed him the ropes."

The conversation detoured to other members, away from me, but Nick kept tossing glances my way. I acted like I didn't notice, but my stomach jumped under his gaze each time.

CHAPTER 15

NICK

By the time we got back on the road, I was exhausted. I learned fast that when Dave got going, he didn't stop. Thankfully, when Greg offered him a ride home, he took it without complaint. Dave was hammered, and I was willing to take his keys if he had tried to drive home. Still took us thirty minutes to escape his talking so we could all get in our cars, though. I chuckled, recalling Greg yanking him away while he talked on, oblivious to his surroundings and griping about getting his car the next day.

Taka glanced at me, his face lit by the lights on the dash. "What's so funny?"

"Man, that guy is a talker. You should warn people before you take them out with him," I said as Taka pulled up behind my dorm.

Taka broke into a laugh as he parked in the maintenance

parking lot behind my building. "I didn't expect you to keep talking with him."

"I didn't want to be rude. You should've saved me." I laughed and playfully shoved him on the shoulder. "It's all your fault."

He pulled the e-brake and turned to me. "My fault? I don't run your life." A smile dimpled his cheeks as he checked his phone. The smile faded a little.

"Are your parents worried?" I asked.

He shook his head. "They know I'll be home late tonight."

"Well, I had a lot of fun. Be sure to invite me next time." I gripped the door handle, pushing the door open.

"Sure. I'm glad you came with me. It was fun," Taka said, leaning over the center console as I rose from the seat.

I closed the car door with a wave and turned away. I fought with myself; I wanted to invite him up. Instead, I wandered around the building, my footsteps echoing off the walls until I took the stairs to my dorm.

I should've listened to Sky. How far was I willing to let this go? Eliminating Taka from my life would be the smart option. Even if he'd broken up with his girlfriend, it still wasn't clear he was into me the way I hoped.

I pushed through the front door and flopped on the sofa, releasing a heavy breath, running my hands over my face. It was barely two hours into our adventure when I realized Taka was someone I could have a dog, a nice house and yard with; someone with whom I could visit my family, go out for dinners, spend holidays; someone to come home to after a long day of work, his smiling face relieving all the stress and frustration of the day, our lives filling with happy memories. He was someone

I could plan a future with, and I hated myself for picturing it.

After all these years of being interested in nobody, why did he have to be the one?

• • •

Birds chirped outside the window as the sun crept over the horizon. I hadn't made it to my bedroom after getting home. I lay there, staring at the ceiling from the sofa, contemplating my actions. Should I cut Taka from my life or suffer as only a friend? I'd never understood how people could remain friends with someone they thought of romantically, but now I think I could. It was a sickening thought that I would stoop that low.

My phone sprung to life in my pocket, immediately rubbing on my nerves in the worst way. I relaxed as I read the name. My younger brother, Harper, was one of the few individuals in this world who would receive my unconditional love and attention.

"Harp? Everything okay?"

"Everything's fine," he said. "Mom was wondering when you were coming home. I told her you're busy, but she wants to see you."

"Well, I don't know." I sighed and ran my fingers through my hair. "When's the next long weekend? Memorial Day, maybe?"

"Is that coming up?" Harp paused a moment, and I could hear him flipping through the calendar that hung on the wall over his desk. "Oh, I guess it is. Do you want to come up that Friday?"

"I'll have to check with River on my work schedule. I signed up for the summer this year since I need the extra money. When I find out, I'll text you."

"Okay. Sure."

"Was that all you called for?"

"Yeah."

With a chuckle, I propped my feet on the arm of the sofa. "You know that could've been a text, right?"

"Who knows if you would've responded any time soon."

"Fair point." I sat up with a groan. "By the way, you would be happy to hear that I did something cool with a new friend yesterday."

"Friend?"

"Yes, a *friend*. I met him recently, and he invited me to a car meet. It was so damn cool, Harp. I'll have to take you to one sometime."

"A car meet? Doesn't sound like you."

"It was better than I thought it would be. We had breakfast at this cute diner and then went to a raceway down here. I rode with my friend on the circuit in his souped-up car, and then we watched drag racing until dark."

"Who are you, and what have you done with my brother?"

"Seriously, Harp. It was fun. I'm planning to go again with him."

"And you're not dating this guy?"

Ice formed in my gut because I knew what I wanted and couldn't have it. "No, we're friends."

"You never make new friends. This is weird for you."

"Way to kill my happiness, bro. I can make new friends and it not be the end of the world."

"Sure, Nick. If you say so."

"The hell, Harp?"

"Your track record speaks for itself. You have Sky and

River, but other than that, you're a loner, and you mean to tell me you met someone and want to be besties with them out of nowhere?"

My brother knew me too well. Called me out too fast. For a seventeen-year-old kid, he was more like a father to me than I ever had been to him.

"God, you could've let me enjoy the fucking moment."

"I can't do that. You sounded way too excited. Who is this guy?"

"Someone I met by pure accident on campus. I helped him with his assignment in the lab, and we clicked."

"So, where is the problem?"

"He's not gay."

"And you still want to be friends with him?"

"I do. He's nice and fun to be around."

"You sure that's all there is to it?"

This fucking kid. "I'm sure."

"I don't believe you, but you do what you want. I'm sure Sky already warned you enough for the both of us."

"Jesus, do the pair of you talk or something?"

Harp fell into an exaggerated chuckle.

I missed him. Christmas was the last time I was home.

"Anything new with you, Harp?"

"Nothing much. I've been applying to colleges since the first pick rejected me."

"Good. Just because the first didn't work out, doesn't mean you will lose out on a great college. Let me know if you need help with anything."

We talked for over an hour. Harper caught me up on his school life and his college plans. The kid was the most put-together of the whole family; I envied him for it.

I often thought about what my life would be like if I had my shit together, but it could never be me. Compared to everyone else, I felt like a failure, always struggling to keep up with others. Struggling to keep up with myself. The only thing I was good at was art: put me anywhere else, I would fall flat. My family, peers, and professors praised me for my talent, but they never saw how I would flounder to get there. They never saw the struggle inside, the raging storm in my dark heart, the front I put on for the world. Sometimes even I believed my lie. Sky was the only one who noticed that side of me. Even my mother was left in the dark, mostly unaware of it all.

Since my father left and I was the oldest son, I was the man of the house. Lori was the oldest sibling and took on the brunt of helping Mom, but they both expected me to take on the father role and help raise Harp to be a man. The catch was that I was still learning to be a man myself. Who was supposed to teach me? There was no one; I figured it out as I went.

I traced my thumb over the leather bracelet, trying to push the darkest memories of my life away, but they crawled back. Like a roach infestation, these memories would never leave. From a very young age, I was aware of my sexuality, but I kept it hidden from those around me. Until I met Adam.

I was fifteen when the worst day of my life happened.

Adam and I met in sixth grade. He was an artist too. He also played the piano and had a beautiful voice. His dream was to be a music producer in California. We planned our future together, how we would take on the world.

I loved him more than anyone. When we fell, we fell hard. We were inseparable and lifted each other up, supported each other's dreams. And we did all of this under the guise of being best friends. But Adam was my first love. The deepest love I ever experienced. Something I doubted I would feel again.

His family was deeply religious, so we kept our relationship secret. We were both scared about what others would think and do if they found out. One day, in tenth grade, we were a couple of horny teenage boys. We couldn't stop ourselves. Usually, we were careful about where we were, but Adam was more carefree that day. I remember it so clearly. We were in his bedroom like usual. No one but us in the house. His parents were at work, and Adam insisted we would be fine. I was no match for him and gave in.

The moment his bedroom door flew open, my world crashed down around me. His father flew into a rage. Their shouting back and forth was something I would never forget. It was etched on my mind forever. I had never seen such anger, and it was the first time someone had punched me so hard I lost consciousness. That was the last day I ever saw Adam.

I waited for him to come to school for a week. He didn't answer my calls, and no one had heard from him. Then, one day, a bunch of girls from his music class were crying in an empty classroom. When I asked them about it, Adam's friend was the only one to respond.

"Adam's dead," Jessica said through heavy sobs.

Instinctively, I laughed. It had to be a cruel joke.

"No. It's true," Jessica said.

Another girl added, "He hanged himself."

"You're lying!" My voice trembled as I stood in that big classroom, listening to the sobs of Adam's friends. "There's no way."

Jessica wiped her eyes and shook her head. More tears ran down her red cheeks. "I heard it from his mom. She wouldn't lie."

My knees hit the floor, and my soul shattered into a million pieces. Sounds became muffled. My breath burned as it escaped my lungs, but no matter how hard I tried, I couldn't refill them; I couldn't breathe. Never in my life had I felt so much pain. Not even when my father abandoned us.

That day I found out Adam was gone, a part of me died too.

Losing Adam sent me into a spiral. I wasn't allowed to attend his funeral because his family refused to let me see him. They blamed me for it all.

Mom had to pull me out of school and send me to therapy. The anti-depressants they put me on made me a zombie. When they sent me back to school after six months, I was a shell of my former self.

What sent me over the edge was the sad looks. The comments about how sorry they were that I lost my best friend. But Adam was more than my best friend–far more than they could ever imagine. Even the teachers gave me a wide berth, keeping their distance. Their behavior only made me feel worse.

Most of the time I felt nothing, but when I could feel through the medications, it was never anything good. On days when memories of our time together forced their way into my thoughts, I would sit in the tub, marking my skin. In those moments, I could feel more than internal pain. I could feel the razor slice through my skin and, as it did so, the physical pain dulled the heartache.

I couldn't continue to live that way; I was a ghost trapped in human skin. Life no longer had meaning.

I wanted to join Adam.

I even failed to do that.

CHAPTER 16

TAKA

"Good morning," Mom said from behind the stove. Her yellow apron was crooked and covered in flour, and a yellow clip held her silky black hair away from her face.

"Morning," I said as I approached the island and rested my hip against the edge. The pan held three perfectly round pancakes with chocolate chips melting in the browning batter. I took a whiff before releasing a groan. "Do you want help?"

"No, I have it."

"Are you sure? I can make eggs or something."

"I'm sure," she said, flipping the pancakes over.

"Yum, pancakes." Tami's squeal rang through the kitchen. She bounced in. Her cute, rounded face was soft, and her pink pajamas were wrinkled from sleep. Her hair was tied in a side ponytail that rested on one shoulder. "Taka, Dad wants to see you before we eat."

"Okay," I said, pushing away from the counter and wandering toward my father's office. He lived in that room. There was no need to ask where he was. It would always be the office.

Warm sunlight poured through the cracked door of his office, and I slipped inside, closing the door behind me. "Hi, Dad. Tami said you wanted to speak to me about something."

He glanced up from his computer with a smile. He motioned to the white chair across from him, and I sat.

His short black hair was growing evermore peppered with white. It was hard to ignore the color change. I hated the thought of my father growing older. His fiftieth birthday was in December, but I struggled to think of him as that age.

He placed his glasses on the desk and turned away from the computer screen. The chair creaked as he leaned back and folded his hands in his lap. "I have a friend with a daughter I would like you to meet."

Here we go again.

"She's a nice young lady. Attends your university on a student visa. She's the daughter of a business partner in Japan, and her father and I would like it if the two of you met. We are hoping you get along well." He twirled his thumbs together as he eyed me, waiting for my reaction, or maybe my agreement. "I know you recently ended your relationship with Isobel, but the least you could do is meet this young woman."

It was like a truck slammed into me. The breath I had taken was gone. I was stuck, frozen, and unable to move.

"Her name is Maeko Yamamura." He held a paper up and slipped his glasses back on. "She's nineteen and studying political science. She wants to be a diplomat."

What the hell is this? This wasn't the first time he had tried to set me up with someone, but I couldn't help feeling that this time was different.

"All I ask is that you meet her once and, if you get along, think about dating." He placed the paper back on the desk and looked at me over the rim of his glasses. "The mess with Isobel is unfortunate, but you don't appear to be too upset over it. Tami may disagree, but I think meeting someone new would be good for you."

My breath finally came back. It was like my father had pressed the play button on my bodily functions again. Clearing my throat, I stared through the bay windows overlooking the backyard. The grass was clean cut. Perfect. Matched every other home that surrounded us. The American Dream.

What a farce.

"I take your silence as acceptance," he said.

A shiver rolled down my spine. I couldn't defy him. "When do you want me to meet her?" I forced the words from my lips, and it felt like acid ran down my throat.

"Saturday night. I will set it up with her father."

Six days away. I was in for a long week.

• • •

I spent the morning in a foggy haze before Alex Bennett called me. He wanted to meet on campus to discuss our group project, but I didn't expect several people to join us. I arrived to find a conversation in full swing.

"Okay, but we won the game." Zack Lowe chuckled before stuffing a handful of fries in his mouth.

"But you almost broke my knee, Lowe," Kiran Hayden

yelled. His piercing eyes sparked with rage as he glared at Zack.

"Shit happens," Zack said, tying his shoulder-length dreads back. "I didn't mean for you to take the fall."

Zack wasn't a big guy, but on the soccer field, he was a beast. Luckily, I missed the game the day before and had no standing on who was at fault. Not that I cared much about sports.

"Alex," I said, "we were supposed to work on our group project, not hang out with our friends."

He shrugged at me. "Relax, T. We have plenty of time to work on our project." Strands of his long black hair fell into his bright blue eyes.

"You're too relaxed, Al." William Greene jumped into the conversation for the first time since I had sat down.

I met Will a few times through my mom, but it wasn't until I started college that I saw him more often and hung out with him. Zack and Will ended up as roommates in their freshman year, but Will and Kiran were friends from the start, so our groups merged naturally.

I hadn't had a large friend group before, but it was nice. Casey normally tagged along, but I hadn't spoken to him in a few days. I had tried to keep him at a distance since the incident with Nick. No one questioned Casey's disappearance from our lives, and I didn't want to talk about it. I was even dodging the DGZ meetings, but Casey wasn't pursuing me too hard, so I got away with it, and I was lucky to have Jax as my Big. He was covering for me and sometimes even forging my signature at meetings. He was risking a lot on my behalf, but I couldn't bring myself to be around them right now. Casey had mentioned Nick to my brothers. From the sound of it, he had gotten his Big, Charlie, riled up. Apparently, Charlie and a few other seniors had gotten into a fight with Nick and his friends during a Greek Row party a couple of years ago. It was so bad that they all were threatened with expulsion if it ever happened again.

Will's phone buzzed on the table, and I turned back to Alex. My patience was wearing thin. My father's attempt at setting me up that morning already had my nerves frayed, and now Alex was wasting my time.

"Alex, we don't have time to play around. This project is thirty percent of our grade."

"I know. I've got you." He flashed me a wink and leaned back in his chair.

"You guys mind if a friend joins us for a bit? He was already coming this way for lunch," Will said and flipped open a book before anyone could answer.

He wasn't asking permission; he was telling us, which was unlike him.

"Whatever, dude." Zack waved him off as he returned to arguing with Kiran.

My heart fluttered as Nick approached our table moments later. He had on a black hoodie, and his hair was in a state, like he had recently gotten out of bed. It had been mere hours since I dropped him off at his dorm, and I couldn't help but get excited at the prospect of speaking with him. Seeing him. Simply being near him.

Beside Nick was his friend Sky. I hadn't really met him before, not officially, at least.

When Will reached them, he was all smiles. Loose and relaxed, I had never seen him that comfortable before. He was usually stiff and stern whenever I was around him, always reading a book or on his phone, and whenever he spoke, he was terse.

Will touched Sky's arm so briefly that no one would have noticed. I only caught that gentle greeting because I was staring them down. Observing every moment and interaction. All because of the man beside them.

Nick was staring at me. He stood beside Sky and Will, off in their own world a few feet away from the table of my rowdy friends. A blank expression covered his face, but his eyes didn't leave me. Our eyes were locked together, and neither of us could tear away; we were bound by an invisible force.

My heart pounded. My breath was heavy. What would people think if they caught us staring at each other like this? My breath lodged in my throat, and I fought to swallow before breaking eye contact, refocusing my attention on my notebook, and diving into my group project.

Nick's gaze was a tangible touch on my skin. Even if I wasn't looking anymore, I couldn't shake the feeling of his eyes on me. Surely, if I looked up, he would still be staring. The question was why. Why was he looking at me like that? What was he thinking?

Will's large body appeared next to me as he cleared his throat. "Guys, this is Sky and Nick," he said, pointing to the pair.

Zack gave a nod.

"Hey, aren't you the guy that got that really hard-to-get art scholarship?" Kiran asked.

Nick tilted his head. "How do you know about that?"

"I knew it! That's so cool. I'm in the BFA program. You were huge news when you got that. We thought someone going for their BFA would get the scholarship for sure, but then this digital art guy swooped in and got it instead."

Nick's brows pulled together. "I didn't realize it was news."

Sky nudged Nick with his elbow. "Nick here is an amazing artist. Y'all should feel blessed to be attending the same school as him."

"Shut up, Sky," Nick said and grabbed a chair from the table behind us, dragging it beside me. "Hi, Taka. How're you?"

His cologne wafted over me, latching onto my senses. "I'm good. You?"

"Good." He flashed a smirk and shoved his hands in his pants pockets. "What is everyone doing here, anyway? It's a Sunday afternoon."

"I was supposed to meet Alex to work on our group project. But that turned into lunch with our friends, so not a single thing for our project has been done," I said, glancing at Alex, who was now bickering with Zack and Kiran.

"Your friends seem lively," Nick said.

"They are. The one with the long black hair is Alex. He's a business major like me. The guy with the dreads is Zack, and the skinny blond guy that looks like he could crack bones with his jaw is Kiran."

"Interesting group of people."

"How do you two know Will?" I asked.

Nick shifted his body and then cast a glance toward Sky and Will. "They met during freshman orientation and dragged me into the friendship because Sky is my best friend. Will is cool. He's quiet and doesn't annoy me, so hanging out with him is easy."

"You say that, but have you met your best friend?"

Based on the limited interactions I had with Sky, he appeared to be a boisterous and outgoing person, and when I saw him standing next to Nick, I couldn't help but wonder how they even crossed paths.

"Sky is special. I don't mind his annoying tendencies because I love him."

"Noted." I laughed. "You can handle annoying people as long as there is love."

"It depends." Nick chuckled. "Sometimes, annoying is simply annoying."

"You two seem chummy," Zack said as he, Kiran, and Alex pulled their attention back to the rest of the table. "I didn't know you knew people from the art department, T. Outside of Kiran."

"I met Nick in the computer lab. He helped me with a project for my marketing class."

"Oh, you're that guy," Kiran said, propping his elbows on the table and resting his chin in his hands. "Dude, you have a lot of piercings. Any tattoos?"

"I do."

"That's so cool. I always wanted one. Can I see?"

"No."

"What? Why not? Is it ugly? Embarrassing?" Kiran leaned over the table, his eyes glistening with excitement as he raced through each question.

"I don't like to show it to people I don't know."

"Damn." Kiran pouted like a child. "I'll just have to get to know you." He winked before shifting his attention to Sky. "So, you're Skylar? I haven't seen you around, but you're kind of famous. What department are you in?"

"Graphic design."

"Respectable. Excellent direction." Kiran nodded. "My parents didn't want me to get my BFA, but I begged them. I don't like digital art, but you both are smart for going into it. I don't know how I'll make money when I graduate. Painting doesn't sell these days."

"Your skills can translate to something," Sky suggested.

"They can, sure, but digital art is more lucrative. There are so many jobs for people who know how to do what you're both doing."

"Why did you choose it then?" Nick asked.

Kiran shrugged. "I guess I wanted to spend my last four years of freedom enjoying myself before I need to break my back as another corporate cogwheel." He slumped forward, his head making a dull thud when it connected with the table. He lifted it again and asked, "What about you two?"

"Marketing," Sky said.

"Freelance," Nick mumbled, like he didn't want to participate in the conversation.

"Freelance? So, like, what do you plan to do?"

"I do digital painting mostly, but I can do animation, 3D modeling, and video editing. Pick one, and I can do it."

"Do you have a favorite?"

"Digital painting."

"That's cool, dude. I tip my hat to you. No wonder you got the scholarship. You can do all kinds of things." Kiran released a sigh as he rested his head on his arm.

"You okay, buddy?" Zack asked, patting Kiran on the shoulder.

"I'm fine. Just seeing someone skilled and with plans is depressing."

Alex released a sound between a grunt and a laugh. "If you planned ahead instead of trying to enjoy your college life, you could be like them."

"Not a chance. That isn't for me. I know I can't make a living from art. That dream was crushed long ago."

"Depends on what you want, I guess," Nick said.

Kiran whimpered, looking over his shoulder at Zack. "This guy." He pointed his thumb roughly toward Nick.

"Alex." I was fed up with him wasting my time. "If you won't work with me on this project, then I'm finding a new partner."

"Hey, T," he pleaded, drawing the words out. "Don't be like that. You know we're just having good fun right now. We can get serious after we're done here."

I had a feeling we wouldn't be "done here" any time soon.

CHAPTER 17

NICK

When Sky asked me to join him for lunch, it didn't turn out to be what I expected. We found ourselves in the one study area on campus next to a food court that wasn't the Ellis Center. This side of the campus was out of the way for most, but the business students hung out in this spot because it was secluded and closest to the business department buildings.

While Taka and Alex worked on their project, I sat with Taka's friends for nearly an hour. Zack and Kiran bickered like a married couple. They were both friendly, but Zack only talked about soccer, and Kiran talked about anything and everything all at once. He was the type of person gags were invented for. I should have told him he would be great in sales. I couldn't believe that he had already given up on a career in art. Giving up on art was unimaginable to me. What would my life be composed of after that?

Alex groaned, interrupting the group's heated discussion about which soccer team would win some world championship. I didn't know the first thing about soccer, or any sport, and their conversation continued for longer than I had wished. They even pulled in Sky, whose favorite pastime was soccer.

"I'm so bored, T. Can we call it quits?"

"Alex, you barely lasted an hour."

I glanced up from my phone, holding back my smile. Their dynamic was interesting, and I was having fun listening in.

"Yeah, an hour too long."

Taka dropped his pen and leaned back in his chair with a huff. "Fine. I give up."

"Yes!" Alex jumped up and ran circles around the table. "Freedom!"

"You're like a child," Taka grumbled.

"T." Kiran leaned over the table with a grin. "Do you want to go to a rave on Saturday? You two are invited too." He pointed to Sky and me.

"I can't," Taka replied.

"T, you never come out. I'm begging you to come this time," Kiran said.

Taka shook his head. "I have something planned Saturday evening."

"We won't go out until ten," Kiran persisted.

"I won't want to go out afterward."

"Got a hot date?" Zack asked. "You and Izzie broke up two weeks ago, but is our little guy ready to get back in the game?"

Taka chewed the inside of his cheek, glancing at me out of the corner of his eye.

My chest tightened, and my stomach dropped to the floor.

Why would he look at me like that?

"My dad set me up on a blind date. I can't reschedule it."

"Shit," Alex said, dropping back into his chair. "Can't imagine liking anyone my dad thinks is a good match."

While his friends were lit up with excitement, Taka was stiff and clearly uncomfortable.

"So, if your dad set you up, is she a family friend or something?" Zack asked.

"His business partner's daughter. She's a student here."

The inevitable disappointment I had been fighting off finally took over. I knew he would never be interested in me. I knew it, but I held onto the sliver of hope and let that hope consume me. I thought for once, after all these years, I could finally connect with someone on a deeper level. I was wrong to allow myself to think it. It was almost laughable.

"Let's look her up on Facebook. I want to see what she looks like!" Kiran nearly threw his phone at Taka. "Search her for me. Let's look at who your father thinks is a good match for you."

"I would rather not." Taka tried to give the phone back, but no one would take it from him.

Alex said, "Have you seen her yet? Come on, give us a look-see."

Taka groaned and tapped away on the phone screen before handing it back to Kiran.

"Yessss," Kiran hissed, gripping the phone like it held treasure. He looked at the image and gave a low whistle. "Fuck, she's hot."

Everyone jumped up from their seats and piled around Kiran, even Sky, the damned traitor. I couldn't move. I didn't want to see my competition. Our relationship was supposed to be based on friendship, but here I was, jealous of his next girlfriend. Who was I kidding this whole time?

"Dude, she's gorgeous." Zack gaped at the phone, looking between the phone and Taka. "Your dad has amazing taste."

Taka sunk into his chair further and chewed the inside of his cheek with renewed intensity.

"Nick, wanna see what T's future wifey looks like?" Kiran waved over with a silly smirk.

Not at all, but I stood up anyway. Taka shifted and covered his face with his hands as I hovered behind Kiran, my hand on the back of his chair providing me some stability. She was gorgeous. Petite with long black hair. Beautiful dark-brown eyes, high cheekbones, plump lips, and hips accentuated by tight jeans that rode low.

"Dude, Nick, anyone ever tell you that you smell like sex?" Kiran laughed, then sucked in a deep breath, hovering his face inches from my throat.

I stepped back. "The fuck does that mean?"

"Your cologne is amazing. What is it?"

I smiled and sat back down.

"Not even I know what it is," Sky said.

He had begged me for the name for years, but I never told anyone what it was.

"Why don't you tell anyone?" Kiran asked. "It's the most amazing smell I've ever encountered. Makes you want to throw a woman down and make love to her for hours."

I laughed and ran my fingers through my hair. "It's my trade secret."

Alex appeared beside me and sniffed the crook of my neck,

sending a chill down my spine. I jerked away.

"Don't be creepy," Taka warned Alex.

"Oh my God, it's amazing. How can someone smell . . . *that sexy*?"

"I would honestly prefer if you all don't sniff me." I retreated in on myself, crossing my arms and lifting my shoulders to protect my neck.

Why was I still here? Taka was going on a date with a gorgeous woman, and I was being sniffed by a bunch of straight dudes in heat.

As the group looked through the girl's Facebook profile, I sat beside Taka in silence, their attention finally off my cologne. An international student from Japan, she wanted to be a diplomat, apparently. Taka's friends had been right: his dad picked out a good match for him. I was sure they would be happy together.

While they were busy with another heated discussion about soccer, I pulled myself to my feet, needing to get away. As I stopped behind Sky, I patted him on the shoulder and said, "I'm heading out. I have homework to start." To everyone else, I said, "It was nice to meet everyone. Maybe I'll see you around."

I headed for the door, looking forward to the fifteen-minute walk to the dorm. I wanted to curl up in bed and drown myself in misery for the rest of the day.

"Nick?" Sky called after me.

"Yeah?"

"Are you okay?" he asked, matching my fast pace.

"I'm fine, Sky. I have homework, like I said."

"You're such a liar."

"I don't want to talk about it."

He sighed and paused a moment. "I know you're hurting. After the time you spent together, I know you were holding onto that hope that Will had given you, and I'm sorry."

"I said I don't want to talk about it, and I mean it!" I hadn't meant to yell, and it came out harsher than planned. My intention wasn't to snap at him, but the damage was already done.

Sky halted and gave me a wounded look.

"Sorry. I'll go cool off," I whispered, unable to look back at him. I didn't want to see the hurt on his face. Sky had been there for me every moment I needed him, but I was so mad at myself. I would owe him big-time for that.

• • •

The week passed like a slow-moving storm cloud until Saturday evening arrived. The storm was here, and I wanted shelter from it. Yet, somehow, Sky had convinced me to go with Will and his friends to the rave. He practically begged me, and then I begged River to join us so that when Will and Sky ran off to do their thing, I would have company. And that was how it always happened with the two of them. They would come out to a party, go to the dance floor, and then disappear without a word. As predicted, now they huddled at the center of the run-down building, dancing in front of the surprisingly professional DJ.

River gazed out at the sweaty, dancing mass in disgust. "I can't believe I came with you. You know I adore you, and you're a good friend, but..."

Strobe lights flashed over the space, swapping through a rainbow of colors. A bar was set up across the way, and along the edges of the walls were sofas and chairs. It was a professional-looking event, for a change.

"I know, and I want you to know I appreciate you. You're a wonderful friend." I put my arm around her shoulders and pulled her close.

According to Kiran, this place had been used often for raves, but the cops hadn't been called out so far. The theory was that we were too far from civilization for anyone to give a shit. Either that or the fraternities who set this up had connections with the property owners.

"Seeing you dress up is worth it," River said with an appreciative wink.

"Oh, hush," I replied. But she was right. I had gone all out that night and dressed up with everything I had. I pulled my black leather boots from the deepest recess of my closet and paired them with a black dress shirt. The black skinny jeans were my go-to. I had a million of them, but with the other two items, I was looking hot for sure. I dressed with purpose, even if the object of that purpose wasn't here to witness my hotness.

Sky bounced over to my side. His white button-up flopped open, exposing his chest to the world. The last few buttons on the shirt were the only thing keeping the fabric from flying off his body. "Zack secured a table. Let's go!"

Sky clasped my wrist in his clammy fingers and tugged me through the sea of strangers. I clung to River, clearing a safe path for her. When we popped out of the crowd, we squeezed along a wall until we reached the seating area. It wasn't what I expected. There was a well-used coffee table between two full-size purple leather sofas facing each other and two armchairs at either end. One chair was faded red leather; the other a dark blue velvety chair. The sofas appeared less worn than the chairs.

In this back corner, the music sounded deeper and heavier. Zack and Kiran were lounging beside each other on the sofa facing the makeshift dance floor, shot-sized plastic cups already in hand.

Kiran waved as we approached, and I sat across from the pair while Sky settled in the red armchair.

"Where did Will and Alex go?" Sky asked as he picked up a cup filled with green liquid from the table.

"Restroom," Zack yelled. He downed his shot, then asked, "You didn't drive here, did you?"

I pointed to River, who clung to my side. "She's my DD."

"Smart man." Kiran leaned forward with a sly smile. "I love the hair."

River leaned in to meet him. "Thanks. But I'm gay."

"Oh." He leaned back with a smirk.

I grabbed a plastic cup from the pile at the center of the table and downed it. I was going to need a lot more to get through tonight.

As the party continued, so did the conversation. It turned in the direction I wished it hadn't. Of course, it was about Taka and his date. Of course they were curious about it. As they took turns guessing what Taka was doing, I drank and kept drinking until the room was a spinning blur of shadows and flashing lights.

Did Taka like the girl? If he liked her, he probably took her back to her dorm. Did he kiss her, all polite and respectable? Or did he fall into bed with his date, like I would? My imagination ran wild with that thought, of him in bed with that woman, his hands running over her body. I wished I were her. I wanted to know what it would be like to be the focus of his full attention in the most intimate way.

I grabbed another shot off the table and drank it down. It was sweet, cutting through my bitter thoughts.

"You may want to slow down," Zack said as he leaned toward me, resting his elbows on his knees.

"Don't worry about me. I'll be fine." I slurred as I flashed him a cheesy and no-doubt crooked grin.

Riv patted my thigh as she leaned close to my ear. "Tell me when you want to leave."

I looked down at her worried expression and her face swam in my vision. "Don't worry Riv, I haven't forgotten my name yet." I laughed, reaching for another shot and pressed the thin plastic cup to my lips. "When I forget my name, we can go." I poured it down my throat, savoring the heat.

CHAPTER 18

TAKA

Maeko Yamamura stood before me with a sweet smile and bright eyes. The boys were right; she was stunningly beautiful. She came up to my shoulder, the perfect height for pulling her into a hug and resting my chin on top of her head. She smelled divine, too. I held the passenger door of my car open, and she cooed her thanks. I closed the door and rushed around, sliding into the driver's seat.

When I looked over at her, I felt nothing. I should have been excited. Nervous, even. Would this be my future? Empty relationships? Was that what life would be about now?

The restaurant was busy, but my father had made reservations. I didn't have to worry about a thing that night except ruining his business relationship.

"Keep a respectable head on your shoulders," Dad said as he saw me off.

It was his way of telling me not to shame him. Not that I could ever dream of it, even if she wasn't his business partner's daughter.

The hostess showed us to a back corner, which provided a sense of seclusion from prying eyes. Dad was a romantic, and I knew he loved this sort of thing. There was no question that this was his choice of table.

The conversation with Maeko was boring. She spoke of her future aspirations to be a diplomat and how her mother wanted her to return to Japan and settle down, but she had other plans and wanted to travel the world.

Even if I had been interested in her, I mused, I wouldn't be happy with a partner who was never around. When I took over my family business, I would be busy and want to come home to my lover and relax after a long day.

"Do you want to settle down and start a family?" I asked, hoping the question would give me the excuse to reject this match-up.

She nibbled her lip as she surveyed me. "I do, but not right away. I want to experience the world for a few years. Make a name for myself."

It would be hard to make a name for herself fresh out of college; what she was thinking was far more than a few years. I had my reason for rejection on those simple terms. I needed nothing more than that, but I had to finish the night, or Dad would be upset.

She flipped open the menu, perusing the options before her. As the evening progressed, Maeko dominated the conversation, and I sat comfortably on the sideline, providing the expected responses. It was everything I was used to, and I hated it. Dinner went on far longer than I would have liked. Maeko ordered dessert and talked my ear off. By the time we left, I was drained.

Students ogled my car as I pulled up to Maeko's dorm entrance. It was after eleven, and I wanted to escape from her incessant talking. Respectable, gorgeous, and intelligent, she was everything she was supposed to be. Everything my father wanted in a partner for me. But what I wanted, yearned for, was a spark. I had never felt a spark before Nick and could not be sure it was even real. Perhaps a spark was only something we dreamed of because reality was too dull. Nick's face flashed in my head, and I tried to suppress it, pretending that it had never popped into my thoughts.

I accompanied her to the door. "Thank you for a lovely night, Maeko," I said, then gently kissed her on the cheek before I left.

• • •

I called Rylee after I dropped Maeko at her dorm, sitting in my car.

"T, how could you go out with her?" she demanded.

Of course, she was beyond confused. I had told her only last week that I would embrace my feelings for Nick, but I hadn't; I had run like a dog, tail between its legs. Disappointment filled me. What was I doing with my life? Was I going to let my father dictate every aspect of my future, even down to the woman I would marry?

"I didn't have much of an option," I replied.

"I know you think you can't say no, but you could."

"And risk angering my family?"

Her sigh was heavy before she spoke again. "I think you need to stand up for yourself more. If you're unhappy, say it. Don't let people run over you."

"Ry, I–"

"You are an amazing person. You deserve to be happy. No matter what that happiness looks like. T, I want you to think about the things you want. The things that make you happy and fucking embrace them."

"I'll try," I said. "I'm grateful for your advice."

Rylee meant well, of course. But she did not truly understand my life, my family. It was not as easy as she implied. But her words had seeped into my mind. As I hung up, a bubble of rebelliousness ignited in my chest, warm and filled with something I couldn't place. I drove away from Maeko's dorm.

Several minutes later, I climbed out of the car and walked along the gravel path that led to a rundown building that emitted a deep thrum. The rave was in full swing.

I walked into the building, wandering through the crowded floor in search of my friends. Alex had texted me, letting me know their general location, but I hadn't told them I would come because I didn't think I would. But after that date, something in me needed to get out. I needed an escape from my cage.

I didn't know what I was expecting when I found the group, but Nick was not it. His hair was freshly cut and styled. Chains linking over and around his ear between his multiple piercings replaced his usual earrings. The sleeves of his dress shirt were rolled up to his elbow, exposing his leather bracelet and smooth skin. He relaxed against the sofa, tossing back a shot before setting the plastic cup heavily on the wooden table.

Alex beckoned me toward them from his place in an armchair. "T, you made it."

When Nick turned his head, the warmth in his eyes evaporated and he looked at me coldly.

"How was the date?" Zack asked as he motioned for me to sit in the empty spot beside Nick.

"I want to hear all about it." Kiran grinned from ear to ear.

Will sat in a red armchair, with Sky resting comfortably on his knee. The pair of them were staring at Nick, acting as if I wasn't there. River, the girl with pink hair from the lab, peeked around Nick with a polite wave. I waved back.

"So, spill, dude," Zack said. "We've been waiting all night."

I groaned and plucked one of the flimsy plastic shot cups from the table. The burn of alcohol hit me, and I sunk into the sofa. The back of my head touched Nick's forearm, which rested along the back of the sofa, but he didn't acknowledge it or move. No one else seemed to notice the weird intimacy between us as they waited for me to tell them about my date. "She was nice, just not for me."

"Woah, say what?" Kiran exclaimed. "You didn't like her?"

"She was . . ."

I wanted to complete my sentence with "not Nick." I also wanted Nick to have some kind of reaction to my revelation, but he was blank. No emotion. No movement. Nothing. "She was okay, but we didn't click."

"Shit, one date and she's done already? Maybe give it another try, dude."

"Where did you go?" River asked.

"A restaurant my father picked out."

I was already tired of the questions and ready to forget the evening so far. "How does a person get a drink around here?"

"A sorority volunteered to handle drink deliveries," Alex said, grinning.

"I need another drink. I can order for you." Nick pulled his arm from behind my head and got up.

I wasn't sure what I wanted or what variety of alcohol this rave offered, so I said I would go with him. He nodded, and I followed close on his heels as we pushed through the crowd in the direction of the bar. The warmth of fingers brushed mine, and he turned to me, deep brown eyes gazing back inches from me.

"Sorry it's so crowded. I don't want to lose track of you."

"It's okay," I stammered and continued forward, my fingers entwined with his. At the bar, he let go.

The counter was packed with people standing shoulder to shoulder, squeezed in, hoping to get the bartender's attention. I slid in at the corner against the wall, and Nick hovered close behind me. The warmth of his body and the scent of his cologne teased me. Electricity ran through me as Nick's breath tickled the back of my neck.

It was a mistake to come here tonight.

"I'll have a whiskey, no ice." His voice was rough and thick, and the smell of alcohol was strong on his breath. "Whatever they have is fine."

I fought the urge to lean against him.

"We're table five," he added close to my ear, sending a wave of goose bumps over my skin.

"Got it," I choked.

I waved the bartender down and placed our order for the sorority delivery.

"Done?" Nick asked, still inches from me. If I turned, what would I see? Curiosity got the better of me, and I spun around, meeting his gaze. The sight of Nick and his drunken smirk made my heart skip a beat and my groin ache. He pushed back from the wall and headed back into the crowd before I could answer. I hurried to keep up with him and tripped over something. I lunged forward, catching myself from falling by placing my hands on his back.

He turned around and gripped my elbow. "You okay?"

"I'm fine. It's dark and too crowded over here."

Once again, his fingers laced in mine, and he guided me forward. His heat seeped into my hands, spreading throughout my body, scorching every molecule. My whole body was damp with sweat.

I tightened my grip as I fought to keep up with him. But I held on because I wanted him to hold my hand. I ached for his touch in a way I hadn't craved for anyone before.

Finally, we emerged from the thickest crowd, and he let go.

He chuckled and leaned his face close to mine. "I'm trashed. Can you tell?"

"Do you need to go home?"

"Why? Do you want to take me?"

"If you need to go, I can take you."

"I don't need to, but if you want to, I would."

What was he saying? Did he need a ride or was he suggesting . . . I swallowed through my quickening breath. Did he just ask me to go home with him?

"You're hesitating. Does that mean you're considering it?" He stepped forward until his abdomen was flush with mine, his face looking down into mine. "What do you say, Taka?"

I stepped back. But like a prowling wolf that cornered its prey, he followed me step for step until my back hit a wall. A staircase shrouded us in shadows. My heart was pounding, and my mouth had gone dry. The distance between us was nearly gone. My brain was malfunctioning. I didn't know if I should fight or give in. I was trapped in a mental tug-of-war.

"Are you considering my offer?" he persisted.

I nearly laughed, but the laugh died in my throat as our eyes locked again. There was no joking. No laughing. There was an animalistic need behind those smoldering eyes. I expect he saw the same need in mine.

His eyes raked over my neck like a hungry animal. I wanted to hide. To run for cover. Beg him to leave me alone. Yet, I also wanted to see what he would do next. What would it mean to go home with Nicholas Dawson? I trembled at the thought of us tangled in bed together.

He smirked and ran his fingers through his hair, moving the loose strands out of his eyes. "Do I interest you, Taka?"

The thrum of the music reverberated over my body, drowning out the world. Everything disappeared except pure temptation, dressed in black, standing before me. I still couldn't speak, yet I couldn't look away. I licked my dry lips.

Nick leaned in, dipping his face nearer mine. "You did that on purpose."

"Did what?" I whispered.

He licked his lips, mimicking me, gently mocking me.

The heat of his breath sent a tremble down my spine, and a puff of air escaped my lungs as my mind and body fought in a battle of wills.

His sweet, woodsy cologne flooded me with memories of

his hand covering mine. Of his chest encasing me for a brief moment. I wanted more memories like that. Like this. That spark I dreamed of was unmistakable.

Nick pulled back and looked at me with a heat that pushed through my fears and clawed through my body like a blazing wildfire. He lifted his hand, cupping my chin, then ran his thumb over my jawline and over my lower lip.

The sensation nearly caused my knees to give out. It took everything I had to stay upright against the wall. My chin was tilted up, and his fingers pressed against my skin, forcing me to look into his eyes.

"Are you going to answer me?"

"I haven't decided." I shifted my gaze away from him, trying to avoid eye contact.

"Look at me, Taka." He gripped my chin more firmly. "Don't avoid me."

"I'm not." Even I didn't believe the words as they tumbled out.

"Then why haven't you punched me or pushed me away? Why haven't you told me to fuck off and run from me? You don't think I can see how you act around me? You try to hide it, but occasionally that mask of yours slips away, and I get a glimpse of you."

Was I that bad at hiding the fact that I had craved this moment with an intensity I had never felt before? I wanted him so badly that I was willing to pretend the world didn't exist and it was only the two of us. Even if, for only a moment, I could be who I wanted.

"I thought I imagined it the first couple times, but now, I think I know." Nick traced two fingers down my neck, and I moaned softly when he reached my collarbone. His fingers ghosted over my shoulder before firmly encircling the back of my head, the pressure sending a surge of warmth through my body.

I had never been touched this way. Never felt this wanted by someone. It was like I had been introduced to a new drug, and I was only being given a taste.

"I'm giving you a chance to tell me to stop. If you don't want to, then say it. Punch me, kick me. I don't care." He scanned my face; his eyes darted all over, looking for any sign that I would reject him.

When I didn't protest, he closed the gap, pressing our bodies tight together. His lips brushed over mine, sending a wave of heat erupting through my insides, teasing to the surface something I had suppressed with every ounce of my being. Like a seed sprouting after a long winter, I came to life, and there was no turning back.

His hands slid down my sides to my lower back. His lips were so close I could feel the heat against my skin. A breath passed between us before our lips collided. Desperation hung in the air as his fingers found their way under my shirt, and the moment there was skin-to-skin contact, I knew I could not resist the intense desire that seeped into my soul.

A choked moan escaped me as his hands climbed over my body, and our kiss deepened. When his lips parted, I slid my tongue into his mouth, teasing and dancing with him. It was warm and strong and tasted of alcohol. The fabric of his shirt stretched beneath my grasp as I tugged at it. As I ran my fingers over the front of his shirt, I broke away from him, my breaths coming out in short, heavy bursts. "I want this gone."

Nick smiled. "Is the answer yes, then?"

I scanned our table in the distance. Everyone was laughing and clearly entertained by each other. *Would they even notice if we left? Probably not.*

"Let's go before I change my mind," I said and pulled my keys from my pocket.

"I'm right behind you." His lust-filled voice was pure seduction.

My breath caught as I pushed off the wall and stepped out from the shadow of the staircase.

• • •

The twenty-minute drive back to campus was excruciating, but the walk from the garage to Nick's apartment topped that. We were silent. Not a peep came from Nick since we left the rave. It was like he was afraid of breaking the spell.

Hell, so was I.

If that kiss had happened anywhere but in a public space, I would have stripped him in seconds. Now we had time to contemplate our choices. Nick was sobering up, and I was terrified.

I have actually come home with him. I drove him here.

Nick's phone rang as we stepped into the entrance of his building.

"Hey, Sky," he whispered as we entered the stairwell. "I'm home," he said, placing his hand on my back to nudge me up the stairs faster. "He's with me. He drove me home."

Nick paused a moment, and I could only imagine what Sky was saying on the other end. Words of encouragement? Words of warning? Probably both.

His hand slipped from my back, and a moment later, his

keys jingled. "I'll text you later. Tell Riv that I'm sorry I ditched her, and make sure you and Will keep an eye on her. You understand?" We exited the stairwell and turned the corner. "I'm hanging up now." He slid the phone into his pocket and slotted the key in the door.

"Did they finally notice we left them?"

"They did."

"Are they upset?"

"Sky is telling them I got sick, and you took me home."

I stepped through the threshold into the dimly lit entryway. My heart was racing, and I debated running away.

Nick kicked off his shoes, then turned to me. "Now, if I remember correctly, you wanted my shirt off."

He gripped his shirt, pulling it from the waistline of his pants. I watched him slowly unbutton the shirt until his chest was revealed. His body was lean, and his toned muscles invited me to look. A thin trail of dark hair that started at his navel disappeared beneath his waistband.

He tugged the shirt off and tossed it to the side before closing the distance between us. "Your turn," he whispered.

I struggled to breathe as his fingers swiftly unbuttoned my shirt. He spread it open at the sides and tugged the fabric from my arms. The material settled at our feet, and I felt more exposed than I ever had before. My cheeks flushed with warmth as I dipped my chin to my shoulder, wanting to hide from him.

"Don't look at me like that," I said. My heart fluttered like it couldn't decide on a speed, and my breath was far too light and quick. I was getting lightheaded. His gaze was like a spark, igniting a fire inside me with every lingering look.

"Like what?" He stepped closer.

My pulse quickened, pounding through my veins. "Like you're going to devour me."

A deep chuckle climbed up his throat, raspy and filled with heat. "I'm looking at you like that because I will."

Goose bumps ran down my arms, and the bulge in my pants strained against my slacks.

"Taka," he said, pressing our abdomens together, dipping his head in the crook of my neck as he rubbed his arousal over mine through our pants. Nick's cologne surrounded me, dissolving what little resistance I still had. If I let go, gave in, would I be happy? If I released myself from the rules and expectations, could I satisfy this longing?

I knew what I was doing went against everything I was supposed to be. If people found out . . .

Fuck it.

I gripped his waist, and my palms slid over his soft skin. He teased me with a gentle thrust.

"Is this your first time with a man?" His breath was a warm whisper against my skin, heating me in the coldest parts of my heart.

I shook my head.

But this wasn't the same as before, nowhere near the same. What I had done in the past didn't come close to this intensity. This was entirely different.

"Good," he breathed as his fingers slid to my belt. His skin grazed my navel, sending a shiver through my chest. The button came loose, then the zipper.

I was on fire. Crumbling under the slightest touch.

His breath ran over my shoulder, and I clung to his hips while he loosened my pants. I reached for his waistband, tugging the button free before slipping my finger into the band of his boxers. There was already a dotting of pre-come on the fabric, and I ran my thumb over the area, provoking a groan. He braced himself on the wall, encasing me between his arms.

I had never been in the position of wanting to be devoured by someone, and, at this moment, I was willing to let Nick have me however he wanted.

"When was the last time?" he asked.

It had been a long time. We were boys, inexperienced boys. "Freshman year of high school."

"Okay," he said, dropping a hand to my waistband, tugging my boxers low, exposing my erection.

I mirrored his movement, sliding his waistband down and running my finger up his length. The skin was soft and warm. Heat settled in my abdomen as I touched him.

A grunt came from Nick as his hands cupped my sides. I was off the ground in a flash, wrapping my legs around his waist. His hands braced under my thighs as he moved us into his bedroom, kicking the door shut behind us.

I hadn't been picked up since I was a young boy, and Nick being able to lift me, like it was nothing, turned me on more than I ever could have expected. I grabbed his face and brought our lips together. It was soft at first, like a quiet greeting, then his tongue was rolling over mine.

He sat on the bed, and my knees hit the mattress without breaking our kiss. His hands climbed over my body as he tugged me down until my chest was flush with his.

I reached for our erections, wrapping my hand around our lengths. The heat of the connection seeped into my body, sending warmth crawling up my spine.

Nick dropped his head back, breaking our kiss and thrusting in my grasp. His breath rushed over me as he released a soft groan. The heat of his tongue ran over my skin as he sucked at my throat.

"Nick, don't–" I groaned as he sucked again and thrust in my hand, sliding his length over mine. His touch on my lower back was gentle, but firm, as he held me against him.

In a blur, I was rolled onto my back, sinking into the soft bed, and Nick braced himself above me with a sly smile.

"What are you–"

His mouth was on mine, his tongue breaching and entering my space.

Blazing heat trailed over my chest as his fingertips slid over my skin, tracing my collarbone, sternum, and navel. He brushed my hand to the side with a smirk that sent a shiver down my spine before trailing kisses down my chest. My arousal throbbed, leaking onto my abdomen, aching for attention. Fingers gripped my wrist, pinning my hand on the bed near my head. A rush of adrenaline pounded through my veins, and my chest tightened with need as rapid breaths forced their way from my lungs.

"Let it out. Make all the noise you want." Nick's voice was hoarse, full of desire. "No one but me will hear you."

He slid his fingers down my abdomen, past my navel, to the tip of my arousal, and I gasped at the contact.

"Stop teasing," I begged.

"But that's half the fun." His lips trailed over my body as he licked and bit me all over.

"I can't take it."

He trailed his tongue to my navel, his chin and throat

pressing against my erection as he dropped further.

"You're such a tease."

"You want it that bad, huh?"

I bit my lip, nodding as my body begged for more.

"If that's what you want, I'll let you have it."

His lips descended on mine, and his hand wrapped around our erections. It was warm and slick with pre-come. I wrapped my legs around his waist and thrust with him.

A moan poured from him as he dropped his face into my neck and cupped my ass. He released our arousals and pressed me tight against his abdomen as we continued our rocking. Another groan spread through him as his palm braced my lower back, holding me so that our bodies were as close as they could get. We thrust in time with each other, sliding between skin coated in our pre-come, losing ourselves in desperation and pleasure.

I clung to him as my climax rocked through me, spilling over my abdomen.

"Shit," Nick breathed as he thrust against me, sliding in my come. The heat of his climax joined mine, and it pooled between us.

Our breathing was heavy as we sank to the bed, and reality crept in.

I had never been handled like that before. It was the most exhilarating experience I had in years.

What did I just do?

I wanted more.

CHAPTER 19

NICK

Taka seemed to be panicking, even regretting it. I didn't exactly ask the important questions before ripping clothes off.

I was too scared to speak. I could feel the tension in the air as we came down from the lust-filled high.

The only light came from my clock on the nightstand, giving enough illumination to see traces of my room. I pulled back, resting on my heels between his thighs. His pants were tugged down past his ass, exposing him in the most delicious way.

My heart sank at the thought of him leaving here, regretting this moment, and never speaking to me again. I couldn't let that happen. But first, I needed to clean up the mess. He was covered in our cum. It pooled on his abdomen, filling the valleys between his defined abs. He was lean and full of muscle. I bet he hit the gym daily to look like that. Would he hate me if I licked . . .

Fucking hell, Nick. What are you thinking?

"Don't move. I'll get a towel." I rushed to the bathroom, grabbed a hand towel, and then rushed back to the bedroom, where I prayed Taka was still lying.

To my surprise, he hadn't disappeared. He was in the same position I left him in. I flicked on the side table lamp and counted to ten, gathering myself enough to face him. The bed dipped as I sat beside him and touched the cloth to his skin. My hand shook as I ran the towel over his body. Was he angry? Upset? I wasn't sure what to do.

"Thanks," Taka whispered, dropping his arm over his eyes.

"Sure." I tugged his waistband back up, then focused on my own mess. It had mostly dried already, so I put myself back together and sat beside him. "You okay?"

He clenched his jaw before saying, "No."

I held my breath as panic raced like lightning through my veins. I had told him to hit me, punch me, whatever if he didn't want to go through with it. At no point did he tell me he didn't want this.

"I, um," he whispered through a shudder. His chest dipped like he was fighting back a sob.

I fought the urge to pull him into my lap and hold him. What the hell was happening?

"Is it my fault?"

"No."

Relief settled the storm that had been brewing, quickly replacing panic with concern. "Do you want to talk about it?"

"I don't know." His chest caved, and a sob rocked through the silence.

"Woah, this is a first for me. I've never been so good that

I made someone cry," I said through a strained laugh, hoping to relieve some of the tension.

Chuckles broke through his sobs as he turned on his side, facing away from me. "There aren't many people in this world that know I'm bi. In fact, you make four."

"Oh," I said, leaning against the headboard while keeping an eye on his shrinking figure.

Taka curled into a ball as if trying to hide from the world. I hated seeing him like this, but I understood. I understood more than most.

"Two people were my boyfriends, but it's been so long since I ever spoke to either of them, and I broke it off in such harsh ways that they probably wouldn't care if I were alive or dead."

"Hurt them that bad, huh?"

He nodded and sniffed.

I wanted to comfort him, rub his back while he let it all out, tell him everything was going to be okay and he could rely on me. But there was this wall between us that hadn't collapsed yet.

I told him, "I came out to my mom and siblings in eleventh grade. I was beyond terrified, but Sky convinced me I needed to accept who I was, and if no one else in this world accepted me for me, then they could fuck off, and I could find a new family. A family that I make of people that love me without limitation."

"What happened?" he asked in a tiny voice, like my personal history somehow had weight.

"My mom said she'd always known and had been waiting for me to tell her on my own terms. My sister loved me no matter what. My little brother was too young to fully understand."

"What about your dad?"

"I wouldn't know."

"What do you mean?" He flipped over to look at me with tear-filled eyes.

"My father left when I was in elementary school. I haven't seen or spoken to him since."

Taka's eyes grew wide, tears spilling onto his cheeks as he sat up to face me. "I'm sorry. I didn't mean to bring up something like that."

I shrugged. "It's not your fault. How could you know without me telling you?"

His sobs had stopped, and he looked like he might be okay.

"Can you tell me why you're so upset?" I asked.

He wiped his tears and crossed his legs. "My family immigrated to the States when I was five. I was born in Chiba but have no memories of living there. My sister was born here, so she and I are very Americanized, but my family is holding onto many traditions and expect us to follow them as well."

"That's pretty cool. I couldn't even tell you where my family is from. We're all a bunch of mutts."

He laughed, and the smile lit up his face. "As the eldest and the first-born son, there is a lot of expectation on my shoulders. My sister, Tami, is fifteen. It's only the four of us in the States. We don't have any family here." He ran his hands through his hair, pushing the loose strands from his face. The strands fell right back into his eyes, and I resisted pushing them back for him. "My father wants me to go into the family business, marry a woman, and continue—"

"The family name." I nodded. "Fathers can be like that. They want the bloodline and family name passed through their children. Society tells us that the responsibility falls on men.

It puts pressure on us to meet those expectations, and if we don't, then we're failures."

"Exactly," he breathed, his voice cracking. "But that isn't the only reason. My father—" He paused, sucking in a deep breath. "When there was talk of legalizing same-sex marriage, he lost it. He was furious. I know it isn't legal yet, but knowing how he felt about people he didn't know or would never meet scared me. I was terrified he would disown me."

"So you never thought about telling your family?"

He shook his head. "I've thought about it plenty. The problem is that I can never see a positive outcome."

"Family can surprise you. People who love you, *truly* love you, can often overlook their own issues. But you'll never know how they'll act until you're in the situation."

"It terrifies me."

"It isn't a simple thing to talk about. Not yet. I hope that one day we can simply be ourselves without limitation, but we aren't there yet. Not even close." Tears welled up in his eyes again. I looped my hand around his and gently pulled him toward me, then wrapped him in a hug. As he settled his cheek against my chest, I combed my fingers through his hair, hoping I could help ease his fears. "Taka, you don't have to pretend around me. Be yourself."

His tears hit my skin, and I tightened my hold around him, burying my face in his hair.

I wasn't sure how long we clung to each other, but it felt like hours. Taka's breath was soft against my skin. His face was red, eyes swollen from crying. He'd fallen asleep curled up against me, but I was getting cold, and we needed to shower.

"Taka." I stroked his head.

He groaned and nestled into my neck.

"We should shower, and do your parents know you aren't going home tonight?"

His sleep-filled eyes blinked through his exhaustion. "What time is it?" He pushed off me and rubbed his eyes before fishing his phone from his pocket.

His hair was disheveled, and his skin was covered in pink blotches from the kisses and bites I'd left. I thought I'd gone easy on him, but damn.

"Crap, it's after two."

"Spend the night. Let your parents know you won't be home."

His eyes flicked back to his phone. "Are you sure?" He dipped his head and tapped the screen.

"Stay the night."

I wasn't sure how to handle this situation. At the beginning of the night, I still thought he was straight. But when he arrived at the club, I was so trashed that my filter was shot. Completely gone. At that point, I thought I had nothing left to lose. If someone had told me this was how my night would turn out, I wouldn't have believed them.

"I'll get you a change of clothes so you can shower," I said, then headed for the closet.

I sifted through my drawers and grabbed him a shirt, sweatpants, and boxers. Warmth wrapped around my heart, tightening around my chest as I reflected on this moment. Taka was about to shower in my house and wear my clothes. God, I was lucky. A smile crept over my face as I pulled fresh towels from the linen closet.

When I found him, he was hanging around the counter in

the kitchen. I took in the sight of him standing in my space, shirtless, disheveled, and rubbing his sleepy eyes as I sauntered to the kitchen. *I could get used to this*, I thought, but I had a feeling this was a delicate situation. Was he willing to date me, or did he still want to hide this side of himself? Could we be boyfriends? Lovers? Life partners?

I shocked myself at the thought. I hadn't wanted to date someone since Adam, and here I was, hoping Taka would want to be with me.

"I left you a change of clothes and fresh towels in the bathroom. Let me know if you need anything else."

"Thanks, Nick, I appreciate it." He set his phone on the counter and shuffled to the bathroom.

Damn, I knew he was trouble the moment I laid eyes on him, but this night lifted me to cloud nine. Whatever happened next, I hoped it would be worth it.

CHAPTER 20

TAKA

Before I entered the shower, I couldn't stop looking in the mirror. The man reflected there looked precisely how I felt. Guilty. I dried myself and slid into the clothes Nick had left me. What the hell had I done tonight? After all these years, I let myself cave . . . and then I cried in front of him! With a sigh, I ran my hands over my face. What was I supposed to do now?

Sinking to the floor, I tucked my head between my knees. Not once in my life had I ever been treated like that. But the way Nick was, how he . . . *Oh, God.* I buried my face in my hands.

"Taka, you okay in there?" Nick asked through the door.

A throaty noise escaped me as I lifted myself up. "I'm fine," I said, opening the door.

He held a mug in his hands with a crooked smile. "Have some tea," he said, offering the cup. "I ran to the convenience store just off campus and grabbed you a toothbrush and some snacks. If you're hungry, we could always drop by Jay's. But first, I'm gonna hop in the shower."

I slipped past him, glancing at my watch. "At this hour? It's nearly three."

"Hunger doesn't have a time limit," he said, closing the bathroom door behind him.

Leaning against the kitchen counter, I gripped the mug like it had the answers I was looking for. I listened to the shower running and eyed the chips and candy bars Nick had bought. After a few minutes of contemplation, I chose a bag of chips, quickly opened the package and stuffed a few in my mouth.

My phone rang on the counter, drawing me out of a daze. I drew in a deep breath, then slowly released it before hitting the answer icon, dreading my next moments as I lifted the phone to my ear. "Hi, Mom."

"Taka, what friend? You never stay out like this."

"I know, Mom. One of my friends was very drunk, and I brought him home. I didn't realize the time until it was two, so I stayed here."

"This isn't like you. Is something going on? What happened to your date?"

I blinked, confused. Then I remembered Maeko. "Oh, I was tired and didn't want to continue to drive. I'm sleeping on his couch for the night. There's nothing to worry about."

She pestered me with questions, and I diligently answered. I was exhausted, but I could have driven home.

Nick breezed out of the bathroom, a towel wrapped around his waist. My breath hitched at the sight of him before he disappeared into his bedroom. He was sauntering toward me a moment later, shirtless and glistening with beads of water on his shoulders. His hair was wet and wavy. Sweatpants slung low on his waist, sparking images of what we had done in my mind.

Nick was handsome and stood out from the crowd. Something about him, though, was mysterious, unknowable, like there was a darkness in his heart, covered by his friendly demeanor. A darkness that mirrored my own. It drew me in.

"Taka!" Mom barked, yanking me back to our conversation.

"Yes, I'm here."

She continued, but my focus was on Nick as he spun on the barstool across from me, looking at his phone and eating a candy bar. The tattoo that had teased me was on full display as he spun. It was breathtaking. Covering his pale skin was a black-ink masterpiece of a bird, emerging from flames, gripping a clock in its talons, one hand pointing to four and the other to seven. The wings spanned across his back, curling over each shoulder. The tail feathers wrapped around his left side, ending around his waistline.

"Please let me know these things ahead of time. Your father and I worry about you."

"Yes, Mom. I'm sorry. I won't do it again."

She said her goodbyes and hung up.

Nick was flipping through a magazine. On the counter, next to the glossy pages, was the empty candy bar wrapper. "Finally," he said, dropping the page he was about to turn. He was so relaxed. Like he was unaffected by tonight's events. Or was he that good at pretending?

"We could still go to Jay's if you're hungry."

I shook my head. "I don't want to eat a meal. The chips were fine for me."

He slid from the barstool with a shrug. "Suit yourself. By

the way, you'll need clean clothes. I'll put yours in the wash."

"There's no point with mine. Dry-clean only."

He hopped to the front door and grabbed my button-up off the floor. "We could iron it, but—" He stuffed his nose in the cloth and took a whiff. "It doesn't stink or anything." He folded it and set the shirt on the counter before returning to the barstool.

"My pants are another story," I said.

"You could always leave in my clothes tomorrow."

I glanced down at the sweatpants and T-shirt that hung loosely over my body. "Too bad my dress shoes don't mix well with this look."

"How tall are you?"

"Six-foot."

"On the dot?"

I nodded, slightly puzzled.

"I'm six-three. It may not work." He lifted his phone off the counter and tapped the screen a few times. A moment later, he smiled and said, "Sky, my best friend ever." He listened as Sky spoke to him and then said, "Taka is sleeping over and will need a change of clothes. Can he borrow yours?" He eyed me while Sky replied. "Probably just some jeans—oh, and maybe some shoes." He mouthed at me, "What shoe size are you?"

"Eleven and a half," I whispered.

"Sky, I'll pick out shoes too." Nick paused a moment as he listened before chuckling and running his fingers through his hair. "Okay, see you in a few," he said and set his phone on the counter.

"Sky is coming home? It could wait until tomorrow."

"He won't be home tomorrow. He spends the weekends

with Will. Since his room is locked, he's coming to grab clothes for you. He's five-eleven and wears the same shoe size. The jeans should fit you well enough." He tapped the counter and slid from the barstool. "Let's hang out on the sofa while we wait for him. It will only be a few minutes."

As we relaxed beside each other, I realized my mom was right about one thing. This wasn't normal for me. I didn't spend the night with friends. And I especially didn't spend the night with a lover. And never had I fallen into bed with someone I wasn't dating.

"Can I ask you something?"

Nick tilted his head to the side and set his phone on the coffee table. "Shoot."

"What does your tattoo represent?"

His gaze flicked to his left shoulder. "It's a phoenix rising again."

"And the clock?"

"Four for April and seven for 2007." His lips formed a wistful smile. "The month and year I came out to my family. The month and year that Nicholas Dawson was reborn to the world. The day that I told the world that I wasn't afraid."

"I envy you."

"Don't. There are a lot of scars hidden under this exterior," he said, rubbing his thumb over the leather bracelet on his wrist.

"But–"

"Nicholas!"

Nick and I jumped out of our skins as the owner of the voice barreled into the apartment. Nick hopped to his feet and greeted his friend with a hug. Sky's eyes landed on me. "Nick," he scolded, wrapping his arm around his shoulder and tugging him close. I couldn't hear what they said, but assumed he was whispering about me.

"My God, Sky." Nick pulled away with a laugh. "Unlock your room already."

"Fine." He crossed his arms and stared me down. "What style of clothes do you like, Taka?"

"Anything will be fine."

Sky shrugged, briefly disappearing into his bedroom, then reappearing with black jeans and dark sneakers. "Try these on. I hope after all this, they actually fit."

I took them and headed to the bathroom, listening to the pair laugh and bicker. They had a relationship that I was envious of. Even though I had close friends, like the guys and Rylee, I never felt the bond Nick and Sky appeared to have.

The jeans hugged me tighter than I was used to, but they were comfortable. I always thought tight jeans would cut in all the wrong places, but they were surprisingly comfy. I slipped out of them and back into the sweatpants before returning to the living room.

"Did they fit?" Nick asked as I set the jeans on the coffee table.

"They did. A lot better than I expected."

Sky smiled. "Give it all back when you can. Follow the directions when you wash the jeans or buy me a new pair if they shrink."

"Get out of here," Nick said, ruffling Sky's hair as he opened the door. The action brought memories of what I do to Tami, a kind fondness toward someone, gentle and laced with adoration.

Sky tossed him the bird over his shoulder as he disappeared into the hallway, closing the door behind him. Nick sank onto the sofa and dropped his head back. "Sorry about him. He can be a bit to get used to."

"It's fine," I said, joining Nick on the sofa. "It's good to have reliable people in your life like him. Who else would rush back home without hesitation at three in the morning?"

He nodded. "And that is why I consider him my brother."

"You're lucky to have that."

"Don't you think of the guys like that? I thought Alex, Zack, and Kiran were your friends."

"I'm close to them, but it's not quite the same as what you and Sky seem to have."

As I said it, I felt the emptiness in my heart that needed to be filled by someone who truly understood me. Maybe I had found that someone in Nick.

CHAPTER 21

NICK

The sun crept through the blinds, accompanied by the comforting sounds of birds chirping near the window. Taka was peaceful, his face mushed against the pillow, hair tangled and fluffy. He was even more adorable in his sleep, as if the weight of life's expectations didn't follow him into his dreams.

"Hey, Taka," I said, resting my chin in my hand as I rolled onto my side. He didn't stir.

It was one o'clock, according to the clock on the side table. We'd slept the day away, and I couldn't believe I had him beside me like this. Would he stay with me today? Could I convince him to sleep over a second night? I wanted to try.

"Taka," I said, inching closer until I was millimeters from him, sharing in his space. I could get used to this. Going to bed beside him. Waking up to his sleeping face. Those long black lashes and soft lips. His slender neck, begging me to kiss it.

"Wake up," I whispered. *Please wake up.* I wanted to see that groggy look from him.

I ran my fingers through his hair, down his neck, and over the cotton shirt, but he still didn't stir.

"Taka, I'll kiss you if you don't wake up."

Still nothing. Only his gentle breath puffed against my cheek.

I leaned in, closing the gap, brushing my lips over his cheek and nose. Wrapping my hand around his waist, I tugged him close, pressing him against me. A slight noise rose from him, but he was still dead to the world. I kissed his cheek again, sliding my hand under his shirt and stroking his warm, smooth skin.

"Taka, wake up so we can play," I whispered in his ear. "Come on. Wake up." I trailed my tongue along his jawline.

He stirred with a groan that sent my heart fluttering into the clouds. I kissed his cheek again, trailing soft kisses to the corner of his mouth. Heat raced to my groin, and my cock strained against the fabric of my pants. "Please wake up." I slid my hand down the curve of his spine to the waistband of the sweatpants. Last night was hurried. Desperate. Right now, I wanted to treasure him.

He moved and stretched against me, his thick lashes parting as he blinked away his sleep.

"Morning," I said.

"Why are you so close? It's too early for this," he groaned, pressing his palm against my bare chest.

"It's after one. We slept the day away." Sliding my fingers further down his back, I slipped beneath the waistband. "But the man beside me was so cute, I couldn't help but beg him to wake up and pay attention to me."

"And what kind of attention are you seeking?" he asked, coyly.

"I think you can guess." I kissed his chin and slid my hand further, cupping his ass and kneading my fingers in the muscle.

A soft moan fell from his lips, and he hid his face in my neck. "I've never done that."

"That's okay," I whispered, kissing the top of his head. "Would you want to with me, or is it out of the question?"

"I would try with you."

My heart slammed against my rib cage as I tried to rein in my nervous excitement. I half expected him to shoot me down and tell me he would never consider it.

"Do you want to try with me now?"

His dark eyes glistened with heat as he gave the slightest nod.

His flushed cheeks and groggy morning look had me melting inside. My heart fluttered, leaving me nearly breathless. "I promise I won't do anything unless you're comfortable with it. You tell me to stop, and we stop."

He nodded, tracing his fingers up my chest, caressing my neck, then his fingers slid through my hair. Heat spread down my neck and spine, evidence of his touch. Then he pulled me into a deep kiss.

My cock grew harder, aching for him. I pressed closer, rubbing against his abdomen.

He wrapped a leg over mine, hooking us together. The position opened him to me, and I took advantage, running my fingers down his crevice and over his hole. A soft gasp caught in the air before I was on my back, pinned beneath him. The sun poured through the window, lighting him up as if the heavens were shining down, claiming him as theirs; rays of sunlight lit his skin like a statue, shadowing the curves and crevices as if sculpted by God himself.

He lifted the shirt over his head, achingly slow as he straddled me. I ran my fingers over his skin, taking in every inch of him. Committing his every breath, curve, and touch to memory.

He dipped his head, bracing his hands on my chest as he ground against the aching bulge in my pants. Pulling him close, I closed my lips around a nipple, twirling my tongue and sucking until his breath was heavy and his hands clung to my shoulders. I released the nub, gently caressing Taka's skin with my lips. I slid my hand up to the back of his neck and brought him into a kiss. Wrapping my arms around him, I rolled him onto his back, pinning him beneath me. He was panting, and my nerves were tingling.

"One moment." I reached over him and dug through the side table for the lube and condoms.

"Nick." Trembling hands held my hips. "Is it true?"

"Is what true?" I asked as I settled back between his legs.

"Will it hurt?"

I let out a breath and set the tube and packet beside us. "I won't lie to you. Many people experience some pain, especially for their first time. It can depend on the individual and the prep."

His features fell into a frown, and he stared at me.

"I swear to you, I will do everything in my power to avoid hurting you. I want you to crawl back to me, begging me to do it again and again." I placed a tender kiss on his collarbone, relishing the sensation of his body so close to mine. "I want to make you feel so good that you never want to leave."

"I can't believe you said that," he said, grinning.

"Taka, that's tame compared to the things inside my head."

"I think I'm afraid of your mind."

"You should be." I pressed our foreheads together. "I want you addicted to me because I'm already addicted to you."

"You're so corny," Taka whispered, cupping his hand on the back of my neck and pulling me into a kiss.

I pressed my lips to his heated body as I made my way to his navel. Then, hooking my fingers in the waistband of the sweatpants, I tugged them down along with the boxers, tossing them to the side. Before slipping out of my clothes, I took a moment to admire him. I could finally understand why artists would paint their lovers. I wanted to capture this image forever. The golden sunlight danced over his skin like rivulets of honey. It was something I never wanted to forget.

I settled between his thighs, positioning his ass on a pillow.

"What's the pillow for?"

"Some people say it helps. We'll try it," I said, opening the lube and covering my fingers. "Please tell me if it hurts." Rubbing my fingers over his hole, I lathered it before slowly inching the first finger inside of him. His breath hitched as I slid deeper. "Try to relax," I said.

"It feels odd."

I snorted. "Well, my finger's in your ass. I would think it feels weird."

He erupted in a deep laugh, and I slid my finger further.

"There, see, when you're relaxed, it's easy to get in." I slowly moved around inside him, being as gentle as possible.

"This isn't so bad," he said.

"Good. I'm trying another finger." Slowly pulling my finger out, I poured another glob of lube. "Remember, keep relaxed, and trust me." I ran my thumb over his hole, hoping the sensation would relax him.

A quiet moan puffed from Taka's lips. His eyes were wide, like he hadn't expected it to feel good. Swirling my fingers around the opening, I bent over him, running my tongue down the center of his abdomen until I reached his erection. I ran my tongue over the tip as I slid two fingers into his hole. He tightened as I entered, so I paused and licked his length before taking him into my mouth.

His fingers settled in my hair as I took him all the way in and waited for his muscles to relax. As he loosened, I moved, provoking a soft moan from him. I kept inching inside while distracting him with my mouth. When he felt relaxed enough, I began the hunt for the prostate. When I finally found the smooth ball, I paused and released his cock from my mouth with a smile. "Got you." I moved up and captured his lips with mine, stroking the soft, round ball that rested against my fingertips. His nails dug into my back as I caressed his warm walls. When I released his mouth from my assault, he cursed at me.

I couldn't help but laugh as I teased the soft gland again.

After working his hole, I reached for the condom. "I'm turning you over, okay?"

"Why?"

"It's hopefully going to be easier to enter you this way."

"If you say so," he said, eyeing me as I slid on the condom.

"Tell me if it hurts. Discomfort is one thing, but pain is something I don't want you to have." I slid my hands up his thighs to his hips. "Okay, turn over for me." He did as I asked, and I tugged the pillow out from under him. His back was smooth and muscled. His legs were spread, waiting for me. I lathered my cock with lube before rubbing some around his hole again. I was taking no chances today.

Bending over him, I kissed the center of his back before

nudging at his hole. It was slick, but I moved slowly, inching my way inside, looking for any sign that it hurt him.

His fingers were clenching the blanket, and he buried his face in a pillow. I didn't like to start in this position. I wanted to see his face as I entered him, but this would have to do.

He groaned as I sunk deeper. His fingers tightened on the blanket as I filled him until he completely encased me. I bent over his back, wrapping my arms around his waist. "Are you feeling okay?"

He nodded with quick, heavy breaths.

"Does it hurt?"

"A little."

"Do you want me to stop?"

"No," he breathed.

I rocked inside him, letting him grow accustomed to me before sliding out slowly. He gasped as I pushed back inside just as slowly. A shiver rolled through his body as I passed over that soft, little gland. My fingers spread over the center of his back as I rocked, taking in the sight of my cock sliding in until his ass was pressed against me. I slid my fingers over his toned back, packed with lean muscle. My other hand cupped his hip, digging into his skin. The view of it made me harder. I pulled my hand from his back and bent over him, reaching around and sliding my palm over his length until a deep moan poured from his chest.

"Don't be so gentle," he groaned.

I obeyed his request, pulling him up, cupping his face with my palm, and capturing him with my mouth. His hands flew behind us, gripping my ass in his tight hold. I held him close, but I wanted him facing me.

Taka broke our kiss as he released a breathy moan. He tried

to drop back down to the bed, but I held him in place and kissed the back of his neck. Just behind his ear, I sucked on the soft skin. His moaning carried in the room, and I wanted to hear more. My hand held tight to his abdomen, and his cock bounced against my knuckles as I thrust inside him, provoking a string of moans.

Slipping out of him, I let him drop to his hands, his breath heavy as he glanced back at me.

"Face me. I want to see you better."

He turned around and wrapped his arms around my neck, drawing me into a sensual kiss. I pulled him close and pushed him to the bed. His legs wrapped around me, opening himself to my cock once more. I entered him slowly, careful not to hurt him, rocking until I found the gland again. Not everyone can orgasm from only stimulation of the prostate, but I was going to try.

We moved in time with one another. Each time I passed over Taka's gland, he shivered. His face fell to my shoulder, and his heated breath rushed over my neck as I pushed inside him again. His moans were soft but growing more frequent. I was sure if I touched his dripping cock, he would climax. But I wanted to give him something he would never forget.

I ran over the gland again, and Taka's body shivered beneath me as a deep groan fell from his lips, his eyes rolled back, and his body went limp. I stroked his cock, forcing a breathy whimper from him as he erupted in my hand. He clenched around me, his hole pulsating. The mix of sensations sent me over the edge, and deep inside his warmth, I came.

We collapsed, and I rolled to the side, catching my breath.

"What the hell kind of orgasm did I just have?"

I chuckled and rolled to face him. "Amazing?"

"Amazing doesn't even come close to how that felt."

We lay there for a minute, catching our breath and staring at the ceiling. The sun rained in from the window, reminding me we had done absolutely nothing today. Though it was worth every moment.

"Nick," Taka whispered.

"Yeah?"

"Get me a towel."

I chuckled. "I have something better." I climbed over him and placed a soft kiss on his forehead before scooping him into my arms.

"Hey, what are you doing?"

"You'll see."

I slid off the bed and carried him into the bathroom, where I set him on the edge of the bathtub and flipped on the water. Tugging the condom off, I tied it and tossed it in the trash before grabbing a washcloth from the linen closet.

"I could've walked, you know."

"I know, but why walk when I can carry you?"

"Are you going to carry me everywhere now?"

"If you want me to." I wiggled my brows, then checked the temperature of the water before swishing the washcloth under the stream. I wiped the cloth over Taka's stomach and tossed it in the hamper.

"Hey, Nick," Taka breathed.

"Hmm?"

"I think that was the best sex I've ever had."

"Seriously?" I tried to hide my smile but failed.

He nodded. "Without a doubt."

"You're not just saying that, right?"

"I'm serious."

"If you wanna do it again, say the word." I chuckled and looked at my reflection in the mirror. A huge red bite mark was on the left side of my neck. Perfectly in view for the world to see, and lines of blood were oozing out of tiny punctures. "You bit me!"

Taka flinched and covered his mouth. "It was your fault."

"How was it my fault?"

"You made me come right after I had already gone through that explosive orgasm, and I was so full of pleasure that it almost hurt. I didn't know what to do with myself. I was feeling so much, so I bit something, and it happened to be you."

I laughed. "Happened to be me?" Another chuckle fell from my lips as I looked at the bite mark. "Man, how did this not hurt? You drew blood. Are you a fucking vampire?"

Taka bent over himself with laughter as I rubbed water over the wound.

"Oh my God. People are going to talk so much shit about me," I said.

"Just tell them you fucked someone so good they tried to kill you."

I spun around, gaping at him. "You're so bad. I knew you would be bad for my health the first moment I met you."

Taka stood quickly, closing the distance between us. "Don't be mad. We can get makeup or something to cover it up."

"You kidding? I'm wearing this proudly. Besides, you aren't without your own marks." I motioned for him to look in the mirror. His neck was covered in hickeys from last night and today.

"Shit, my parents will kill me if they see this."

"Wanna stay over again tonight?"

He glanced back at himself in the mirror. "What will I tell my parents?"

"Tell them I invited you to dinner with our friends, and we're all gonna crash at my place, then go to class from here tomorrow since I live on campus."

"It might work, but my parents will be suspicious of this new friend of mine."

Sliding my hand around his hip, I tugged him close. "Friend, huh?"

"Do you want to be something else?" he asked.

"I like the term lover. Or partner. Boyfriend. Any of those would do."

"Is this you asking to be that with me?"

"And if I say yes, how would you respond?"

He chewed the inside of his cheek. "You know I'm not out, right?"

"If you're worried about me keeping it secret, then there are a couple of rules I have for a secret relationship."

He gave me a quick once-over before slipping his arms around my neck. "Go on."

"I do not keep my family in the dark. They will be told when I want."

"I sense an and."

"Clever boy," I said with a smirk. "Sky, of course, will know. The only issue is that Sky and Will are a thing, so by default, he will be in the loop."

"Naturally."

"And you're cool with that?"

"I am."

CHAPTER 22

TAKA

Monday morning greeted me with the alarm on my phone blaring in my ear. I quickly tapped snooze. There was no way I would go to the gym this morning, and my first class didn't start until nine.

"Nick," I groaned. "What time is your class?"

"Eleven," he said in a sleepy grumble.

I moved my alarm to seven-thirty, thinking that should be enough time to shower, grab breakfast, and walk to class.

Nick's arms wrapped around me, pulling me close.

I snuggled against him and sank back to sleep until my seven-thirty alarm jolted me awake.

The practice of pulling myself away from Nick's embrace proved harder than the theory. I didn't want to return to the reality of my life. The last two days had been the freedom I never knew existed.

After a steamy shower, I put on the jeans I borrowed from Sky, as well as a T-shirt and hoodie from Nick. Last night, our bruises had turned deep shades of blue and purple. Wearing a hoodie for a few days would hide the hickeys until they faded, but the bite mark on Nick's neck was still quite visible. I felt like an asshole for biting him as hard as I did, but as I looked in the mirror at the small blotches all over my neck, my guilt quickly vanished in a wave of pleasure.

I borrowed his deodorant and hair cream, but having the status of boyfriend, I felt it entirely acceptable to spritz myself with his signature cologne. He was sneaky, hiding it under the sink behind his extra bottles of body wash. How Sky never noticed it was beyond me.

The sun shone through the window near the bed, bathing the room in a gentle gray light—a stark contrast to the afternoon sun from the day before. I sat on the edge of the bed, lacing up the sneakers Sky lent me; they fit perfectly and looked like they had never been worn.

As I rose to leave, an inaudible rumble came from beneath the covers.

"Did you need something?" I asked.

"Do I not get a goodbye kiss?"

I leaned over him, tugging the covers away from his face. His hair was messy, and his eyes barely opened as he squinted at me, puckering his lips. I brushed my lips over his in a soft kiss, then placed another on his cheek and forehead. "I'll see you later," I whispered and backed away.

His muffled reply had my heart swelling, and I wondered when the last time I was this happy had been.

As I walked toward the Ellis Center to grab breakfast, I

called Rylee. I was flying high and needed to share in my happiness, maybe get dragged down back to earth from the heavenly cloud I was in.

On the fifth ring, she answered. "T," she said. "Meet me for breakfast?"

"You read my mind. Ellis Center?"

She agreed, and I picked up my pace as we hung up.

Breezing into the small bagel shop on the basement level, I tugged at the neckline of Nick's hoodie. I couldn't remember the last time I had to worry about hickeys, but I remembered why I always kept people from giving them. It's not like they're inherently bad, but I always felt people judged me for having them, like I was a sexual deviant. The looks and stares as if I did something wrong never sat well with me.

I ordered the bacon and egg bagel for Rylee and a regular for myself. The girl passed me a cup for coffee, and I thanked her before turning to their coffee counter set up in the corner. As I poured the sugar, slender arms wrapped around my waist.

"Good morning," Rylee said, squeezing me tight.

I patted her hands as she clung to me. "Morning." I dropped the empty sugar packet into the trash and took a sip of the steaming, dark liquid. "I ordered for us already."

The girl at the register called for me, and I quickly grabbed the paper bag with Rylee hot on my tail. I laughed. "Watering at the mouth, as usual, I see."

We sat at a small square table, and I handed her the bag.

"Food is the best thing in my life other than you." She unwrapped her breakfast and sank her teeth into the sandwich.

"Ry, I have something to confess."

She glanced up from her meal. "Oh yeah?"

I told her everything, spilled my guts, and somehow it made me feel even more secure in my actions. She didn't judge me. Instead, she was proud that I was finally embracing the side of me I had denied. The part of me I pretended didn't exist.

"I know you're probably scared of how this will turn out, but I'm so happy you let him into your life," she said.

I nodded as I finished the last of my coffee. "He makes me feel accepted. I don't know how to describe it."

"You've needed someone like him. I know you have me, and I support you completely, but let's face it, I'm not like you. It's not possible for me to share the same perspective. I can imagine, but I don't know what you've experienced."

She was right. It was important to have someone understand what it's like to live in society from a perspective like mine. I hadn't ever spoken to anyone about it, and the times I met people like me, I had never confided in them. Not once.

Talking with Rylee gave me the courage to face the day. The courage to fully embrace my decision. This was right for me.

• • •

"T, what the hell are you wearing?" Kiran asked as I sat at the table with him, Alex, and Zack at lunchtime.

"Clothes."

"Dude, those are not your clothes. You almost never wear hoodies, and I have seen all of your shoes. Those are not your shoes," Zack said.

"Don't forget that this is the guy that said he would never in his life be caught in skinny jeans." Alex laughed as he poked my thigh.

"I borrowed my clothes from some friends."

"Which friends?" Zack asked, eyeing me.

"Where did you disappear to all weekend?" Kiran asked, leaning forward, resting his chin in his hands.

I was not expecting my friends to be so intrusive. I cleared my throat and stood a little too fast, sending the chair sliding across the floor. "I'm grabbing lunch."

They jumped into their speculations as soon as I walked away. By the time I returned to the table, three sets of eyes silently stared me down. They would not let this go.

Kiran scooted closer until he was nearly touching me. "T, tell us! We're your best friends. We deserve to know where you were and why you had to borrow clothes."

My heart raced as he rested his head on my shoulder. I hadn't thought about an excuse or explanation. It had been the furthest thing from my mind.

Kiran shot up immediately, squinting at me. "No way." He leaned in and breathed deeply. "Nick?"

Shit, the cologne was a mistake.

"What?" Alex joined in, sniffing me. "Oh, that cologne is recognizable anywhere."

"For real?" Zack asked, crossing his arms over his chest. "Were you at his place since Saturday night?"

I dropped my head in my hand and rubbed my face.

"Fucking hell," Kiran breathed as he stood over me. "How did you get a hickey on the back of your neck, dude?"

I groaned and hid my face in my hands. This was not going as planned.

"How drunk were you Saturday?" Alex asked, as if being drunk would be the logical explanation.

"Wait a second. We need some clarification here. Was it Nick that gave you the hickey?" Zack broke into a chuckle and leaned back in his chair. "'Cuz, uh, that would be a big deal."

"Oh, ho. T, look at you. You got another one right behind the ear. My God, what kind of shit did you do?" Kiran was tugging at the collar of the hoodie as he investigated my skin. "Oh shit, you won't be able to wear normal shirts for a while. You've got a ton." Finally, he released me and sat down, clearly satisfied with himself. "Taka's a freak in the sheets."

I groaned, resting my forehead on the table and tugging the hood over my head. I wanted to sink into the floor and hit the restart button on today. My fingers hit the phone screen and opened my conversation with Nick.

Me: *My friends are annoyingly clever.*

In seconds, he replied.

Nick: *Why?*

Me: *Kiran smelled your cologne on me, then noticed a hickey on my neck and lost his mind. Alex, Zack, and Kiran have already guessed, and I haven't said a damn word.*

Nick: *You used my cologne?*

Me: *The cologne is not the important point.*

Nick: *Using my cologne without asking says a lot about how comfortable you are with me :) And it's like I've marked you as mine, and I didn't even have to do anything. Even your friends knew immediately, lol.*

Me: *This isn't funny.*

Nick: *I know you're freaked out. Where are you?*

Me: *Ellis Center food court. Please come save me.*

"T, come on. Give us something here," Kiran begged as he shook my arm.

"We're so curious, dude," Zack said.

"I don't want to talk about it," I grumbled. I slipped my phone back in my pocket and kept my forehead pressed to the table, knowing my boyfriend was likely on his way to rescue me from this horrible fate.

My boyfriend. I still couldn't believe it.

The table fell silent. They probably realized they had gone too far. As smart as they were, they were not subtle. Multiple phones vibrated on the table, and Kiran scoffed. They had moved to texting. Like I couldn't tell.

My food was getting cold, but I refused to lift my head. How could I face them like this?

I let the minutes pass by, hiding my face and refusing to speak to anyone even after their conversation returned to normal.

A breath caught beside me.

"Oh, shit. Did he force himself on you?" Alex asked.

"No!" I shot up, glaring at him with a snarl. "What the hell is wrong with you?"

"It was consensual!" Kiran bounced in his chair.

"What was?" Nick's smooth voice silenced their teasing.

Kiran stilled beside me, but a smile still dimpled his cheeks. He sucked his teeth and glanced between the two of us. "Yo, you know you got a thing." He pointed to his neck, where the giant bruise from the bite mark showed on Nick's neck.

"A vampire bit me."

"Oh." Kiran laughed and scooted his chair away from me. "I see."

"Looks like it hurt," Alex whispered. "Right, Zack?"

Zack cleared his throat. "Yeah, lucky you made it out alive."

Nick pulled up a chair from an empty table nearby, straddling it and resting his arms on the back. "Yeah, lucky."

"So, I'm going to ask because we're dying to know," Zack said, but hesitation filled the air. "You two are a thing, right?" He pointed to us and made a together motion with his hands.

Nick stayed silent, smiling at the curious faces around us. He was keeping his side of our promise. But they already guessed it. What was the use of hiding it from them?

"Yes." I grabbed my plate of food, pulling it closer. "Anyone have a problem with it?"

Heads shook as I dug into my food, reveling in the odd comfort telling them had brought me.

"So, Nick," Kiran said. "Can you tell us something? What's the deal with Will and Sky? Are they together too?"

Nick laced his fingers together and cocked his head to the side. "They're complicated. It's best to leave a label off them."

"And what about you two? Do we ignore the label too?" Zack asked.

I hated my friends. They were the absolute worst.

"Boyfriend," I said.

"Since when?" Alex asked. "Weren't you just on a date with a girl Saturday night?"

God, I hated them.

"I'll ask it since no one else is." Kiran leaned over the table and stared at me. "Have you always liked guys?"

"Jesus," Zack groaned.

"What? It's a valid question," Kiran huffed.

"Yes. Nick is not my first boyfriend."

"For real?" Alex asked, the most shocked out of them.

"Please don't tell people. I don't run around telling the

world I'm bisexual. Okay?"

"Of course, dude. Keeping it hush-hush," Kiran promised. "I guess that means Nick is an official member of the group now. Can I get your number to add you to our group chat?"

Nick froze, like he wasn't sure how to respond.

I nudged his thigh with my knee so he would look at me. Our eyes locked, and I gave him a nod. "Nick doesn't always reply to texts, but he will see them." I gave Nick another nod, encouraging him to go with it. "Go on, Nick. It won't kill you."

He glared at me before handing his phone over to an eager Kiran. "If you annoy me, I'll block you."

Kiran laughed, taking the phone. "So testy."

"What's up, guys?" Will said as he came up behind Zack, with Sky following close behind.

"Nicholas," Sky said when his eyes fell on his friend.

Nick instinctively covered his neck with his hand.

New rule. No biting or sucking of necks so that it leaves marks.

"Nick," I whispered. "Maybe we should run."

"There's no escaping it now. We'll suffer through." Beneath the table, he ran his hand over my thigh in a quick, comforting gesture before returning it to prop his chin up over the back of the chair.

Sky rushed to Nick's side, grabbing at him until he could see the bite mark in clear view. "Nicholas, what on earth is this?"

"He was bit by a vampire." Zack sent a devilish smirk my way. "Lucky to be alive."

"It's true." Nick chuckled.

"It looks terrible. I can't believe you let that happen."

Nick dropped his face with a grin. "It was worth it."

The table erupted into noises of shock and mocking.

Sky took advantage of the moment and whispered something in Nick's ear. I heard him tell Sky that the guys knew about him and me.

"So, are the two of you dating now?"

"Yes," we said in unison.

"Good. So, this biting thing, is this a new kink? You need to be careful. The pair of you look like you were a smidge rough."

"We weren't rough," Nick said. "They're love bites."

"Well, I'm happy for you two." Sky offered Nick a gentle pat on the shoulder before taking a seat beside Will in a chair, which was tightly wedged between Alex and Zack.

Did I honestly sit here and tell my friends I had a boyfriend? And they accepted it? I mean, sure, they teased me a little, but that was nothing new. Before today, when Will would come by, Sky would always leave. He never hung out with us like this. And now, Nick was by my side, making small talk with my friends, laughing. Smiling. Everyone was smiling.

"Hey, Nick, will you walk with me to my car? I need to go home, but I need to give you something."

He looked over at me, a little puzzled. "Of course. Did you wanna go now?"

I nodded. It was time I went home before my parents grew suspicious of my behavior.

• • •

In the parking garage, I popped the trunk of my car open, and grabbed the infamous black bag. "Nick, now that we're dating, I fully expect you to accept this. It isn't an apology gift anymore. This is your boyfriend giving you a gift."

"Sneaky little fuck."

"I was never going to return it. I was contemplating different ideas that could entice you to take it."

"It's way too expensive. I can't."

"Do you want to hurt your boyfriend's feelings?"

"Asshole," he said, and slid his hands around my waist, tugging me close to him.

"Nick, people could see."

"We're on the top floor. Do you see anyone around?"

It was empty, and I hadn't seen anyone up here. It seemed relatively safe.

"Besides, what would some random who doesn't know us do?"

"I don't know. But I don't want my family to find out from someone else."

He released a breath of disappointment. "Okay. I won't do anything obvious in public anymore." His hands slipped from my waist as he stepped back to a less intimate distance.

"Here, take it and enjoy." I handed Nick the bag.

He groaned, but took the bag from me. "Fine. You're lucky you're my boyfriend."

My chest tightened, catching my breath in my throat.

I wasn't sure why, but Nick calling me that out loud had butterflies dancing in my stomach.

"Why do you look like that?" He chuckled. "It's like I just told you I was an alien or something."

I shook my head, unsure of what to say. *How do I express these feelings?*

"Are you okay?" His voice dropped as he closed the gap

between us again and rested his forehead on mine. "Come on. Talk to me."

My entire body was warm and tingly as I tugged him close, brushing my lips over his. I wrapped my arms around his neck and teased my tongue over his lips until he opened them to me. My back hit the concrete wall, and fingers slid under the fabric of my shirt, caressing my skin.

Just then, the elevator door dinged on the opposite side of the garage. Our breath was heavy in the air as footsteps entered the space. I was too into the kiss to care at first, but then I reluctantly pulled away, breaking our kiss. Nick stepped back a few feet, running his fingers through his hair, the bag still clutched in his hand. My own actions and desires shocked me. In that brief moment, I wanted Nick to fuck me against the wall in the middle of a parking garage. What kind of person was I?

A car near the elevator started, and I was awash with embarrassment. "I should go."

"Good idea, or else I'm taking you back to my room, and I won't ever let you leave."

The prospect was enticing. I wanted to accept.

CHAPTER 23

NICK

I had made it through the week only seeing Taka for lunch or if he stopped by the lab while I was working. I could finally cut my hours back down to normal because I caved and took the stupid laptop. How could I have said no at that point?

"Are you coming out to Crystal Cat tonight?" Alex asked. "Last time, you and T left before the night even started."

It was an odd experience to be accepted into a group of people in a matter of days. Sky, Riv, and I couldn't escape their friendship even if we tried. We were sucked in and made to feel like we had always been friends with them.

Zack was in his soccer jersey, soaked in sweat with a ball resting in his lap, and Kiran was transfixed by his phone, scrolling away.

"You'll have to check with Taka. I'll go if he goes."

"Aw, he'll for sure say no," Alex said.

I chuckled and leaned back in the chair. The business department's food court had quickly become my daily destination. I met these guys every day for lunch. We would be there for hours until someone else had a class, event, or sports activity. I somehow managed to finish my work, even with them chatting around me. Sometimes, I felt like a different person. I'd already changed in the short time I'd known Takahiro Akiyama, and I liked this new version of myself. He was happier, more adventurous, and more sociable too.

"Hey, guys," Taka said as he sat beside me, setting a plate of food in front of him.

Kiran set his phone down and turned his full attention to Taka. "So, T, I asked Nick earlier, but do you want to go to Crystal Cat with us tonight? It's Friday night, and we want to party."

"What did Nick tell you?"

"He would go if you go."

"Nick?" Taka's curious eyes turned to me, and my heart filled with warmth.

I grinned. "You decide. I'll do whatever you want to."

"I do like seeing you all dressed up." He bit his lip, trying to hide his grin. "We'll go."

• • •

The last time I was there, I didn't know that the abandoned dump had been dubbed Crystal Cat—it was more like the Mangey Cat. Since Taka had been so taken with my outfit the first night, I wore a similar style. This time, however, under the black button-up was a mesh tank. The moment Taka saw it in my closet, his eyes lit up, and I knew he would enjoy it. It was mostly hidden under the shirt, but knowing that it was there had Taka constantly touching my back and running his fingers over the fabric.

He had changed into one of Sky's dark blue button-ups, and his prominent collarbones were peeking through the neckline. It was hot, and I wished we were home instead. He also borrowed Sky's skinny jeans again, and the boys were picking on him when we arrived. Apparently, Taka had been heavily against skinny jeans for years. Sky and I found it hilarious; Taka, not so much.

"Okay, boys, we're grabbing some drinks, and then we can hit the dance floor," River said as she led her girlfriend, Sarah, toward the bar. They came in the skimpiest dresses I had ever seen and were itching to ditch us.

"Have fun, ladies. Come get us if any creeps bother you," Kiran shouted after them, then turned to the rest of us. The whole group was there, but all I wanted to do was get Taka on the dance floor and maybe back to the dark corner we had found last time. "Let's secure a table and get ourselves some drinks."

Zack shouted and charged forward, leading the way. "Don't forget you're DD, Alex!"

Alex grunted, rolling his eyes. "I know."

Alex's parents let him borrow their minivan so we could all fit in a single car. Will and Sky came separately, and so did River and Sarah. Taka and I wanted to drink, so we relied on Alex to keep his word and not get drunk.

Taka kept his hand on my lower back as we maneuvered through the crowd until we found a table.

"What number is this?" I asked, looking for the painted

number that was usually on the coffee tables. "Taka and I can order the drinks."

"Six, I think," Kiran said, studying the table.

"Taka?" a deep voice came from behind us. His voice sounded familiar, immediately sending a chill down my spine.

I turned to the man, and silence descended on the group. Casey was standing next to Taka with a couple of his friends and Izzie. Her glare was like ice rays shooting toward me as they approached.

Taka greeted them with a nod, and that fake smile he put on when he was uncomfortable appeared.

"So, you hang around this thing a lot these days," Casey said.

"I've been upgraded to thing. That's nice," I replied.

"No one was talking to you." One of Casey's friends spit the words like venom.

I laughed, inching closer to Taka.

"If you're going to insult my friend, you can leave," Taka said in a parental tone, like a father scolding his child. "Your hate isn't welcome here."

"You haven't been around the frat lately," Casey said, stepping closer to Taka. "Are you trying to get kicked out?"

"My business with our fraternity is none of your concern."

"You missed the fundraiser. Daddy donated for you. Should've seen him apologize for his son's lack of responsibility as he wrote us a fat check."

"You don't have to be so mean," Izzie said, tugging on Casey's arm as she glanced between Taka and me.

Her eyes lingered on my neck, looking for the mark I was sure she had heard about. There had been rumors spreading around campus about the two of us running around with hickeys and bite marks. No one had approached us about it, but we had a rule now to not leave marks. It didn't help that we weren't very good at this whole secret relationship thing. We hung out as one big group now that we were official, and I was sure people had noticed our two very different friend groups had merged seemingly overnight. College was no different than high school in the way rumors and gossip spread.

Casey looked at me with loathing in his eyes; his lip curled up in a sneer. "T, you one of them now? Batting for the other side?"

Taka's shoulders tightened up as he looked back at me. His eyes, full of worry, sparked a blazing fury in me. I stepped forward, placing myself between Taka and Casey, but I was conflicted. If I was reported for another fight, I would lose my scholarship. But there was a deep desire to defend Taka from that asshole.

"Back off," I growled through gritted teeth.

"You think Taka needs your protection?" Casey asked as he released a laugh. "Do you treat him like a woman? Huh?" Casey looked back at his friends and Izzie. When his gaze returned to me, a smirk filled with hate made my blood run cold.

I clenched my jaw so hard I thought my teeth would shatter. But I didn't want to issue any threats. "Homophobia and misogyny. You're single, I assume."

"I'd rather cut my dick off than be touched by something like you," Casey replied, clearly flustered.

"The entire human race would thank you if you cut your dick off," I said. I stepped closer, staring into his eyes. My fingers clenched at my sides as I fought the itch to punch him. "I'll bring the knife."

Sky popped up out of the shadows. "If you and your frat buddies want a repeat of freshman year, bring it on; otherwise, I suggest you leave."

"Fuck off, fairy," Casey said.

"This little fairy would be happy to put you in your place," Sky said, excitement emanating from his body as he stepped closer to Casey.

Sky was a fighter. It was how we got into the mess back in freshman year. He never backed down from a fight. Enjoyed them, even.

Will grabbed the back of Sky's shirt, yanking him back. "Don't."

"Back off, Casey," Kiran warned as he and the others swarmed around us.

Alex appeared at my right side, arms crossed. "No one wants a hateful piece of shit like you around, anyway."

"I bet you're all a bunch of fags," Casey yelled. He was getting increasingly red in the face, but there was something in his eyes I couldn't identify. It was something more—or different—than hate.

Zack crossed in front of us, stepping up to Casey's face. "You should leave before I decide to report you to the university for harassment and hate speech. Let's see how that lawyer daddy of yours would feel seeing you get kicked out of school for this shit."

"Casey, let's go," Izzie said, pulling on his arm. "They aren't worth getting into trouble for."

"We don't need the attention right now," one of the guys tagging along with Casey said.

Casey allowed himself to be dragged away by his crew, disappearing into the crowd with a final scowl in our direction,

Izzie hot on his tail.

"Way to kill the mood," Kiran said as he flopped onto the sofa.

I laced my fingers with Taka's and tugged him onto the sofa beside Kiran. "Thanks, everyone."

"It was nothing," Zack said and dropped into a chair.

"I'll grab the drinks," Alex said, slipping away.

Sky stood in front of Taka, his eyes full of concern. "Are you okay?"

Taka nodded but didn't say anything.

His hand was warm and clammy, and I gave it another reassuring squeeze. "Don't let them get to you."

Sky kneeled down, glancing between us. "Taka, if you want to go home, we can take you."

He shook his head and smiled. "I don't want to go. I don't want to let him ruin our night."

"That's the spirit," Sky laughed and tapped Taka's knee. "Assholes like them don't deserve any headspace. If they want to call me a fairy, let them. I'm a blazing, demonic bastard of a fairy!"

"Fucking hot," Kiran said as he laughed. "I wanna be a demonic fairy, too."

"Trust me, Kiran, you are your own category," I said.

Zack snorted, covering his face.

"What does that mean?" Kiran asked, pressing his hand to his chest in mock offense.

"It's a compliment, man. You defy standard categorization," I said, smiling.

Kiran crossed his arms, puffing his cheeks. "I feel like I should be wholeheartedly offended."

"It's okay, buddy," Taka said. "We love you no matter what kind of mythical creature you are."

"What did I come back to?" Alex asked, carrying a tray full of plastic shot glasses.

Kiran pouted, grumbling, "I don't even know." He shot a look at Sky like he had thought of something important. "Can I be a pixie? They're cool, right?"

"Okay, Tinkerbell," Sky said, holding back his laugh.

"No, not that," Kiran grumbled again. "You guys are the worst." He grabbed a plastic shot glass, quickly downing the drink and crushing the tiny cup in his hand. "Give it all to me. I'll be the greedy fucking pixie. Don't give them anything."

Alex scanned the group, confused as hell. "Why?"

"They're jerks."

"Share the drinks, Tinkerbell," Zack said, rising to his feet and grabbing some cups off the tray.

CHAPTER 24

TAKA

"Guys, we've been sitting here for an hour nursing these drinks. Let's get our asses on the dance floor," Sky said as he stood, chugging another shot and pulling Will from his chair.

"That's the idea." Kiran leaped to his feet, following on Sky's heels.

"Nick, do you want to join them?" I asked.

"As long as you dance with me."

"But people will see us."

"Will they?" he asked, scanning the dimly lit dance floor. He leaned in close until his lips brushed against my ear. "I don't think they'll notice us."

I wished I could let go and not care, but every fiber of my being screamed that it was risky. Someone would notice. Someone would judge us.

"If you're that worried, we can stay here."

It was like a moment from a movie as I wrestled with the devil and angel on my shoulders. The devil won.

I took hold of Nick's hand and led him to the middle of the dance floor. It was dark and crowded. Heat surrounded us like a cloud of steam created by people pressed together. Not one of them gave us a single moment of their attention. When I spun around, Nick was biting his lip and he stared at my face with a dark intensity that sparked a bonfire of desire. Did he know how provocative he looked?

"You picked a good spot," Nick said, dipping his face and resting his cheek against mine. His lips brushed my jaw as he spoke. The heat from his hands seeped through my shirt, searing my skin as he slid them over my body until his palm rested flat on my lower back.

I mirrored him, pressing our abdomens together as we swayed to the music. My fingers made their way under his button-up and found the soft fabric of the mesh shirt.

Nick's tongue trailed up my neck, and I moaned, curling my fingers in the mesh and running them over his skin. His lips brushed my earlobe as he slid his palm lower on my spine. The pressure sparked a memory of his hand pressing on my back as he rocked inside me. Fuck. Why didn't we drive here?

"Nick?"

"Yes?" he asked as he pressed his forehead to mine, swaying his hips with the music.

"I want you right now," I said.

A sly smirk formed on his lips, and he pulled me closer, rubbing our arousal against each other through the thick fabric of our jeans. "What do you want me to do?" He scanned the room with smoldering eyes.

"Have you ever done it in the woods?" I asked. I didn't want to suffer through this torture anymore.

I did not need to repeat my question. He understood. His hand took mine, and he pulled me through the sea of people. The music vibrated the air, electrifying my sensitive nerves. Nick's hand slammed against the door, shoving it open. The chilly night air hit us like an ice bath after the heat of the dance floor. Yet, it did nothing to soothe the heat that had engulfed me.

Nick was like a hunter, scanning the tree line for the ideal place. We dipped around the back of the building and disappeared into the dense trees. When we were far enough that the lights and sound barely reached us, my back hit a tree, and desperate lips descended on mine.

I fumbled with the buttons on his shirt. Shaking as I opened it to the world, displaying that mesh covering. I slid my fingers down his chest, reaching his navel, stopping at his buckle. His arms braced against the trunk of the tree. The fabric of his shirt draped around my hands like a tent, creating a barrier that blocked our actions from sight.

As my fingers tugged his belt loose, he watched every movement. When his button released, a smile crossed his lips, and his hand dropped to my waist, hooking a finger in my waistband and sliding across my heated skin until he reached for the button. With a snap, it released, and he tugged the zipper down.

My heart pounded with a mixture of arousal and fear. Fear of being seen. Yet, the idea of someone watching was equally enticing. Being with Nick released a side of me I never knew I had. A primal and out-of-control version of me.

My breath was heavy as I ran a finger along the inside of his boxers, sliding against his skin until I reached his erection. "Can you enter me here?"

"Did you think I wouldn't?"

"Do we have what we need?"

"Don't worry," he said, trailing his thumb over my chin, lifting my lips to his as he slid his tongue into my mouth, devouring me within an inch of my life. When he pulled away, he whispered, "Open your mouth for me." I was confused but didn't question it. His fingers found their way into my mouth, stroking the tip of my tongue. "Suck." He kissed my forehead and tugged my pants down past my ass with his free hand. I did as he asked, licking and sucking on his fingers until he pulled them from my grasp. "Good," he said as his fingers found their way to my hole, stroking in circles.

I muffled a moan and clung to his shirt.

"Relax more, don't tighten on me."

"I'm not meaning to."

"Do I need to distract you like last time?"

"No, you don't have to."

"I can distract you another way." He cupped my arousal in his palm and pressed his erection against mine. The warmth hit me as his fingers tightened around us before he slowly stroked over our lengths. As he moved his palm over us, his fingers inched their way inside me.

Pure pleasure hit me as he slid deeper in combination with his strokes. "Stop," I stammered between heavy breaths. "You'll make me come."

"Are you that sensitive today?"

I nodded against his shoulder and whispered, "Yes."

"Fuck, why did we have to come here tonight? If you're this sensitive, I want to be in the privacy of my room."

"It was a stupid choice. I'll never make it again."

He chuckled against my neck as he slid his fingers deeper.

My body flooded with a wave of pleasure, like a tingling heat that electrified my skin and muscles with such intensity that it was almost painful. A deep moan forced its way through me as I fell into Nick's arms, and he pushed further inside until the base of his knuckles hit my skin.

He slid his finger out, releasing me from the intense pleasure. "I'll stretch you more, but can you hold out like this?"

"I don't know."

"Fuck it." Nick's hands slid down my sides until he reached my thighs, scooping me up in a swift motion, wrapping my legs around his waist. His mouth was hot on mine. His tongue chased after mine in a lustful dance. My knees hit the ground, and he tugged my pants lower, and the cool air ran over my skin.

Nick released me from the kiss, and I pulled back. Our breath was heavy, filling the silence of the night. The deep thrum of the music in the distance was barely audible. From this spot, the moon provided enough light to see. Nick's eyes raked over me with a palpable hunger, but I was focused on the soft, thin mesh that covered his chest. It teased me, and I ran my fingers over it. He shuddered under my touch, and a soft grunt fell from his lips as I traced my thumb over the smooth, warm skin of his arousal.

"I have to say, you're much stronger than you look. It's not even like I'm small, and here you are, carrying me all over the place."

"Gotta be able to handle any situation."

"Does that mean you like to fuck standing up?"

"Yes."

"I look forward to it."

His crooked smile was a promise.

Straddling was quickly becoming my favorite position. "Can I ride you?"

Nick's brow raised as he bit his lip. "Whatever you want." He fumbled in his pocket before revealing a condom and tiny ketchup-like packets. "Let me prep you first."

I picked up a packet, eyeing it. "What is this?"

"To-go lube."

"They make that?" I laughed as he took the packet from me and ripped it open, pouring the contents over his fingers.

He pulled me down so that I was lying flat over him. His fingers were swift as they found my hole, slowly stroking the sensitive skin. I was impatient for the feeling. I wanted more. I wanted to lose myself in it. A breath of relief escaped me when his finger slid inside. My body moved on its own as I pushed against him, forcing him deeper. I muffled a moan as tingling heat spread up my spine.

"So eager tonight."

"I've never wanted to be touched more by someone in my life." The words came out breathy and barely audible. I said it without thinking and without embarrassment.

Nick's breath hitched beneath me, and his heart thundered against my skin. "You really know how to turn me on." He kissed my shoulder, climbing my neck until his lips reached my chin. Slipping a second finger in, he ran his hands and mouth over my body, creating nothing but pleasure with each touch. "Don't freak out when I say this." His breathing was heavy. "I knew I could fall for you hard and fast the moment I saw you walk into the computer lab. You're like gravity that was made just for me. You pull me to you, and I can't escape."

My chest tightened, and an uncontrollable flow of tears began as his words replayed in my head. Nick's thumb ran over my cheek, wiping away an escaped tear.

"Don't cry. That wasn't supposed to make you cry."

I couldn't hold them back. They crashed through the wall I was holding them behind and spilled over. "I'm not sure why that hit me so hard."

Nick sat up, taking me with him, holding me in a hug as the unexpected tears flowed. "What's wrong?"

"Nothing's wrong. Everything's right. I don't think I've ever felt so cared for. It's like you see me; you hear me and listen. You don't pressure me. You encourage me to be myself. You let me be me."

I had never been in a position where I felt I could simply be me.

His eyes ran over my face as he wiped the tears from my cheeks. "I never want you to be anything else but yourself. God, I didn't mean to ruin the mood."

"You didn't ruin anything," I said, cupping his face in my hands. "You blindsided me, that's all."

Nick laughed and squeezed me tight. "Sorry."

I wiggled in his embrace, kissing his chin as I ached to have his touch again.

"Want to continue?" Nick said, running his hands down my back.

I nodded eagerly.

His fingers squeezed my ass before circling my hole. "Still nice and slick. Are you still overly sensitive?"

"Yes," I gasped as his fingers pushed inside with ease.

His lips caught mine as he circled his fingers inside me, inducing a swirl of heat that coiled up my spine. Nick played with me until I was incapable of taking any more teasing. I grabbed the condom packet and tore it open with my teeth as I pushed him down. His hands released me as he relaxed and bit his lip.

"You're so sexy when you're on top of me like this."

As I slid the condom over him, I shot him a smirk. Then I positioned myself and sank onto him. I bit back a cry from the sharp pain I had caused myself, but I didn't want to wait any longer. Nick's groan of pleasure only enticed me more as I settled on him, letting him fill me. It was unlike any other experience. The sensation of him deep inside me was erotic and mind-numbingly good. The initial pain died down, and I took a sharp breath before moving. I moved slowly, testing myself. Every nerve was screaming in pleasure as I moved over Nick's length.

His hands slid over my waist, gripping my sides as I rode him under the moonlight. A soft moan escaped me at his touch, and I dropped heavily, taking him all the way in, producing in him a grunt of satisfaction. His hands clamped down around my hips, holding me in place, forcing me to rock with him. I dropped my head to his chest as he ran over my prostate. An indescribable sensation rolled through me, forcing a deep moan from my chest.

"Have you had enough?" he asked as he thrust inside me, rolling over the sensitive gland again. How did he manage to find it every time?

"Do it. Please."

My back hit the ground in an instant, and Nick held my

hips, keeping me pressed tight against him. I ran my fingers over that enticing mesh, licking my lips as he slid out of me, achingly slow.

"Take off your shirt, or it's gonna get destroyed." I tugged my shirt off and tossed it to the ground a few feet away. He climbed over me, pressing his forehead to mine, and entered me again. Our breaths mingled as Nick pleasured me, over and over, until my body felt like it would catch fire if I didn't have release.

"Let me come," I begged, as his lips trailed over my jaw.

"As you wish," he breathed, raising up, tightening his hold on my hips, and thrusting into that tiny gland again. My body was screaming for that indescribable orgasm again. I needed it. I was addicted to that feeling, and somehow, Nick knew how to provide it.

My nerves tingled. Every cell in my body cried in pleasure as a rush of heat and ecstasy rolled through me. My muscles tightened, and my head flew back as the rush took control.

Nick dropped his head to my shoulder, groaning as he rocked inside me, easing us down. Then, before I could take another breath and collect myself, he slid out of me, and his lips descended on my arousal, setting me off. My release poured into his mouth, and he swallowed with a satisfied groan.

He fell to the ground beside me, panting. He rolled onto his back. "That was fucking amazing."

We gazed up at the night sky for a few minutes before gathering ourselves and finding our way back to the car. We were a disaster. Covered in dirt and leaves, we couldn't show our faces inside. I had texted Alex to let us in the van; we were ready to go home, but everyone else was still partying the night away.

"What happened to you two?" Alex asked as he unlocked the van.

"You don't actually want that answer," Nick said as he climbed into the back of the van with a chuckle.

"You guys look like you got into a fight."

I laughed. "Alex, let your precious little mind keep thinking that and go back to the party." I climbed in beside Nick. "We'll be out here, probably asleep."

"Suit yourself." Alex closed the door and marched back to the building, glancing back a few times before he was out of sight.

Nick pulled me close, and I nestled into his side. "I can't believe we did that."

A chuckle came from him. "Neither can I. But I loved it."

CHAPTER 25

NICK

After the night at Crystal Cat, Taka stayed at my dorm for the weekend, and I started hanging out with his friends on my own. I would seek them out, enjoy their company, and liked them as people. Sky was beside himself, not sure if he should be worried or happy that I was making friends. For years, my only friend had been Sky, and when I came to SCU, the only new person I let into my world was River.

I hadn't told my family about Taka; I wasn't ready yet, but I knew I needed to tell them soon.

"Which one do you want today?" Kiran asked as he scanned the food court. "I'm tired of this crap."

I hummed, letting my eyes wander, but nothing stood out. "Not sure. I feel like we've eaten from each one this week."

He scoffed and shoved his hands in his front pockets. "I bet we have."

"Tinkerbell," Zack called from a few feet away. The nickname had stuck; Kiran embraced it in stride.

"Zack, pick something to eat. Neither of us knows what we want."

He tossed his soccer ball in his hands and glanced around the food court. "Why don't we go to the small place that opened up in the basement of the library. That little grill?"

I squinted, not sure what he was talking about.

"Isn't it expensive, like a real restaurant?" Kiran asked, chewing on his lip as he grabbed the ball from Zack.

"I don't know. I've never been there."

"Bad idea. Next time, know if it's expensive or not before offering the idea." Kiran spun on his heels and pointed at a food stall. "I choose you."

I couldn't help but chuckle as I watched him march toward the same pizza place he had patronized twice that week. "Pizza it is," I said, following him to the line.

When we sat, we dove into what was now standard conversation for us. We talked about random things. Zack and Kiran would talk about soccer, mostly. Sometimes I would sit quietly, but they never cared if I spoke or not. It was nice to never feel pressured to be someone I wasn't.

Kiran's head sunk deeper into his phone, and he released a confused groan. "Hey, Nick?" He slid his phone to me. "Is that you and T?"

"What?" When I lifted the phone, there was a picture of me kissing someone in a parking garage. It was dark and grainy. I couldn't make out Taka's face; he had been wearing my clothes that day, so it wasn't like anyone could confirm it was him, but we were beside his car, and if anyone knew Taka well, they would know his car. I backed out of the photo and stared at the name of the person who posted it. Her post was more concerning than the image. She didn't call him out, but it was obvious who she was referring to.

Izzie: *I found out the reason I was dumped. Apparently, he likes men. I've never felt so betrayed in my life. Was he using me as a cover this whole time?*

My heart raced as I scrolled down to the comments. No one had used names yet, but her close friends knew who she was talking about. She had outed him for revenge.

My phone vibrated in my pocket. "Here, take the phone back, Kiran." I handed it to him, then fished mine from my pocket. Sky's name lit up the screen. "Hey, man."

"Don't 'hey, man' me. Have you seen the Facebook post from Taka's ex?" he said.

"I have."

"I private messaged her already, asking her to take it down. She told me she can post whatever she wants because it's her account."

I figured as much. "No one has specifically called out names yet. You think Taka's safe?"

"Nick, you know people will recognize the two of you. The guy has been so deep in the closet that anyone who knows him will flip when they see that photo. And what if his family sees it once he gets tagged in the comments? Dude, we have to get this photo taken down ASAP."

"Sky, don't panic, okay? Relax. Is Will with you?"

"Yeah."

"Good. I'll see you both when you get here."

"Okay, fine. See you in a few."

"Taka will freak when he sees this," Zack said, handing Kiran back his phone. "We need to get ahead of this." Zack pulled out his phone and started tapping away.

He wasn't wrong. None of them were wrong, but it was already out on the internet, where things lived forever.

"Why will Taka freak?" Alex asked as he sat on my left, sliding a smoothie across the table to Kiran.

"Thanks," Kiran said, taking a gulp and smacking his lips. "Taka's family aren't in the loop. Izzie is trying to fuck Taka's life up."

Kiran sipped on the smoothie and slid his phone to Alex so he could read the post.

"Hey, someone tagged you in a comment, Nick," Alex said.

These boys were legitimately worried for us. It was comforting to know that they cared.

"Who tagged me?"

"A Mia Woods. Oh, she's cute."

Mia was in a few classes with me. I knew her in passing, but she wasn't a close friend or anything.

My Facebook was minimal. I mainly had family and some friends on it. Barely posted any photos and rarely ever updated my status. It wasn't my thing. I had one notification and swiftly clicked on it. Sure enough, Mia had tagged me in a comment on the post in question.

At least this allowed me to see the post easily from my account.

Mia: *Nick Dawson is out and proud, Izzie, but you don't know anything about who he's with. Take this down. What you're doing is wrong. You can't out people like this.*

She had good intentions, but tagging me was not the best

move. It opened the door for me to say something, though.

Me: *I don't know you or why you're posting a photo like this of me, but I would appreciate it if you didn't keep this picture up. I don't like pictures of me on the internet, and the other person in this photo will be upset when they find out. Please take it down.*

"Oh, Nick, good move," Kiran said.

"Should we jump in too?" Alex asked.

"No. No one has mentioned Taka by name. I don't want you all jumping in and making it obvious who else is in this photo." So I went to work screen-shotting the entire thread and the photo. Once the post was deleted, I wanted evidence.

"Hey, guys," Taka said as he sat beside me, setting a plate of food in front of him like nothing was happening.

The table was silent, everyone wondering what to say. There was a problem, and he was clearly unaware.

Zack cleared his throat and glanced at Kiran and me. "Have you been on Facebook today?"

"Hm? Me?" Taka shook his head. "I've been in class. Why?"

"Oh, nothing."

Taka shrugged like the question wasn't suspicious and dug into his food.

"What are you all sitting around for?" Sky's voice interrupted the temporary peace. "Also, nice try, Nick, but the bitch doesn't care." Everyone turned on him, motioning for him to shut up. But Sky wouldn't let something like this go, and he sure as hell was not one to lie—two qualities I loved and hated about him. "Taka, have you seen what your shitty ex is doing?"

Will, Sky, and Riv all found a seat at the table and stared at a confused Taka. My poor boyfriend.

Taka set his fork down and glanced around the table. All eyes were on him. "What are you talking about?"

"There's a Facebook post you need to see," Kiran said and handed his phone to his friend. "We tried to get her to take it down, but she's stubborn."

Taka's face dropped as he looked at the photo and read through the comments. "Why would she do something like this?"

"Revenge," Zack said.

"Would it get removed if enough of us report it?" River asked.

"I don't think so. Does it violate their policies?" Alex asked. Leave it to the business law guy to crush our hopes. "Although I'd have to look it up, it could be defamation or something."

"I don't think it would work for that either," Will replied.

"Shit. Casey tagged me," Taka said.

The table went silent, and I opened the app on my phone. Sure enough, a few comments down from the one I was tagged in, Casey had tagged Taka.

Casey: *Taka Akiyama, is this you?*

Such a simple question, and yet it could ruin Taka's life in an instant. The gang took that as their turn to jump in on the conversation. Now that their friend had officially been outed by name, they went to work. They flooded the comment section with their replies.

"Taka, you can't reply to Casey. You'll basically confirm that it's you," Alex warned.

"But he tagged me, and anyone who has seen my car knows it's mine. Why on earth wouldn't anyone think it was me?"

"We know that, but if you respond, you will confirm their

suspicions. Nick could've been making out with someone who owned the car beside yours. It doesn't have to be you."

"People are smarter than you give them credit for, Alex." Taka's shoulders sagged, and the look in his eyes was something I had seen before. It was chilling to think of what could come of this. We couldn't let this get any further.

"The point is not that they know in their minds that it's you. The point is that there is room for them to be wrong. Once you reply and confirm it is you, then their suspicion will be truth."

"Alex is right," I said. "Don't reply to him and just let it go. We will handle the post. Act like you haven't seen it and don't know what any of us are talking about."

"But–"

"We've got your back." Kiran set his phone on the table. "I think you need to call Izzie, though. Maybe talk to her about this."

Taka nodded and pulled out his phone, found the contact, and placed the phone to his ear.

"Izzie, what have you done?"

I cringed at the tone he took with her. It was as if he scolded people every day. Yet, the confidence that bloomed from him lit my heart. I knew one thing at that moment, crossing Taka was something I never wanted to do. I never wanted to hear him take that tone with me.

"Take the post down, or you and I will have bigger problems." His fist curled into a ball on his lap, his knuckles turning white as he stared at the table. "It's none of your business." His breath caught before he released a sigh. "I never cheated on you and didn't break up with you because I was in love with anyone else. Don't make up stories to make me the bad guy." He paused, and I grabbed his hand, lacing my fingers in his. He gave me a squeeze as he listened to her reply. "Stop. You're wrong, and it is no one's business what my sexuality is. No one deserves or requires an answer. Please take the post down."

Zack chuckled across the table like a child watching their sibling getting scolded.

Taka tightened his grip on my hand, and my heart ached for him. "You're being spiteful, and it's ugly. Take it down, or I will contact a lawyer to see what legal action I can take against you."

"Shit, dude," Kiran breathed and nudged Sky in the side with a smile. "Our boy is not having it."

Sky wiggled his eyebrows with a huge grin, but I wasn't feeling their sense of victory. Taka's fingertips were growing cold and the slight tremble of his hand made me want to yank him into a hug.

"Thank you. I'll be checking to make sure it has been deleted." Taka paused and dropped his gaze to our interlaced fingers. "One last thing. Who took the photo?" A moment passed in silence as he listened. "Please tell her to never do that again. This kind of behavior is harmful." He pulled the phone away from his ear and set it on the table. He was shaking and pale, but a warm smile spread over his features. "She's deleting it."

The table broke into celebration before everyone hopped on their phones to check the post.

It was gone.

"Thank God you called her. I was so worried about you," Kiran said.

"It may be taken down, but the damage has been done," I said, squeezing Taka's hand. "Let's hope it doesn't resurface."

• • •

The campus was a ghost town as I walked through the quad, tugging my sleeves down as a damp breeze ran over my exposed wrists; a storm had come through in the night, bringing in a cold front.

"How are exams going, honey?" Mom asked as the Ellis Center came into view.

"It's hell since most are projects instead of tests, but I'll be done on the sixteenth."

The door handle to the main entrance was wet with rainwater, and I wiped my hand on my jeans. I loved the quiet of the morning during exam week; the campus was always empty since students were studying in the library or sitting through an exam. It would only be back to normal during evening meals.

As an art student, I didn't have written exams like other departments. Instead, I had projects, each assigned weeks before exams. My exam slot was to present the assignment to the class and get my professor's critique. I had an art history class to study for, but I didn't care about that exam as much as my other courses. A forty-hour project was much more complicated than studying for a multiple-choice exam. And I had two projects to complete for this week; luckily, I had until the last day of exams before I had to present them.

The smell of bread grew stronger as I neared the source. Yellow light filled the bagel shop. A girl was standing at the register, ready to take my order. When she greeted me, I waved and headed toward a table.

"You're still coming home for Memorial Day weekend, right?" Mom asked.

"I'll leave that Friday before," I said, dropping into a chair. "I got the entire week off since it will be right after the semester ends, but I have to be back for the summer classes in June."

"Good, tell River I said thank you. And Lori will bring Tom. Will you be bringing your new friend?"

"Harper told you about him?"

"He did. I would love to meet him. Are you two dating yet?"

"We are," I said, rubbing my forehead.

"How'd you meet?"

"The computer lab. We've been dating for a few weeks."

"I would love for you to bring him. Tell him he's invited."

"You know he has a family, right? They'll probably want him to spend the holiday with them."

"It doesn't hurt to ask, Nicholas."

"Fine, fine. I'll ask."

"Good. Text me his response. If you forget, I'll pester you."

I quickly agreed and said my goodbyes before the line went silent. Droplets of water sat on the windows, and the gray cloudy sky hid the sun, though it was trying to peek through. Would Taka even be interested in meeting my family right now? A week-long trip would be a big deal.

Sky dropped into the chair across from me. "How's your project coming along?"

I slid my phone into my pocket. "It's coming. I'm almost done with the animation, but I'm worried about the modeling portfolio. It's taking longer than I thought."

"Let me know if you need help. I finished my projects last night, so I'm free." He glanced over his shoulder at the menu on the wall behind the counter. "You want anything?"

I shook my head. "Not yet. I'll wait for Taka before I order, but you can go ahead."

Sky scrunched his nose and chewed his lip. A sure sign he wanted to ask me something.

"What's the face for?"

"We haven't really talked about it, but I think we should."

"Talked about what?"

"You and Taka."

I rolled my eyes, leaning back in the chair. "Are you about to give me relationship advice?" His eye twitched at my question, and I knew I had him. "What's the problem?"

"Are you really okay with a hidden relationship?"

"We already set rules; obviously, it isn't that hidden. Our friends know. My family knows. The issue is on his side."

"Are you okay with being introduced to his family as a friend?"

"It wouldn't be the first time. I'm not hung up on it. I understand his family situation."

Sky eyed me like I was a liar. "What if you're a friend for the next ten years? Twenty years? What if you move in together? There are so many things to think about."

"Taka and I have talked about his family. They're strict and put a lot of pressure on him. Also, his dad seems like a raging homophobe, so it's probably best to keep it secret for as long as possible."

"But that means you always have to be careful how you act in public."

"I already know this. We're already doing what we need to. Having the photo taken was a harsh lesson, so we're extra careful now."

"You don't find it exhausting?"

I shook my head. "It isn't exhausting because I really like him." I knew Sky was looking out for me and meant well, but I didn't like that he thought of my relationship in a negative light. "What about you and Will?"

"What about him?"

I tilted the chair onto its back legs. "Don't pretend you don't know what I'm asking."

He groaned and laced his fingers, setting his hands on the table.

"Don't sit here and lecture me on my relationship when you do what you do," I said.

"Shut up. I'm not like you. This commitment thing is hard for me. And I'm not hiding anything from anyone."

"You say that, but here you are, essentially dating him but not dating him."

He stood as he glared at me. "I'm getting food."

"Not so fun when others judge your relationship, right?"

His glare lingered on my skin. "Point taken."

I chuckled as I watched him trot away. A few minutes later, he came back with a coffee and two bagels, still glaring at me like I had killed his pet.

"By the way, are we going to pride in DC?" Sky asked before sipping from the to-go cup.

"I was thinking about it. The first march is the weekend of the thirtieth, right?"

"I think so. I can check."

Approaching footsteps drew my attention away from a sulking Sky. My heart fluttered at the sight of him. Something about him today looked sexy, even with his bedhead, the worst I'd seen. White and black lettering for a band covered his bright red hoodie, and his lime green lanyard hung from his pocket.

"Someone looks exhausted," I said.

Taka frowned. "My exams are killing me. I pulled another all-nighter."

I motioned for him to sit beside me. "Do you want to nap in my room?"

He sat with a quiet sigh and shoved his hands in the pocket of his hoodie.

"After my exam this morning, I have free time until one."

"Good, that'll give you some time to nap."

"What subject is your first exam?" Sky asked.

"Accounting. My brain feels like it will explode if I look at any more numbers."

"You'll do great," I said, offering some encouragement. "Do you want me to order you a coffee and breakfast?" His weak nod tugged at my heart, and I patted his shoulder as I stood. "Bacon and egg sandwich?" Another tired nod.

Moments later, I dropped into the seat beside Taka and placed the coffee in his eager hands. It was like looking at a zombie. He would sway every few seconds like his body was struggling to stay upright and as if sleep was only a moment away.

"When was the last time you slept?"

He slowly sipped the coffee and closed his eyes. "I slept for two hours yesterday." He swayed and took another sip. "Or maybe the day before? My days are blending, and I don't know anymore."

"You drove like this?"

His eyes flicked to me. "I did."

"Dummy," I scolded and settled into the chair, sliding my knee against his. It was our version of holding hands in public.

A seemingly accidental touch.

Sky pulled his face away from his phone with a smile. "It is that weekend, Nick."

It took my brain a moment to find what he was referring to. Then it clicked. Pride. "Nice. We'll still be in town for that."

"What?" Taka asked through a mouthful of his breakfast.

"We're going to a Pride parade in DC at the end of May."

"You're going home?"

I hadn't talked to him about my plans yet. Guess this was as good a time as any. "I was hoping you would come home with me for Memorial Day weekend and the following week."

"To your home? Like to meet your family?"

I had a feeling this was too soon. We barely knew each other and hadn't discussed meeting family yet. I felt bad dropping this on him. "My mom asked me to invite you up."

Taka let out a breath as he bit into his sandwich, a crumb of bacon falling onto the table. He fixed his gaze on the wasted crumb. "Let me think about it."

My stomach somersaulted with hope. There was a chance he would come home with me. The idea catapulted me into the clouds. "Let me know what you decide. I'm fine either way."

• • •

Memorial Day weekend arrived in the blink of an eye, and the drive home was absolute hell on earth. Accident after accident caused hours of traffic jams. I took as many back roads as I could, but there was always a point where the highway was the only way to go. A six-hour drive turned into ten. Taka was cranky, and I couldn't blame him; I felt the same. I wanted to arrive, curl up in bed, and sleep.

Taka grumbled as he got out of the car. I quickly followed him, trying not to laugh at how cute he was when grumpy. "I hate this already. Why did I come?" he said as he pulled our bags from the trunk. "I'm hungry. Thirsty. Sleepy. Annoyed at everyone who has a driver's license."

I bit back my chuckle as I walked up to him, pulling him into my arms. "Is someone in a mood?"

"Yes," he said with a sharp tone as he tried to turn away, but I pulled him back.

"Want me to make you feel better?" I kissed his cheek and stroked his back.

"No. I just want to eat and be left alone for, like, ten days."

I couldn't hold back my laugh at his pouty face as he declared his hate for the world.

"Stop. Just get our shit, and let's go." He tugged himself free of my grasp, and I grabbed one of the bags from him, slinging it over my shoulder before searching for the house key in my pocket.

The front door flew open, releasing the shriek of a harpy as Lori came rushing out. Hot pink leggings and lime green T-shirt assaulted my eyes, and as her bare feet hit the pavement, they slapped on the ground joyously before she leaped toward me. A mixture of terror and joy swirled through me. I resisted the urge to duck out of her way and instead caught the crazy woman flying through the air.

"Nick," Lori screeched in my ear as her body smashed against me. "I missed you." She buried her face in my neck and clung to me with more strength than I thought physically possible.

I squeezed her tight. It had been nearly six months since

I'd seen her. Maybe longer. "I missed you too." I gave her one last squeeze before lowering her to the ground and kissing her forehead. "Lori, this is Taka."

She spun around and leaped toward Taka, pulling him into a hug. "I'm so glad you came," she said as she stepped back, giving him a once-over. "You look exhausted. Let's get you guys inside."

When the door opened, laughter tickled my ears, and the smell of food brought a swell of warmth to my heart.

"Here, Taka, give that bag to Nick and come with me to meet everyone."

The twitch of his lip as he smiled was the only sign he was nervous. My family was welcoming, loud, and loved with all their hearts, but I knew this was a big step for him. A big step for us.

I planted my lips in a kiss on his temple as I took the bag from him. "They don't bite," I whispered before heading up the stairs to my bedroom.

My room hadn't changed since middle school. The familiar navy-blue walls welcomed me as I dropped the bags at the foot of the bed. My black sheets and comforter were pristine, likely freshly made. Mom was particular about cleaning my sheets before I came home, even if we had washed them the last time I was here.

Laughter climbed the stairs, and I wandered through the house until I found everyone crowded around Taka in the kitchen. He smiled at them with his fake smile that gave me chills. It made my heart sink. It tied my stomach in knots to know he was uncomfortable enough to put on that fake smile. As I approached, Tom's eyes met mine, and I gave him a nod before pulling my mom into a hug. I breathed her in as she patted my back. The warmth I felt when I came into the house was amplified, spreading through every cold crevice of my body, filling me with the love of my family, leaving so much light in my heart that I forgot what darkness was for a moment.

"Hi, baby," she said in that warm, loving tone I adored. "Welcome home." She squeezed my hand and rested her head on my chest.

"I missed you." I squeezed tighter before releasing her and setting my sights on Harper. He squinted and backed away as I marched toward him. His gangly teenage body was filling out; he was looking more grown now. "Harp." I spread my arms wide, urging him toward me with a wave of my fingers. "Give me a hug, or I'll chase you down until I get one."

"I don't want to. You're going to squeeze me until my ribs shatter."

I released an exasperated breath. "I would never. You're exaggerating."

"No. Your hugs hurt."

"I want you to feel my love. Come here!"

A soft chuckle pulled my attention away from Harper, allowing him to escape behind Lori. Taka's cheeks were red, his eyes bright with laughter. "Are you laughing at me?" I shot him a shocked expression, pretending to be offended, which only made him laugh more.

There it was. The relaxed version of the man I loved. That smile melted my heart.

"Enough playing around. Nick, you and Taka go shower and relax before dinner. You've had a long day." Mom waved us away, then turned back to the stove.

CHAPTER 26

TAKA

Nick's family had shown me nothing but love and acceptance since I arrived. With his family, I didn't need to hide. I didn't think about how they would feel if Nick and I held hands or kissed in front of them.

Tom, Lori's fiancé, and I ended up bonding over cars the first night I arrived. Nick's sister and brother were immediately accepting of me, welcoming me with open arms. It was hard for me to wrap my head around the family dynamic and lack of rigidity. Their mom, Evelyn, was probably the kindest person I had ever met. It was no wonder Nick turned out the way he had.

I turned over, looking at Nick as he slept. His cheek was on the pillow, lips parted slightly, and drool pooled under his mouth. Under normal circumstances, I would've found it disgusting, but seeing Nick like this made my heart tighten.

I think I'm falling in love.

A smile tugged at my cheeks as I rolled out of bed. Nick slept through the morning most days, and I was used to waking up for the gym at four, so I naturally woke up hours before him. While in his childhood home, I fell into a simple ritual of waking up and having coffee with Evelyn while the family slept. I looked forward to our morning chats. I could talk to her about anything. Evelyn and I talked about things I had never voiced before, and she offered guidance where she could. But mostly, she listened. Talking to a parental figure and receiving a non-judgmental response reassured and calmed a deep part of me that had felt cold for a long time.

The kitchen was filled with an unexpected silence. Did I beat Evelyn this morning? Pouring water into the coffeemaker, I hummed to myself, then grabbed a paper filter and coffee grounds. Making coffee was a simple thing, but this new routine made me brim with joy. I continued to hum as I switched on the coffeemaker and stared through the kitchen window, listening to the water brew while the sun crept over the horizon.

"Taka, honey," Evelyn's soft voice floated on the air like a blanket of love. "You beat me to it this morning."

Her hair was in a state of disarray, and she had puffiness around her eyes. "You deserve at least one morning to have the coffee made for you." I smiled and motioned for her to sit as I grabbed two mugs from the cabinet. "Did you sleep well?"

"I wish. My back was hurting, so I had trouble falling asleep." She puffed out a quiet chuckle as she sat at the kitchen table. "The joys of getting old."

"You aren't old," I said, pouring her coffee and handing her the mug.

"You don't have to lie." She cupped the mug with both hands and sipped. "Are you all still going to the parade tonight?"

"We are." I sat across from her in our usual position. "I'm nervous."

"Bah, you'll have the time of your life. From what Sky and Nick always tell me, it's the only time they truly feel free to be themselves." She turned her gaze to the window and sipped her coffee. I followed her gaze, looking out at the grassy yard too. "I know that not everyone suffers in the same way, but what you boys and others like you have to go through, with the judgment of society weighing heavily on your shoulders. I wish I could erase the cruelty of others."

I couldn't help but look at her, those words cutting deep, hitting the spot in my heart that desired the real me to be loved unconditionally.

"You know Nick is only the way he is because of you," I said.

Her tired eyes met mine.

I continued, "He can love so openly. I didn't understand how he could always be so hopeful and kind until I came here. He can hear slurs and hate, be surrounded by people who wish those like us would disappear from this world, and still smile." My throat tightened as I slid my hand over hers. "You taught him to love. Thank you."

"Goodness," she said, wiping tears from her cheeks. "My dear, thank you. I know your situation with your family is weighing on you, and it can be scary, but understand that this home is always available to you. I don't care if you and Nick break up and hate each other in the end. This home will always be a safe space for you. Please remember that."

"What are you two being all sappy for this early in the

morning?" Lori asked as she breezed into the kitchen in a loose tank top and shorts. "Anyone want bacon, eggs, and waffles?"

"Make enough for everyone," Evelyn said.

Nick's family burst to life around me. I sat in their kitchen, listening to their lively banter and bickering as each individual woke up and converged on the kitchen. When Nick finally came down, he was sleepy-eyed and grumpy, searching for coffee and food.

"Hi, Taka," he said, stopping beside me and running his fingers through my hair. "Lori, be careful not to burn the eggs. Every damn time you char them until they're inedible."

"I second that," Harper chimed in without pulling his nose from the pages of his book.

"Shut up, you two," Lori said, "or nothing for either of you."

Nick cupped my cheek in his palm, and his lips brushed over my hair. "Morning."

I glanced up at him, in awe that this was my reality.

• • •

"Sky, hold up a second," Nick grumbled as Sky ran down the street.

The fluorescent streetlamps caught him as he hopped down the sidewalk, weaving through the crowd. Sky spun around and walked backward. "We're almost to Will. Come on!"

"I don't want to run. If you're in such a rush, you go ahead."

Clicking his tongue, Sky pouted and grumbled, "You're such a bore."

Nick grabbed my hand, lacing his fingers with mine; the smile he showed me could light up the night sky.

Police lights flashed ahead of us, and orange traffic cones blocked the street behind them. The closer we got, the louder the music became.

"Sky, turn around. He's over there." Nick nodded toward the police cars; sure enough, Will was talking to a police officer. His rainbow T-shirt glowed like a beacon, and he flashed a bright smile I'd never seen cross his face before.

Sky rushed to him, leaping into his arms. The pair clung to each other, kissing in the street for everyone to see. I scanned the crowd, searching for any sign of danger to them. But there was nothing. Instead of disgust, people were smiling and cheering them on. Others ignored it like it was nothing as they went about their business.

As we passed through the cone barrier, it was like entering another world. A world of people like me. Rainbows filled the street; flags hung around shoulders; glow sticks encircled necks and wrists; drag queens danced past us, vibrant and full of life. Laughter carried through the night air between the thrum of music in the distance. Food trucks flew rainbow flags. Some vendors were dressed in drag and others wore rainbows on their clothes or painted them on their bodies. Their smiles lit up as we walked by, and their greetings were filled with joy.

As we got closer to the epicenter of the event, it was remarkable to observe the crowd around the stage. The music thundered through the street, and the crowd's cheers were so loud it was like a physical force. The man at the center of the stage announced the next show, and gorgeous queens walked out. Sparkly and bright, glowing with joy, they broke into song, and the crowd sang with them.

"Having fun?" Nick asked as he pulled me into a hug.

A group of young teens rushed by, raising their pride flags high.

"I don't know what to say. It's incredible that something like this exists."

"I'm glad you're here to witness it for yourself," he said as he kissed my forehead.

A rush of warm tingles ran through my body at the tender gesture.

We danced, then watched a fashion show. It was like a festival. I stuffed my belly with street tacos handed out by someone covered in rainbows. Their smile was infectious, and they refused to take money for the food. "Happy pride," they said before running off to the next group.

I was seeing a community for the first time. I finally felt I belonged. Like I wasn't different. I had found a place where I didn't have to hide. Somewhere I didn't want to hide.

A woman walked onto the stage and grabbed the mic. "Are you all ready for the flag march?"

The crowd erupted and moved away from the center, spreading to the edges like they all knew exactly what was next.

"What's the flag march?" I asked Nick, who only grabbed my hand, tugging me to the edge with the rest of the crowd.

"You'll see," Sky offered before he and Will fell in with the crowd.

The woman on stage made way for five people with a giant bag. They dropped it and got to work, unzipping and pulling out a massive roll of rainbow cloth. They tossed the roll over the edge of the stage, and the crowd cheered as it unrolled through the clearing. It must've been over sixty feet long. People at the edges closest to the fabric grabbed the sides, pulling it until it lay flat on the ground.

The woman on the mic asked everyone to grab a side and start the march. I was still confused until the crowd did as she asked and picked it up, holding it overhead, creating a canopy out of the colorful fabric. It picked up the breeze and lifted higher. Under the stage lights and streetlamps, it was like the sky had filled with color. The crowd headed off with the massive flag in tow. Some people ducked under the enormous canvas. Singing poured through the street, and people danced beneath the canopy as we walked down the road.

"This is something you can't miss." Nick grabbed my hand and drew me into the fray, guiding me under the rainbow. Sky and Will followed us, laughing and holding hands, occasionally dancing among the crowd.

I was overwhelmed by the sight of the flags waving and the sound of chanting as we marched through the street. The crowd cheered louder than before when we all reached another stage where a DJ played dance music and mashups of famous songs. The people holding the pride flag walked to the front of the stage and raised the rainbow-colored canopy up over them, making a shelter for the dancers. As the music changed, people ran beneath the giant flag to dance.

A pickup truck was parked on the side of the street, the truck bed piled high with paint cans. Cloth bags full of paintbrushes hung from a contraption attached to the tailgate. Someone stood on the back of the truck, opening the paint cans and handing them to people on the ground. A woman received her can and ran into the crowd, laughing as she aimed at her friends and tossed paint onto them. Another person slung their can up, shooting paint into the sky, which rained down, landing on anyone within its radius. Some people grabbed paintbrushes and smeared color over their bodies; before I knew it, the road was lit with glow-in-the-dark paint, shrouded by the giant rainbow overhead.

Nick brought me close to him and stared into my eyes. "Happy Pride," he said, resting his forehead on mine.

"Get over here," Sky screamed, chasing Will with a bucket of paint and a brush in hand. "We're doing it."

Cold, goopy paint splashed Nick and me. "Happy Pride, bitches," a smug Sky said before sashaying away and picking up a new bucket.

I could only stare in shock, but Nick hadn't budged. Instead, he kept hold of me, keeping me close, as red, glowing paint dripped down his head. The smoldering heat in his eyes teased me and stirred something deep within.

"I never want this to end," he said as he cupped my face in his palms, paint sliding between our skin.

"I love you," I blurted.

The confession spilled from my lips, and I worried it was too soon, but Nick's grin filled my heart. He held me in a sensual kiss. It was like he was making love to me in front of the world with that kiss. Time ceased to exist, and I fell into a world that belonged to me. A place where I felt more love than ever before. When we finally broke apart, his lips brushed my ear, and his voice sailed through my heart. "I love you too, Taka."

• • •

We tiptoed through the house, careful not to wake anyone as we rushed to the bathroom. I stripped the clothes stained with paint and flicked on the shower. Nick popped into the bathroom carrying towels. His smile hadn't wavered since the night began. He set the towels on the counter next to the sink and climbed out of his clothes.

He moved close to me, sliding his hands over my waist. "Taka, I don't know a better way to say this, but I want you to fuck me."

My heart stopped, and my breath lodged in my throat. "You what?"

He guided my hand over his hip, sliding my palm over his ass. "I want you inside me."

I stammered through unintelligible words, unable to form complete thoughts.

"Do you not want to? I'm happy to do it our usual way."

"It's not that," I breathed, backing into the wall.

"Are you doubting yourself right now? Really?" He guided me into the shower and kissed me. "Don't be worried." His hands slid over my body as the paint ran down our skin, spattering the shower walls with the colors of pride.

"Right here?"

"Mm-hm," he murmured.

The cold tiles on my back shocked me as his mouth dipped to my collarbone. His tongue ran over my skin before he sucked hard, filling me with pain and pleasure, and he rubbed his erection against mine, sending a wave of heat through me. "Right now. Don't hold back."

"I'm nervous. I don't know why."

"Come here." Nick pulled me under the water with him. He poured shampoo into the palm of his hand and ran his fingers through my hair. "We can take it to the bedroom instead." He rubbed my scalp, massaging me in slow, swirling motions. "But I want you to know how much I want you to fuck me against this wall right now." He tipped my head back, so water streamed down my face. "I want you so bad, I can taste it." His lips trailed down my throat as he continued to rinse my hair. "Your cock, sliding inside me. Hot water streaming down our backs as you shove me against the wall."

The image he conjured in my mind, I knew, came nowhere near to reality. It would not be that simple. I bit my lip, feeling the water run down my body, pooling and diverging around Nick's lips as he caressed them over my skin, begging me to fulfill his need. My nerves threatened to overwhelm me, but I grabbed his face, bringing him back to me. I did as he wanted, pushed him against the cold tile, and slid my hand over his ass as I pressed my body close to his. Our tongues danced together, and I slid my fingers between his crevice until I ran over his hole, teasing the sensitive area, and provoking a gasp from him.

"Did you bring the lube in here, at least?"

"Between the towels."

I slid the glass door open and hopped from the shower, fumbling through the towels until my fingers wrapped around the lube and raced back to him. Nick's smoldering eyes followed my every movement, turning me on with each little breath that puffed from his lips. I pulled his face to mine and devoured him while stroking his arousal. Then I poured the lube over my finger and ran over the rim of his hole, swirling and teasing the delicate skin.

I slid my hand to his waist, biting my lip. "Don't think I'm weird for this, okay?"

"I doubt anything you do would be too weird for me."

I eyed him for a moment but quickly gave in to my deepest desires. "Keep quiet. I don't need your family waking up."

"Confident, are we?"

"A little," I whispered, spinning him around, pressing him against the wall. His tattoo stared back at me, calling to me. Droplets slid down his back, leading my eye to the spot I wanted most. I pressed my lips to the feathers on his shoulder, licking and sucking at his skin, making my way down his body, teasing soft moans from him until I kneeled behind him. My nerves faded as I set the lube on the ground and trailed my fingers up his legs, nudging him so he would spread for me. My fingers reached his slicked crevice, and I stroked over his hole with my thumb. A soft gasp fell from his lips. I wanted to hear more of his reactions as I touched him. I leaned in and licked over the tender area, flicking my tongue over the rim.

"Fuck," Nick moaned, and I continued, entering him with my tongue, teasing him until his breathy cry was almost a scream. I sucked and teased, living out my fantasy, encouraged by his soft, breathy moans. I plunged my tongue deeper, sliding over his skin, savoring every moment. When his legs trembled, I pulled my tongue away and grabbed the lube, covering my fingers and sliding one inside him while I licked the rim.

"My God, Taka." Nick reached back, grabbing my hair and pulling me to my feet. His dark eyes were glistening, and his cheeks were flushed. "Please, for the love of God, fuck me."

"Sure," I said, biting back a laugh and readying the pair of us. As I entered him, we were slick with water and lube; he tightened and clenched around me when I nudged deeper. A groan poured from him as I pushed deeper and grabbed his face, taking his mouth in mine to keep him quiet. His warmth enveloped me as I thrust, pressing him harder against the wall, silencing his moans with my kisses. As I sank into his warmth, a deep chill of fear ran through me as I realized my mistake—I had forgotten a condom. It wasn't the end of the world, but I should've known better. Nick didn't seem to care as he pressed himself back, forcing me further inside him.

"We forgot the condom," I breathed as he pressed back again between my thrusts.

"I'm clean. I was recently tested," he said, a smile on his face as he rested his cheek against the tiled wall.

I knew I was clear too, and so I continued with confidence. I had never come inside someone, let alone without a condom, and hearing him say that made me want to bury myself deep and fill him with every last drop I could give.

He moaned as I moved, sliding in his warmth, watching beads of water roll down his back, over his tattoo. Nick had opened my eyes to parts of myself I normally would have been ashamed of. I would have been embarrassed by my thoughts and actions, but each sound that came from him told me he was enjoying it, chasing my unease away.

As I neared my climax, I ran my palm over his arousal, paying him close attention. He bit back his groan as he released, spilling in my hand. Then, when I couldn't hold back anymore, I rocked inside him, biting his shoulder covered in gorgeous feathers until I released. I stepped back into the water, watching him hold on to the wall as he came down from the high.

He turned toward me with a smirk as he stepped into the water, holding me close. "Oh, you're doing that again sometime."

I laughed and pushed him away. "Clean up already before the hot water runs out."

CHAPTER 27

NICK

Taka was in my childhood room, wearing only a white towel. I hoped no one heard us in the bathroom, but I don't think I would care much if they had. It had been an amazing end to the day. He ran a towel over his hair, appearing content. When he glanced up at me, I couldn't help the smirk that crawled up my face.

"What?" he asked as he set the towel on the back of my desk chair.

I shook my head as my heart swelled. "Looking at you over there made me think about what our future could look like."

His head tilted to the side as he eyed me. "What do you mean?"

"I was picturing what it would be like to live together and this," I motioned between us at the simple interaction of getting dressed together, "being our normal." I dropped onto the bed, motioning for him to join me. "Come here." I rolled onto my side and rested my chin on my hand.

Taka ran his fingers through his hair, brushing loose strands from his face before climbing into bed beside me.

"This is something I don't talk about much, and I don't think I'm ready to talk about all of it yet."

He mirrored me, dropping his chin into his palm as he propped his elbow on a pillow. "I won't pressure you to talk about anything."

My throat tightened, and I swallowed through the pain. It had been a long time since I had felt such a strong emotional connection with someone—not since Adam—and I had never expected to be fortunate enough to experience it again.

"It may not seem it, but I'm pretty scared of relationships." I breathed in deeply, fighting the growing tightness in my chest. "I've had one real relationship, and it ended badly."

"We have bad break-ups in common." He laughed.

I knew he was trying to ease my tension, but it was so different. Sometimes the pain would creep in—still raw, like it happened yesterday. The number of times I would replay that day in my head, thinking of different actions I could've taken, said something differently. It was constant.

"I mean, so bad I was pulled out of school for half a year." I offered him a sad smile because I wasn't ready to talk about it completely. I wasn't ready for him to know how broken I was. "You're the first person I've wanted to be serious about since."

"Am I?"

I rolled onto my back, looking up at the ceiling. "I get on Sky a lot for never entering a committed relationship, but I'm just as bad."

“How so?” He sounded worried.

As tears blurred my vision, I closed my eyes, listening to his soft breathing beside me. Taking comfort in him being here. “My relationship ended unexpectedly. Since then, I’ve drifted from person to person, never taking them seriously and avoiding letting anyone in.”

“That must have been lonely.”

I faced him, taking in the sight of his concern. “Sure, it was lonely, but it’s something I’ve gotten used to.” I cleared my throat, fighting back the tightness tugging at my heart. “Besides, it wasn’t that bad. I have a supportive family and Sky.” I leaned in close and whispered, “I’m really happy I met you.”

His breath puffed against my lips as I stared into his eyes. “I’m happy too.” He closed the gap, kissing me softly. The gentleness of it sent warmth through my body, chasing away my bitter memories.

Pulling him into a hug, I breathed him in. It was hard to imagine I had gone so long without this feeling.

Snuggled up together, I played with his hair, twirling the soft strands between my fingers while listening to his breathing slow as he dozed off. “I’m glad you came into my life,” I said.

• • •

The sounds of my family coming to life in the early morning woke me. Taka’s face was buried under the blanket, and the sun was creeping in from the crack in my dark curtains. Last night was amazing, and I was flying high. I didn’t want to return to SCU, and I didn’t want to work during summer break. But I was thankful that Taka lived near campus, so I could see him. They kicked most students out of the dorms for the summer; I was among the few who could stay because I worked on campus all year. Sky was joining me this summer and got a job in the food court so he would have a reason to stay in the dorms with me. I didn't believe it was the only reason, since he and Will had been growing closer this year. Sky wouldn't admit it, but I think he did it to stay near Will.

"Taka," I said, pulling the blanket back to reveal his face before leaning in and kissing his cheek. "Time for us to wake up."

He groaned and rolled away. "I don't wanna."

"I'm sleepy too, but don't you wanna go home?"

A grumble of protest rumbled the bed. "I'd rather stay here."

"Me too, but life is calling us back. Your parents will want you home, and I have work tomorrow to help River prepare for summer classes."

He grumbled again, "This week went by too fast."

In the short time he and I had spent at my house, he'd loosened up almost to the point of being a different person. I loved that he trusted me enough to show me this side of him.

"I don't want it to end either, but you live near campus and can visit me anytime."

He rolled over, facing me with his pouty frown. "You promise?"

"If I could, I'd keep you in my bed for the rest of our lives." I ran my thumb over his cheek, down his soft skin to his lips. The stubble on his jaw dug into my thumb as I slid under his chin, lifting his face to me. "Stop tempting me with that pouty frown." I bent down and kissed him so tenderly that my heart fluttered.

A tap came from my bedroom door, breaking the magic of

the moment. “Nick, stop making out and come have breakfast,” Harper said. “And next time the two of you are home, don’t take up the shared bathroom for an hour in the middle of the night. And maybe be a little quieter when you . . . you know.” The floor creaked as my little brother marched away, scolding me like a father.

Taka’s face flushed as he pulled the covers over his head and rolled himself into the blanket like a burrito. “Harper’s never going to look at me the same again. What have I done?” He groaned as he kicked his feet out and rolled back and forth.

I burst into laughter as I watched him overflow with the embarrassment. “At least he didn’t see it. There’s always a plus side.”

We spent an hour chatting with my family before saying our goodbyes. Taka couldn’t look Harp in the eye all morning, and even the last hug he gave him was awkward.

After hugging Mom tight and telling her how much I loved her, I turned my attention to Lori.

“I’m glad you’ve found someone so good for you,” Lori whispered before I released her from my hold.

I buried my face in her hair as I squeezed her tight. “Me too,” I said, kissing her head and pulling away. “Tom, it was great to see you again.” He gave me his standard nod, and I snuck over to Harper, who was still talking with Mom and Taka. When I came up behind him, I grabbed his shoulders and crushed him against my chest. “Next time, buddy, don’t listen.”

“You shouldn’t do that in the house if you don’t want others to hear you,” he said through my crushing grip.

“You’ll understand when you have a lover. Sometimes you can’t hold back.”

• • •

I cut the car off in Taka's driveway. His house was about four times the size of mine, maybe more. I opened my door reluctantly, glancing back at Taka as he hesitated to leave the car.

"Come on, let's get you home. Yeah?"

The sad look he gave was one I understood. He'd just experienced a lot, and now he was home, where he had to pretend to be someone else. I got out and headed for the trunk as the front door opened and a girl came outside. Her face was bright with a smile. Her glossy black hair hung around her face, which was lightly covered in makeup. I knew he had a younger sister, but I didn't expect her to look so much like him.

"Welcome home," she said as she rushed up to him, wrapping her arms around his waist. "I missed you so much."

Taka's hand pressed against her back as he held her tight. I knew Tami was his little princess. His love for her was immense. We had talked about our siblings once, and while I adored mine, Taka had a deep affection for his baby sister, more than I could ever have for my siblings. I wondered if that was because I was a middle child. If I had been the oldest, would I care differently for my family?

When Tami released Taka from her hold, her bright smile turned to me. "Hi, you're Nick?"

I nodded and walked up to her, giving her my hand to shake. "Nice to meet you, Tami."

She took my hand and held it longer than necessary as she glanced between Taka and me. "Do you want to come in? Mom is in the kitchen, and you must be tired from the long drive. A little break won't hurt, right?"

"Tami, he lives fifteen minutes away. You don't have to invite him in."

She turned on him. "Your friend just drove you home. The least you can do is invite him inside for a break." She spun on her heels and marched inside, shooting a death glare at Taka as she continued through the door.

"Seems I'm going in," I said.

Taka's silence was something I took as shock and uncertainty, but based on how Tami was speaking, I didn't want to cross her or make her angry by refusing the invitation.

"Nothing to worry about. I'll come in for a few minutes and be on my way," I added.

I touched his shoulder, then crossed the driveway to the front door. My heart was thundering in my chest. I'd just met my boyfriend's sister, and now I was going to meet his parents. My stomach sank as I realized I had to be his friend in front of them. This wasn't the warm welcome of my home where anyone could be themselves.

Taka walked past me, likely having the same thoughts as he opened the door and kicked off his shoes. That slimy fake smile of his that I hated appeared. At that moment, a piece of me broke. I wanted to yank him back, tell him how much I loved him, and take him home with me. Instead, I followed him like a shadow. Our joy was stifled the further we made it into the house. By the time we reached the kitchen, all the happiness I had felt from our time together was gone, replaced with a gray cloud I couldn't escape.

The feeling of this home was the same feeling I had in Adam's. An aura told me I wasn't welcome there. That anyone like me wasn't safe. It was cold. I glanced at Taka, my chest tightening at the thought of this being his everyday experience. The place he came home to. The freedom I saw in him during the week at my house was vibrant and beautiful. He was like a butterfly that had unfurled its wings, journeying through life without limitation. But this place was the opposite. The crushing presence of it terrified me.

Tami bounced around her mother at the kitchen island, and his mother glanced up as she noticed us. Taka's shoulders tensed, and I regretted coming here. I didn't want to see it.

His mother hugged him with a warm smile, but deep loneliness festered in the air. When she released him, she waved me over. "Nick? I'm Taka's mother, Chitose. You can call me Chi." She hugged me gently before grabbing my elbow, bringing me deeper into the kitchen. "Do you want to eat some steamed dumplings? Tami requested I make them today. The first batch should be ready soon."

"Sure, I've never had homemade dumplings," I said as Taka pulled out a chair at the kitchen table. I sat beside him and pressed my leg against his. I hoped my presence was comforting, but there was a chill in my gut, and I knew he felt it too.

CHAPTER 28

TAKA

Nick left my house only minutes before, but I was already feeling so alone. Mom and Tami were raving about how nice my new friend was. They asked how my trip went, and I told them about our visit to the National Zoo with Nick's brother, our tour of the streets of Washington, DC. I left out every part that made the trip memorable for me; every part that was the real me. I wondered how I had lived like this before. How did I pretend so easily without even thinking about it? Now, pretending was unbearably difficult. It felt like a chore to lie and skate around the truth.

My father didn't come out of his office at any point to welcome me home. It was typical of him, but it still stung. I slid into bed, cold and alone. An empty bed was tragic after a week with my lover beside me.

A gentle knock came from my bedroom door. "Come in," I called, expecting it to be my mother, but Tami came in, quietly closing the door behind her.

"I wanted to talk away from Mom," she said, climbing onto the bed beside me, crossing her legs while she eyed me. "Nick is more than a friend, isn't he?"

My stomach dropped. I chewed the inside of my cheek, avoiding her eyes.

"You don't have to say anything." She smiled and squeezed my leg. "You've changed since you made your new friend."

"Have I?"

She nodded and scooted closer to me. "You're more laid back. I can see that you've been happier lately. At first, I thought it was because you and Iz broke up. But you stayed overnight at a friend's house—a friend we've never met—then you go on a week-long trip with him." She winked and poked my cheek. "You think you're slick, but I see you."

"Do you think Mom and Dad noticed?"

She flopped onto her side beside me and sighed. "If they have, they haven't mentioned it."

We talked for a long time. I told Tami how Nick and I met, and she pried into my personal life more than ever. It was nice to confide in my sister. After so many years of pretending, even with her, I showed her a side of me that was raw and scared. When she left my room, carrying my secret with her, I thought of the days I spent lounging in bed or laughing with Nick and his family. It all felt so far away.

• • •

The door to my room was thrown open, ripping me awake. My father marched in, dressed in a suit like he was on his way to work. His glasses sat high on his nose, and he looked pissed. In his hand was an envelope, crumpled like he had crushed it before coming to me. "Get up, get dressed, and come to my office." He tossed the envelope at the foot of the bed and slammed the door shut as he left.

My hand shook as I reached for the crumpled paper. A yellow note was stuck to the back of a photo, and I pulled it out, turning the picture over. The grainy photo of Nick and me stared back. My world crashed around me. My pulse raced as I sifted through every scenario of excuses and lies I could devise. Then, I read the note.

Your son has a male lover.

My blood ran cold, chilling my bones. My breath caught, and my body froze. Clutching the photo in my icy fingers, tears stung my eyes and a tightness crushed my throat. I fought back the agony rising to the surface. Curling in on myself, I muffled my sobs. The happy little world I had found for myself had been ripped from my fingers in an instant. All hope for a future with the man I loved was gone. I crushed the photo in my hand, balling it in my fist before tossing it and the envelope in the trash.

The walls Nick had broken through swiftly rebuilt themselves, closing off my heart until I was left with nothing but a cold pit of emptiness settling in my heart like an old, despised friend.

The tears washed away in the shower. I dried myself, shaved, and dressed, going through the motions numbly. I put on the clothes that were expected of me: slacks and a dress shirt. Then, I knocked on his office door. I held my breath, waiting for the "Enter" instruction. Inside the office, I sat in the chair across from him. I didn't cry. Did not beg. Did not ask him to let it go, convincing him I loved Nick and to allow us to be together. Instead, I was silent as we stared each other down.

My father took off his glasses, setting them on his desk before folding his hands on his lap. "I knew you had been acting differently since meeting this new friend. Now I know why." His eyes betrayed his disgust. "I remember seeing marks on your neck and thinking that you had found a girl you liked. But this is not what I expected of my son."

I raised my chin as anger crept in. I fought it back, unwilling to show him any emotion.

"You will stop seeing that boy. You will finish your degree without incident. After you graduate, you will work with me at Akiyama Imports and gain experience alongside me. If you do not do those things, then you will no longer be welcome in this home, and you will have to figure out how to pay your way through life on your own. I will not have a son that disgraces me in this way."

His words were a searing hot knife through my heart. The unfairness of it all burned my throat, scorching my body and leaving scars where no one would ever see them. "I understand." My voice was cold, lifeless.

"Get out of my sight." He waved me off like a disobedient child.

I found myself in the backyard, the hot sun beating down on me mercilessly. My phone sat in my hand, my thumb hovering over Izzie's name in my contact list. She was going to answer for this. I knew it was her. She had been bitter since I broke up with her, but this was a new low I didn't realize she could manage.

I tapped her name and brought the phone to my ear. It rang

longer than I wanted, and I quickly grew impatient. The me that always followed the rules and performed in a respectable manner disappeared. My anger and pain bubbled up when her soft voice came on the other side, and everything I was feeling, everything I was holding back, exploded to the surface.

"You sent my parents that photo. How could you do that?"

"What the hell, T? What are you talking about?"

"You outed me to my parents with that photo. Do you even know what the fuck you've done?"

"Taka, calm down. I don't know what you're talking about. I didn't send anything to anyone. That picture was deleted weeks ago. I never would have sent it to your parents."

"If you didn't send it, then who the fuck did?" I hadn't ever raised my voice at her, and I rarely cussed or got angry with anyone, but rage fueled me, and I needed someone to blame, someone to direct it all toward. "You started all of this—you and that fucking friend of yours. So, you find out who the hell sent that photo to my father."

I hung up before I broke down. I wasn't going to let my family see me crumble, no matter how much I wanted to.

I walked through my house, grabbed my car keys, and entered the garage, hating myself more than anything in this world. Not once had I chosen my happiness over my family, and I wasn't about to start. Heartache wouldn't last forever. Nick and I were still new in our relationship. I could end it now and let us move on while we were young. Then, I would return to the proper son for my family. I would continue to be their rock. I would be there for Tami as she grew up and entered college. It was my duty.

When my engine roared to life, memories of our time

together flooded me. I stared at the passenger seat, remembering how much fun that day at the car meet had been. How easy it was to bring Nick into my life. I backed out of the garage and headed toward campus, my heart shattering with each passing second.

When I pulled into the parking garage, I was like a zombie, wandering through campus until I reached his door. Life was cruel. I was once again the asshole for being the one to end a relationship without warning. I could live with it even if, this time, I didn't want to. My knuckles hit the door like they weren't a part of my body.

When the door swung open, Nick tugged me into his dorm and squeezed me in his arms, kissing my neck as he held me in the doorway. I fought back tears as I pushed him away and stepped back, closing my heart to him and forcing everything deep down in the pit of darkness that held everything inside.

"What's wrong?" he asked, a frown forming as his eyes darted over my face.

"Look, I'll come out and say it. There isn't an easy or nice way for me to do this." My voice was calmer than I thought possible.

He straightened and tilted his head as he eyed me, but he didn't reply. He was probably already aware of what my next words would be. They always knew. I wasn't good at hiding my intentions in this situation.

"This morning, my father brought me an envelope with the picture Izzie posted to Facebook inside of it. Attached was a note. Whoever sent it outed me to my parents."

Nick released a breath and covered his mouth with his hands, waiting for me to continue.

"My father gave me a choice. I could either end my relationship or be kicked out on the street and never allowed home again." I swallowed, hating myself. Hating my father. Hating whoever sent the photo. "I've chosen my family."

His eyes welled up with tears as his hands fell from his mouth. His breath caught before he released quick, sharp breaths. "I have no chance here?" His voice quivered as he spoke, his eyes pleading with me to stop this madness, but I couldn't.

"No."

Tears slid down his cheeks. A deep intake of breath rattled through him. "You won't let us come up with any other options? I would be fine with a secret relationship, more secret than we already have."

I shook my head, knowing that negotiation wouldn't work. I couldn't handle the lies and stress. It would be unfair to us both.

"Just please don't leave me," Nick whispered.

"I have to. I choose my family. The choice is made. You can't convince me otherwise."

"Please, Taka. Please don't leave like this." His eyes were red, and tears ran down his face as he grabbed my hand.

I yanked it away, my heart falling to pieces as I watched the hurt cross his face. "Stop. Nothing you say or do will change my decision." I took a step back, needing to escape from this. Escape from him. I didn't want to face the regret. The pain I was causing was unfair. It made no sense.

"You're giving up just like that?"

I stepped back again, and he dropped to his knees.

"Please don't let this happen again," he begged.

I wasn't sure what he meant and watched him wrap his

arms around himself, lean forward, and press his head to the ground. "I can't go through this again." A sob rolled through him, his body shuddering with the despair I placed in his heart. "Not again."

I couldn't speak. I couldn't breathe. Watching the man I loved fall to his knees in front of me was soul-destroying. I wanted to hold him, tell him I changed my mind, but I knew I couldn't. He would get over me. He would move on. He would find love again.

His cries followed me down the hallway like a demon latching onto my heart, cursing me. When I reached my car, I finally broke. I sunk into the seat and let everything hit me. My heart broke again, and I cried more than I ever had. I screamed and punched and kicked anything I could; I wanted to punish myself for being the shitty human I was. How cruel I was to be this way.

I don't deserve love.

I'm a coward.

I hate myself.

CHAPTER 29

NICK

Voices carried through the hallway and into my apartment, but I didn't register their meaning. My life had been destroyed, and I had been crushed under the weight of it all.

I couldn't say how long had passed since I watched him back away from me. He was the first one to show me his face, never once turning his back on me at the end, and I hated it. The look of anguish in his eyes was the only sign that his words were false. Takahiro Akiyama had crushed me and triggered the parts of me I thought had been locked away for good. Once again, I had been abandoned by someone I had given everything to.

My mind was racing with frightening thoughts. The moment I found out about Adam came back, reopening the wound. The pain I had felt back then returned just as powerfully. Then my mind wandered to the darkest parts of my imagination. Images of someone finding Taka dead in his house. Me getting the phone call that he, too, had left me like Adam had and, once again, family was the cause. Their hate and inability to love their son for who he was had killed him. I hated them. They should feel my pain; know what it was like to love someone so deeply and then have them ripped away from you because others didn't like it; know what it was like to be gay and hated, forced to follow social norms, even if it made you a shell of yourself, even if it left you wishing for death to free you from the agony. Would Taka feel it was too much? Would I find out that he couldn't live like that anymore? I didn't want that news. I wouldn't be able to handle it.

Hands gripped my shoulder, pulling me from the mental abyss. I blinked until reality reappeared and saw Sky's worried face before me.

"What happened? Why is the door wide open? What are you doing on the floor?" he demanded, anxiety clouding his eyes.

I stared at him, the brother who saved me after Adam died. My saving grace in life. The person who gave me a reason to keep trying.

"He broke up with me."

Sky looked confused for a few moments. Then, he closed the door.

"Okay. Um, okay," he said, sitting in front of me. "Look at me." He cupped my face in his hands. "Tell me what happened."

I fumbled through a tear-filled account of Taka's visit, speaking through sobs, sucking in heavy, shuddering breaths as I tried to communicate the events coherently.

"Sky," I said, biting back another sob, "I had promised myself to never let go of someone I love again, but how could

I hold onto him when holding on could risk his life?"

Sky wrapped me in a hug, and he cried in my ear. "I'm so sorry, but I'm glad you let him go. You know he loves you. This was hard for him, too."

"Why does it have to be this way?" I clung to him, holding him close. "Why can't we love each other?"

"I wish I had an answer for you. I really do." Sky ran his fingers through my hair as he held me through wave after wave of sobs.

Life was nothing but cruel.

• • •

The door to the computer lab opened and a young woman walked in, glasses perched low on her nose. She held a paper up to her face.

"Hello," I said, tapping my pen on the desk.

I assumed she was a prospective student touring the building.

River was at lunch, and I had reception duty. River laughed when I tried to get out of it. She didn't give me much room to wallow in my despair. It had been three weeks since Taka had crushed our future together. Three weeks of me wrestling with my demons.

The girl stammered her greeting as she flipped the paper over. "I'm looking for admissions. Do you know where that is?"

I pointed her in the right direction and went back to staring at my laptop. I thought about returning it to him. Then, when I couldn't bring myself to do that, I thought about burning it. And when I couldn't handle the thought, I kept it. This stupid laptop followed me everywhere. I thought of it now as a funny way of apologizing for our breakup before he even knew it would happen. At least, that's how I was excusing my continuing use of it.

"Earth to Nick," River said, setting her bag on the floor beside me and sitting on the desk. She pushed the laptop to the side and placed her foot on my thigh. "When are you going to start looking up? You've been down for almost a month."

"How would you feel if Sarah left you because her parents found out about your relationship and disapproved?"

She looked chastened. "You get a pass. I'm just trying to lighten your mood."

The look on her face brought me back to myself. "I don't mean to be rude, Riv, and I know I'm a downer right now, but can I not have time to be upset?"

She pouted and kicked my leg. "Go home early if you're going to be miserable. I don't want you scaring away the students." She shooed me away from her chair and shoved the laptop at me. "Go work on your art and work through those feelings. I love you, but maybe you need to talk to someone. And if you won't talk to me, I suggest a professional."

I didn't argue. I knew I wasn't nice to be around, and I seemed to keep taking it out on the people I loved, so I placed my laptop in my bag and left the lab. The Ellis Center was mostly empty, only the occasional person here and there. I grabbed food from the food court and wandered through campus, not hungry but knowing I needed to eat. But the idea of taking a bite of anything had me gagging, so I tossed the bag in the trash.

Finding myself standing in my dorm, I looked around, bewildered. Every day was like this. I'd forgotten what I used to do before. What was my life like before Taka entered it? How did I live? What did I do? I couldn't remember.

The group had fallen apart quickly after the breakup, and I was back to Sky and Riv as my only friends. I hadn't realized how lonely I was until they were gone. Until he was gone. I missed him.

My phone vibrated in my pocket, one notification after another. When I opened the screen, I saw several Facebook notifications. I dropped my bag on the bed and opened the app. Will had tagged me in a private photo album with a comment.

I was busy, so I haven't had time to upload these, but Pride was great this year!

Will had gone to Thailand with his parents after Pride. He must've gotten back recently. The display photo on the album was a selfie of him and Sky, covered in that infamous glow-in-the-dark paint. I thought back to Sky splashing the paint over us and couldn't help but smile as I opened the album. What I was met with crushed me.

Will had captured too many pictures of Taka and me. I scrolled through each photo, unable to stop myself. The two of us holding hands under the giant pride flag as we marched together. Picture after picture of those precious memories. My throat tightened as I came to the moment I didn't want to relive: Taka smiling, red paint dripping from his face, wrapped in my arms.

I kept going until I hit the image I knew would break me. The moments after he had said the precious words, "I love you." Our kiss under the pride flag, covered in paint, sharing the moment, embracing the essence of Pride. I enjoyed every moment of that day. We shared a night I would never forget. The memory was burned into my heart, like the indelible ink of my phoenix tattoo.

I grabbed the bottle of vodka from the kitchen and set the phone down on the counter, taking a swig and another until the burn no longer fazed me. Unable to escape my demons, I found myself in the bathroom, sinking into the empty bathtub. I reached for a razor and released the blade from its handle.

Minutes passed in a daze. I jumped backward in time and then back to the present, over and over. Finally, I flicked the clasp of my bracelet open, letting it fall to my lap, and traced my thumb over the old scars that marked my skin. Any feeling other than heartache would be a welcome change if it meant avoiding this crushing despair. The loss I felt was all-consuming. I would do anything to make it stop.

His love haunted me.

Taka's face flashed through my mind, covered in glowing red paint as he told me he loved me. Then I saw the look on his face as I begged him to stay.

"I choose my family." His words echoed in my mind, over and over until I couldn't take it.

Why did they always leave me?

I gulped down the clear alcohol, wishing it would take my memories. I wanted to disappear from this life. I never wanted to feel like this again.

With a trembling hand, I brought the sharp edge of the blade to my old scars, feeling the familiar warmth of blood as I reopened wounds that I thought were long gone. Blood rolled down my wrist, dripping into my lap. It was a release at first, but the pain dulled quickly. It wasn't enough. I ran the blade over my skin again, hoping that it would take my thoughts with it. The last time I saw Adam. The last time I saw Taka. And the last time I saw my father. They all left me. This was my fate: each time I opened myself to someone, they would leave me. I was cursed to lose the ones I loved most. Was Sky next? Would he leave me too?

As my mind raced with memories of them, I fell into darkness, embracing the loss of feeling as my blood seeped from my wounds.

"Nick!" Sky yelled, but he sounded far away. "Nick!" His voice trembled like he was crying.

I must have blacked out. When I opened my eyes, darkness surrounded me, but Sky's face was lit up in front of me, shining with tears as his warm hands cupped my cheeks.

"Hey, buddy. What were you doing in here?" he asked.

Seeing him cry brought fresh tears to the surface, blotting my vision even more. Sky held my head to his chest. His heart was thundering, and his body shook.

Would he think differently of me after seeing me like this?

"Help is on its way, Nick. Hold on."

I mumbled, "I don't want to hurt anymore. I'm so tired of hurting."

"I know you are, but I'm right here with you."

"I don't want to hurt anymore, Sky."

"I wish I could take it all away. I really wish I could." He squeezed me tight, patting my head as he held me. His sobbing vibrated through me as I realized my actions.

"I'm sorry I'm like this."

"Don't apologize to me. We're going to get you help. I promise."

I nodded and closed my eyes. I could hear him talking to Will, and soon there were other voices, but I couldn't respond.

• • •

Shannon, my therapist, sat across from me, scribbling in her notebook as I talked about my feelings, which I had done every other day since Sky found me drunk and covered in blood in the bathtub. The hospital kept me for a few days, and my mother insisted I see a therapist again. She was worried about a repeat of what happened after Adam died. Neither Sky nor I revealed to her that, based on what Sky told me, I had tried to die.

I liked Shannon; she was easy to talk to and didn't press me too much. School was starting back in a few days, and I was finally feeling like my old self again.

"Do you think you're ready to go back?"

I nodded. "I'm ready to get back into the swing of things."

"Good. Since you feel that way, let's reduce our sessions to twice a week, and if you need to meet more than that, call me."

I left her office and called Sky. He answered on the third ring.

"Is your session done?"

"Yup. Are you still interested in lunch?"

"You know it. I'm starving."

I slid into my car and headed for the restaurant near campus. Things were finally looking up.

CHAPTER 30

TAKA

Like an obedient son, I followed my father through the group of people who were standing around, mingling and discussing business. My father called this networking, but it felt like a dick-measuring contest. Who had more money? Who won the government contract? Who had more clients? It was nothing more than a bunch of old men flaunting themselves.

"Son," my father called, motioning for me to stand beside him while he introduced me to a gray-haired man who looked like several others in the room. "This is my son, Takahiro. He will take over Akiyama Imports in a few years, so I can finally retire." His laugh grated on my ears, but I plastered on my perfect business smile and shook the man's hand.

This went on for hours until my father let me retreat to a corner and keep to myself. These people disgusted me. I wished I could leave and never come back.

"Drink, sir?" A server offered me a glass of ruby-colored liquid, which I assumed to be wine. They didn't ask for my ID, probably assuming I was already of legal age.

"Why not?" I grabbed the glass and held it. My father would scold me if I chugged the whole thing in one go, so I sipped it.

My phone rang in my pocket, and I quickly silenced it. A moment later, it went off again, and I looked at the caller ID. Zack? He knew I was at an event. Why would he call me? I ignored the call and turned the phone to vibrate to avoid drawing the attention of the party guests. The phone went off again as I was about to slide it back into my pocket. Zack's name once again appeared on the screen. I hit the answer icon and rested the phone against my ear.

"Zack, you know I'm busy tonight. What do you need?"

"I probably shouldn't be telling you this, but I think you need to know. Will texted me after getting a call from Sky. Sky and Nick are living on campus over summer break. Apparently, Sky found Nick drunk in the bathtub, bleeding."

My heart stopped beating.

"T?"

I cleared my throat. "I'm here," I croaked. "Do you know what happened? Did he slip and fall?"

Zack sighed, as if debating whether to tell me. "From the way it sounded, he had been harming himself."

I scanned the crowded room, holding back my tears. "Do you know why?"

"Not yet, but Will didn't know you two broke up yet since he had been in Thailand, and I'm pretty sure Nick saw his Facebook post."

"What post?"

"Will made it private for our group only. You should see for yourself, T. I just thought you should know."

"Thanks. Please let me know how it turns out. Don't tell them you spoke to me."

"Are you sure?"

"Positive. I'm hanging up now."

I counted my breaths and fought back the tears as I shakily found Will's most recent Facebook post. It was a photo album. He and Sky were in the cover photo. Paint was splattered all over their faces, and rainbow flags flew behind them. Immediately, I knew what had upset Nick. I flipped through the images and stopped at one of us hugging under the rainbow flag. Paint was dripping from my hair and face, and both of us were beaming with joy. Nick's palm print marked my cheek where he had held my face before kissing me. The emotions I had been suppressing burst to the surface. Nick saw this, and what? Did he try to . . . I thought of how much he must have been hurting when he saw this. The best night of my life was captured so perfectly in these pictures. I was so happy. I thought I could escape the expectations placed on me. I thought I could remain like that. I was a fool.

A cry broke through the façade I'd constructed since we split up, and the glass fell from my grasp as my body shook.

"Taka?" my father asked as he strode toward me. Everyone in the room was looking at me. My father was fuming, his face turning bright red as he closed in.

"Sorry to disturb you all." I slid my phone into my pocket and floated in a daze through the building until I reached the exit.

"Come back," my father called from the end of the hallway.

I turned around, released the door, and stepped toward him. Scalding hot tears ran down my face as I stared at the man

I called my father. "What do you want me to say? The truth? You wouldn't care, anyway." I turned back toward the door and pushed it open, disappearing into the night.

• • •

I sat in the first class of the day, waiting for the professor to arrive. It was only the second day of the semester, and I was hoping the professor would let us out early. Since I found out Nick had ended up in the hospital, I worried about him every day, torturing myself before bed, scrolling through Will's photo album of our last night together. I never wanted to forget that night. Never wanted to forget Nick. Life had been a dull gray since I ended our relationship. I had forgotten what it was like to be happy, to laugh from the heart, to smile with joy. The only thing left of me was the outline of a person.

The professor arrived in class and jumped into her introductions. She went around the room, having students introduce themselves. I used to prepare a funny remark or joke to say with my introduction, but today I didn't care.

My phone lit up on the desk. Izzie's name popped up, and I opened it immediately.

Izzie: *I know who sent the photo.*

I held my breath as I waited for her to send the name.

Izzie: *Casey.*

Casey had tried to worm his way into my life again, and I didn't have the energy to fight or care, so I let him hang around me, but it wasn't like it used to be. That morning he brought me coffee and talked about my family like it was nothing. He was sitting beside me, a foot away.

My breath was sharp as I glared at him, sitting in the chair, taking notes as the professor spoke to the class. He had no idea the suffering he caused.

Me: *You're positive?*

Izzie: *He told me himself last night. He was bragging to me while he was drunk.*

He was bragging? I thought. *What kind of person brags about something like that?*

I dropped my phone on the desk, and it clattered loudly. I rose from my chair, and the entire class turned to look at me. My heart was racing. I breathed rapidly as every single moment since June rushed through my thoughts. Every moment of pain and suffering culminated into a single point of focus, and I was staring right at Casey.

"Young man, please sit down," the professor said.

"Taka, what's wrong?" Alex asked.

"It was you," I growled, glaring at Casey.

Casey looked at me, wide-eyed, a blush spreading up his neck. "What was me?"

My voice was cool and laced with something that terrified even me. "Were you the one that sent the photo?" I clenched my fist and chewed the inside of my cheek, hoping Izzie was wrong about this.

Casey glanced at the ground before looking back at me. "What are you talking about, T?"

Something in the way he protested confirmed my suspicion. I swung my fist, landing a perfect punch on his face, knocking him out of the chair. He hit the ground, and chairs scraped the floor as several students leaped to their feet, ready to fight or take flight.

"Don't fucking lie to me," I roared, standing over him. "You even had the nerve to talk to me like nothing happened. Tell me the truth!" I leaned down, grabbing the collar of his shirt and bringing his face close to mine. "Do you even know what you did?"

"I didn't–"

"Don't lie to me," I screamed so loud my throat burned.

The professor hovered nearby, uncertain how to intervene. I ignored her.

"I didn't think it would turn out this way," Casey whined.

"That's right, *you didn't think*. You didn't give a fuck who you hurt."

I pushed him to the ground and turned toward Alex, who was standing, clutching my phone to his chest.

Take a breath. Breathe. Relax, I told myself.

"Casey, tell me why. I need to know why," I said, my voice trembling.

"I don't know."

"That's no answer! I need to know why you would hurt me." I dropped to my knees beside him, bunching his shirt in my fist. "I need to know."

He stared at me, looking up into my eyes, and all I could feel was rage boiling through my veins, begging me to crush him. Never in life had I wanted to hurt someone so badly that I would risk my life and future. I didn't care that the whole class were watching, listening. Right then, only Casey and I existed.

Without breaking eye contact, Casey released a breath and whispered, "Because I liked you first."

"What?"

"I was there first. I liked you first. It isn't fair that he was who you chose when I was beside you this whole time."

A strained laugh bubbled up from deep in my chest. The class of confused and scared students watched me as I laughed uncontrollably, falling apart on the floor. Casey—the exemplary frat boy—had feelings for guys? For me? It was ludicrous. But as funny as it was, I hated him. As if I would choose Casey over Nick, even if I had known of his feelings for me.

Memories of Nick flashed through my mind, breaking my heart again as I kneeled in front of a classroom, outing myself. Through gritted teeth, I hissed, "I love him so much, and you ruined everything. I can never get back what you took from me. It's gone forever."

"T, get up before you get the cops called on you," Alex said, digging his fingers into my shoulder as he helped me to my feet, a sign that I shouldn't take it any further.

"I'm sorry, T. I didn't mean for it to turn out how it did," Casey said.

I laughed again and squatted so I could be close to his face. "How did you think it would turn out? Did you think I would break up with Nick and come running to you? Did you think my father would disapprove of Nick, but approve of you?"

Casey dropped his gaze. As I stood, he reached for me.

"Don't ever speak to me again," I snarled, swatting his hand away.

Alex held tight to my shoulder, keeping me close as he guided me from the classroom. The hallway was full of curious onlookers who gave me room to pass, their whispers of curiosity unintelligible.

"Taka!" Izzie's harsh voice rang in my ears.

"What do you want?" I couldn't help the irritation in my

voice, nor could I hide my anger. I was tired. Too tired to care how I appeared to others. Too tired to show respect to those that never showed any to me. I didn't even care that a crowd had gathered in the hallway, their eyes locked on me, lapping up every moment of my breakdown.

She looked around at the shocked faces staring at us, then said, "I heard you screaming all the way from my classroom."

"What does it matter to you?"

Alex stepped between us. "Izzie, it probably isn't the best time for this conversation."

She chewed her lip, her eyes flicking between us. "Taka, I didn't tell you Casey was the one who sent the photo so you could hurt him. I did it so you would know and maybe feel better knowing who did it."

"Are you joking right now?" I let out a laugh, my fingers trailing through my hair, now damp with sweat. "You didn't think I would hurt him, like he's hurt me?"

She shook her head, her eyes wide with worry as she looked up at me. "This isn't like you. You've changed since you met him." She paused, taking a breath. "That guy. He changed you."

A slow, deep chuckle bubbled up from my chest, and I couldn't control it. "Isobel, you think I changed because you never knew the real me to begin with. None of you know me."

Her breath caught at my harsh tone. My throat was raw and tight from yelling, threatening to lock my voice away. "No one ever cared to know me."

"Don't say that," Alex said, a faint hint of sadness in his voice. "We care. I care."

Izzie reached for my arm, but I could hear the hesitancy in her voice as she said, "I'm sorry, Taka. I posted that picture and said cruel things about you because I was angry and hurt." Her lip trembled as she sucked in a shaky breath. "I'm really sorry for the part I had in causing you pain. Can you forgive me?"

"I don't have an answer for you," I said.

Izzie looked wounded, but she nodded and stepped back, saying, "I understand."

I stalked off down the hallway, Alex close behind me. Sky stood at the end of the hallway, surprise evident on his face. News traveled fast. A quiet moment passed between us before he marched up to me, grabbed my hand, and pulled me through the corridors until we reached an empty classroom.

"Alex, can you give us a minute? I need to talk to him about something," Sky said, his hand holding tight to my forearm as he pulled me toward a desk.

"I'll wait right outside," Alex said, distress written all over his face.

Sky motioned for me to sit at a desk. "I guess you're not doing so well after all." He paused, eyeing me like he was afraid to say anything else. "I need you to know something."

"Is Nick okay?" I asked, worried Nick had done something else to hurt himself.

"He's fine, right now. But it's delicate. And before you do anything dramatic, like getting into fights about him, I think you need to know where Nick's head is at." Sky cleared his throat, looking me up and down. "You never heard these words I'm about to say." I nodded, waiting for him to continue. "Nick had a lover before he and I were friends. His name was Adam, and they had been friends long before they fell in love."

"Go on," I urged. My thoughts rushed back to the night Nick told me he had gone through a nasty breakup. Was Adam who he was referring to?

"Adam's dad walked in on them being intimate and lost his mind. Apparently, Adam's dad was going to send him away, and Adam chose his own way out."

"Way out?"

Sky nodded. His shoulders seemed to sink with the weight of his thoughts. "A few days after, Adam hanged himself."

I swallowed, letting his words sink in.

Adam. I said the name over and over in my head as the feeling I had heard it before ate away at my mind. "Where have I heard that name before?"

"I doubt Nick said anything about him. He almost never talks about it. But he painted Adam for a class assignment, and it affected him more than he thought it would when the professors hung it in the student gallery."

Flashes of a painting flooded my mind. The boy holding a bleeding heart in his hand, staring at me with those determined eyes, begging me to join him with a smile. I resonated with him.

"Oh my God," I said, the tightness in my throat returning. How could I have forgotten? How could I have never put the two together? He painted his dead lover. Chills ran down my arms as I realized the meaning of Nick's artwork. Adam's Apple was Nick's bleeding heart. I jumped to my feet, unable to sit still, as a horrific thought came to mind. "Did Nick think I would do the same thing Adam did?"

"Of course he does, but that isn't why I'm telling you this. Nick tried to do the same as Adam a month later. It took over a year of therapy to get him to a place where he was a person again, where he could laugh and think about falling in love. You were the first person I've ever seen Nick happy with." Sky ran his fingers through his hair. “Before you, Nick had one-night stands or fuck buddies, but never someone he opened up to. Never someone he cared for.”

The floor fell from under me; it was like I was floating in an empty space. My emotions vied for my attention, begging me to hear them. I was the first person Nick had opened up to since his dead lover? Then I hurt him, threw us both off the cliff, and for what? So we could both run around miserable? No. Enough. It was time to take the advice he had given me to choose a family that will love me unconditionally.

My hands shook at my sides as I resolved to do something I never expected. “Thank you, Sky. You’re a great person, and Nick is lucky to have you as a friend.”

• • •

A coldness wrapped around me as I wandered through the empty house, thinking of all the times I had to lie and pretend. Thinking of how scared I was to be myself, how I felt like a stranger in my own home. A stranger to my family.

I closed my bedroom door and quickly packed clothes and necessities into a duffle bag, then I headed to the kitchen and waited for my family to come home.

When my mother arrived, she got to work in the kitchen, and Tami sat with us as usual. I only sat, observing. They eyed me when I didn’t laugh with them and didn’t offer conversation.

Finally, the garage door opened, and my father walked in. He looked old and tired. The gray in his hair was becoming more prominent, and I could only feel sorry for him as I watched him shuffle to his office.

"I need to talk to Dad," I said, pushing away from the table, rushing to his office, and opening the door without knocking. I sat down across from him and waited for him to speak. When he didn't, I did. "Today, I punched someone. I thought he was a friend, but I found out it was him who sent you that picture."

My father folded his hands in his lap but showed no sign of interrupting me.

I continued, feeling bold. "He sent it because he knew how you would react. And, like the obedient son I am, I did what I was supposed to do, right? Follow the rules of society. Never go against the grain. Be a respectable man. Deny myself the one thing in this life that makes me happy. But what makes my suffering worth any of that? What makes it okay for me to give up on my happiness? What gives anyone the right to tell me how to love or who to love?"

I stared at him, waiting for any reaction. Anything at all. But he was silent.

"Dad, I love Nick. And he loves me. He loves me with a tenderness that I've never experienced. His family is welcoming and filled with love. I saw and experienced a world where I was accepted for who I am, not for who someone else wants me to be. You want me to live the way you want me to, but I can't. I refuse to be stifled. I refuse to be crushed by your expectations. If that means you never want to speak to me again, then so be it, but I will not walk away from the love of my life." I pulled a stack of pictures from my pocket and placed them on his desk. "This was the happiest day of my life. I hope you'll be able to see that."

I stood and opened the door before turning back to the man who, despite everything, I loved and respected but whom now I also hated. “I don’t want to hurt you, but I can’t keep hurting myself.”

I stepped back across the threshold of his office, my father’s world, and grabbed the duffle I had left near the stairs. I walked into the kitchen, placed my keys and money on the counter, then silently left my house with Tami and my mother staring after me.

CHAPTER 31

NICK

The smell of food was heavy in the air. Sky was busy in the kitchen preparing dinner, while I was lounging on the sofa and clicking through channels. River had let me out of work early since it was slow, and the administration finally granted the extra headcount we had asked for during the spring semester.

Evidently, my channel hopping irritated Sky. He stopped chopping an onion and sighed. "Don't you have anything you could do right now instead of channel surfing like an old man?"

I felt old, so I shook my head and gave Sky the bird.

A few minutes later, a light tap came from the door, and I tilted my head to Sky. "Expecting Will?"

"He didn't say anything, but it could be. Go answer it, old man." He waved the knife toward the door, motioning for me to go.

I hopped up and swung the door open.

My blood ran cold as I looked at the sad picture before me.

Taka stood there, his T-shirt and jeans soaking wet. A duffle bag sat on the ground, also soaked through. He stared at me, eyes swelling with tears.

"Please, forgive me." His lip quivered as he locked eyes with me, his fists tightly clenched by his sides. Tears spilled down his face as he begged for forgiveness, holding back a sob. "I'm sorry."

My mind reeled. Had he run away from home and come here? Was he choosing me over his family? My heart swelled and broke all in one breath as I yanked him through the door, wrapping him in my arms. "Of course I forgive you." Droplets of water fell from his hair as he rested his chin on my shoulder, clinging to me.

"Nick, what's taking so long over there?"

I craned my neck to look at Sky as he came around the door.

"Taka! Are you okay?" He rushed over and pulled Taka away from me as he looked him over.

Taka nodded, wiping the tears from his eyes and shivering.

"Come in and take a hot shower," Sky said.

I grabbed the duffle off the ground and nudged Taka forward. "Come on, let's get you cleaned up and fed."

Sky smiled. "Guess I should double the recipe now."

I led Taka into the bathroom and handed him a fresh towel. Then I grabbed some sweatpants, quickly returning to him. He seemed fragile, like at any moment, something would break him. "Tell me what happened, but take your time," I said, turning on the shower and setting the change of clothes on the counter.

"I punched Casey today. Then outed myself to the entire class."

I raised my eyebrows. "Why did you do that?"

"He's the one that sent the photo to my father."

Rage boiled in my chest. I regretted not punching the guy myself. Biting back my anger, I pulled Taka close and lifted the hem of his shirt. "What else?"

"I left home. Confronted my father and left." He paused, a shudder coursing through him. "I didn't even say goodbye to Mom or Tami. I said what I needed to say to my father and got the hell out of there." He lifted his gaze to mine. "I didn't even tell them I love them. I just left."

I cupped his face in my palms, happy he was standing in front of me but guilty that he had taken such extreme action for me. "I know that it's hard. I know you hurt. God, I know you hurt." I pressed my forehead to his, stroking his cheeks with my thumbs, wiping his tears away. "I will give you everything I can, but I know it will never replace the love of your family, and I'm so sorry for that."

His shaky hands clawed their way around my waist, clinging to my shirt. He said, "I'm sorry for everything. Breaking up with you was the hardest thing I've ever done. I didn't want to, but I thought it was the only way."

"I was never angry with you. I was scared for you. I didn't want you to fall into the same darkness I've seen before."

He wrapped his arms around my waist and pulled me tight against him. "I never stopped thinking about you. And I never stopped loving you."

I kissed his forehead, the tip of his nose, and his lips. "I love you." I brushed my lips over his once more before tearing myself away. "Now, get in the shower before you get pneumonia." I lifted the shirt over his head and tossed it in the sink.

Taka slid out of his pants, then stepped into the shower. He seemed like he had lost weight in the last few months.

I sat on the toilet while he showered. The silence between us was comforting. Knowing he was there was enough to warm my heart.

Taka's phone rang on the counter beside me. The name that appeared on the screen gave me chills: Mom. I cleared my throat and glanced at the shower before looking back at the phone. "Your mom is calling you."

"Ignore it."

His bitter words cut through the noise of the water like ice. I could never imagine a time when I wouldn't speak to my mother. With a sigh, I ran my hands over my face. "I'm sorry you have to go through this."

"I've made my decision; it was mine to make this time," he said. He sounded more self-assured than I'd ever heard him.

The phone finally quieted and flashed the missed call message, but a moment later, it rang again. His mother gave him only seconds before her next call would come through. Eventually, she stopped calling, but minutes later, Tami's name popped up on the screen, and I was once again told to ignore the call.

As Taka stepped out of the shower, I handed him a towel, and his phone went off again; this time, it was his father. Taka grabbed the phone and hit the power button. "We're going to have silence." He set the phone on the counter.

I cleared my throat as Taka slid into the sweatpants. This wasn't the time to be horny, I warned myself, talking down the bulge straining against my pants. "Let's go eat with Sky. He's a great cook. I'm sure you'll like whatever he's making."

Taka nodded and hung the towel on an empty hook before marching out of the bathroom like new life had been breathed into him. I grabbed his phone from the counter and tucked it into my pocket before trailing after him into the kitchen.

Sky was setting the table and looked up at us with a bright smile. "And the family grows bigger. Welcome to our home. Stay for as long as you like, though, the university may not agree. I'm all for hiding you here."

• • •

While Taka chatted with Sky in the living room, I grabbed his soaking-wet duffle and sifted through the contents. Some clothes had gotten wet, but thankfully his laptop was safe at the center of the clothes. After putting it on the desk next to mine, I returned to the bag. I hung the dry clothes in my closet, making room for his things beside mine. Then, I unpacked the wet clothes and hung them over the dryer. He had brought a toothbrush and was light on toiletries. At the bottom of the bag was an envelope. The flap was tucked in instead of sealed, and I let my curiosity overrule my desire to not invade his privacy. Inside was a pile of thick photo paper.

Seeing the photos he carried with him was like a punch to the gut. He had printed our pictures from the pride march. I cried as I flipped through them, thinking of his pain. The same pain I had suffered through.

I dashed to my desk and quickly took everything off the cork board, tossing it all in a desk drawer; then, I added each photo from Taka's pile until they covered the cork with our faces.

"What are you doing in here?" Taka asked as he came into my room.

I turned to him, wiping my tears. "I was putting your stuff away."

He tilted his head, looking around me. "Why are you crying?" The corners of his mouth turned down when he saw the pictures behind me.

"I found them while cleaning out the duffle. I felt they deserved to be on display."

A soft sigh escaped him as he came closer, a sad smile playing at his lips as he said, "They're beautiful photos. I gave a few to my dad when I left."

"You did what?"

"I told him it was the happiest day of my life and walked away." He ran his fingers over the photo of us hugging. My favorite of them all.

"I would look at these every night before falling asleep," he continued. "I didn't know Will had taken them at the time; I was too caught up in the moment to notice. I might have freaked out if I had known. Scared the pictures would be seen by my family."

I was elated. Guilt-ridden. Consumed by joy. Bursting with love. Yet, anger rolled through me under the surface. The way he had been suppressed infuriated me.

He turned his sad gaze to me. "Zack told me what happened to you after we broke up."

He held my arm in his grasp and ran his thumb over the leather bracelet which hid my scars. "This is because of me."

My stomach clenched and shame rose in my throat like bile.

"No, Taka, it wasn't. That was all on me. I thought I had

gotten over something years ago and moved past that part of my life. But I've been seeing a therapist, and look." I unhooked the bracelet that hid my demons and offered my wrist to him. "Most of my scars are from a time in my life that is long over. Please don't blame yourself for my actions. It wasn't your fault."

"But I hurt you enough to make you do this."

I cupped the back of his head and pulled him close, wrapping my arm around his waist. "Don't ever say or think that again. I did it. Me alone."

"But if I hadn't—"

"Taka, I'm serious, stop. Only I am responsible for my actions."

He nodded, though I knew he would continue thinking he was the cause. I wished Zack hadn't said anything; Taka didn't need to know about that. "How about we get in bed? It's getting late."

We crawled into bed, and I wrapped Taka in my arms, soaking in his warmth as I listened to his soft breathing.

"Nick," Taka said, sliding his arm over my abdomen.

"Yeah?"

He climbed over me, settling himself over my groin. "I know our emotions are a mess, and I'm not in the best mental state right now." I stared at him, lit by the small clock on the nightstand, my cock growing as his heat seeped into me. He looked at me with hooded eyes, like he wanted to consume me. "I've dreamed of us. I've craved you for months." He rolled his hips, running over my erection. "I want you so bad."

There was nothing left to say. No need to question or speak.

CHAPTER 32

TAKA

To say I was nervous would be the understatement of a lifetime. Nick stood beside me, holding my hand as we walked into the Ellis Center. I wasn't comfortable having this conversation in such a public space, even if Sunday mornings were slow on campus and not many people were around. It eased my nerves some, but my heart raced faster with each step closer to the food court.

Nick's worried eyes flicked over me, likely seeing the tension in my body. "You don't have to do this."

"I need to," I replied. I pulled him along, swallowing my fears.

Izzie was at a table. Her eyes pointed at the floor, her lips were tense, and her arms were crossed. Beside her, Casey's face was uncharacteristically scruffy with a five o'clock shadow, and his eyes looked tired and sunken. I squeezed Nick's hand tighter when I realized I was feeling sorry for Casey, even though he tried to ruin my life. Yet, perhaps, he had unknowingly liberated me from the confined world my family had kept me in. Perhaps, even, he deserved my gratitude. Time would tell.

When they noticed us, they looked up with sad, pitiful gazes that tugged at my heart.

"Thanks for coming," Casey said, motioning for us to sit across from them.

Izzie glanced at my hand, locked with Nick's, and I caught what I thought was envy before she looked at our faces.

Nick sat, releasing my hand. He crossed his arms and assumed a defensive yet aggressive posture, sitting low in the chair, his legs wide. I stopped the smile of affection forming on my face, connecting his knee with mine, taking comfort in his touch.

"We aren't in the mood for a discussion about the weather and catching up. Get to the point," Nick said, his voice stern and calm.

Casey straightened and looked me in the eye. I waited for the snarky comment, but it didn't come. "Sorry. I'll try to be fast." He ran his fingers over his chin as he looked at Izzie. "We wanted to apologize."

Izzie nodded, lighting up as she leaned forward. "We both treated you unfairly. I especially–"

"Unfairly?" Nick scoffed. "Gotta do better than that."

"You outed me to my family," I added. Casey's shoulders sank as I spoke. "I was given an unfair choice, but not by you. My *father* is treating me unfairly." I leaned forward, meeting Casey's gaze. "But you. You *betrayed* me. Betrayed my trust and any friendship we once had."

"I'm sorry," Casey whispered. "I was angry and jealous."

"You chose to out me because you were jealous that I found someone to love? But when I was with Izzie, you weren't jealous."

He shook his head. "You and Iz were dating before I met you. The whole time I thought I had no chance, and you were going to marry your girlfriend." He glanced at Nick as he took a breath. "When I took you to the computer lab, I didn't think you would connect with him like that."

"Hold on a second. You have to back up here because Taka and I started out as friends," Nick said, placing his elbow on the table. "When did the jealousy of me start?"

Izzie said softly, "We knew immediately." She looked between us. "I knew immediately."

"How?" I asked. How could she have known?

She dropped her gaze and stared at the table. "You had dinner with him. Twice."

I couldn't help the confusion that contorted my face. "Nick and I were hungry after working in the lab. How does that tell you anything?"

"You hate having dinner with people. You hate taking time to do things unless you want to. I know you more than you think." She sighed, running her hand over her forehead as her gaze flicked between Nick and me. "There was this light in your eyes after you met Nick. I'm not sure how to explain it with words."

Casey nodded as he gripped her hand. "The two of you may have been in denial about your feelings and thought you were friends, but everyone else watching saw the truth. So, yeah, I was jealous. I wanted to be Nick. I wished you had seen me the same way."

"And I thought you were cheating on me. So, when Maddie texted me that picture . . ." Her breath hitched, and she covered her mouth. "You moved on so quickly. I thought you had to have been using me as a cover."

Casey said, "I saw the photo, and I don't know what came over me, T. I fell in love with you shortly after we met our freshman year but felt like I could never tell you the truth. I was worried you'd find out how I felt about you and hate me. The moment I realized I could have had a chance, I also understood my chance was gone because you had already found someone else." He leaned back with a sigh. "Iz and I confided in each other and allowed our anger and jealousy to consume us. It was stupid."

"We're sorry," she said.

A part of me wanted to accept their apology, but it could never be that simple. "Thank you for your honesty and I appreciate you apologizing." I stood, having heard enough. "I may now understand where you were coming from, but I will never understand your actions."

Nick stood with me, and I grabbed his hand, lacing my fingers with his, taking comfort in the little squeeze he gave me as we started walking away. When we were a few feet away, I stopped and turned back toward them. "I will be civil if we run across each other, but we are not friends."

• • •

My fingers danced across the keyboard as I wrapped up my homework assignment. Nick was relaxing in a chair, reading a book, and the rest of my friends were debating soccer as usual. Sky and Will were off in their own world. Over the last two weeks, I'd noticed a change between them. They had been more open in public, and Sky seemed to have taken to the idea of being his boyfriend. Nick thought it had something to do with what happened to us, and maybe it did, but I enjoyed seeing them happy together.

Alex put his pencil down, declaring his boredom.

In moments like this, I realized how important it was to curate a family of people that accept you and stick with you through hell and back. I was thankful that I had found my family.

"You okay?" Nick asked, tapping my knee. "You look spaced out."

"It's nothing. I was only thinking."

He patted my thigh and went back to reading.

Kiran stood, pointing at everyone around the table. "Zack thinks no one will be interested, but who wants to go to the beach one last time before October starts? It's still warm, and I need the sun and sand in my life."

"Kiran," Nick said, shaking his head in disapproval. "Why didn't you offer before the semester started?"

"Are you dumb? You idiot, you and Taka were broken up, and shit was depressing as hell. Who wanted to go to the beach while you two were all doom and gloom?"

Nick chuckled. "My bad, you're right."

Right away, Nick started discussing plans to go out as a group for a weekend trip. After a few minutes, a familiar figure passed our table, and our eyes met before he offered a nod and walked away. I still didn't understand how he thought ruining my happiness was the direction to go, but I felt sorry for him. I surprised myself with my empathy for him. I knew it was not easy for someone like Casey to come out and to express his feelings for another man. He clearly had some way to go before he was comfortable in himself. And for all I knew, his own family might have been keeping him caged, as I had been before I broke free. In a weird twist which I hated myself for, I was grateful for him outing me. While it changed everything I knew, he forced me into a new beginning. A beginning where I was happier.

"Hey, boys," River said as she pulled out a chair and sat beside Nick. "Mind if we join you?"

"We?" Nick asked, glancing up.

Izzie stood behind River. Her timid behavior was unbecoming of her usually assertive nature.

"Don't stand there," I said. "Sit."

Even though Izzie had participated in treating me and Nick like shit, I was giving her a chance at friendship. She and I had a long history, and she was truthfully sorry for her behavior. When River found out that Izzie wanted to be forgiven and work at being friends again, River took her in. To be honest, it was nice to have Izzie back in my life, but it would take time to move past the pain she caused.

My phone lit up on the table, and I grabbed it, opening the screen to the new message. My breath hitched as I read who it was from.

"Taka, you good? You look like you just saw a ghost," Zack said, prompting all eyes to turn to me.

Nick leaned over, looking at the name with me. "Open it."

"I don't want to."

"When was the last time your dad texted you?"

He had called me plenty of times but never once left a

message, and never in my life had he texted me. "Never."

"Exactly, so open it."

I frowned, whispering, "I'm scared."

"What if something happened to your mom or Tami? Open it."

My finger hovered over the new message as I debated deleting it without reading it.

Nick pressed my finger, forcing me to tap the message open. "Hey!" I protested.

But it was too late. The words were there.

I'm sorry. Your mother and I have had many conversations about how we treated you. How I treated you. We want you to come home. We miss you and love you. Please talk to us.

I couldn't believe what I was reading. Did he really send this?

Nick leaned over, reading it with me. "I think it's time to speak to them."

"I'm not ready."

"Would you ever be ready? It's a hard thing to talk about. Speak to them."

Sky came over and kneeled beside me. "Don't push them out of your life if they're willing to accept you. Many of us never get that message. So many of us leave our families behind and never see them again. Don't miss the chance to have your family back. A family that loves and treasures you." He placed his hand on my knee, holding my gaze. "Trust me, you will regret ignoring them one day. By then, it will be too late."

Nick took my hand, laying the phone on the table. "I'll go with you if it makes you more comfortable. I can wait in the car or stand in the doorway. It doesn't matter, but please hear them out."

"If you don't like what they have to say, walk away again," Will said. "No one said you have to like what they want to say. But I agree; hear them out."

"Fine. You guys win."

• • •

I hadn't been home in nearly a month. I ignored all their phone calls and texts until yesterday. Dad seemed relieved to hear from me, but I agreed to meet with them on one condition: Nick could come with me. It shocked me when my father hadn't protested.

Nick pulled into the long driveway. The sun was setting behind us, and I couldn't tell if it was a sign of an ending or the start of a new beginning, but I wanted to run. My pulse pounded through my veins, and my breath was short as I stared at the front door. My house seemed bigger. More intimidating. I was so frightened I could barely breathe.

Nick lifted my hand to his lips and brushed a light kiss over my knuckles. "I'm right here with you," he said.

He hopped out of the car, then opened my door for me when I didn't make a move to get out. I hadn't expected him to pressure me like this. To push me into this. "If they say anything you don't like, we can leave. Come on." He extended his hand, waiting for me to take it.

I finally gave in, grabbing his hand. His warmth was the comfort I needed as we walked up to my house. The front door loomed over me, uninviting. I imagined this was how it had always been. Awareness of it was chilling.

The door swung open, and Tami's bright face stared back

at me, already wet with tears. She bit her lip as she approached me. Her hesitant hug broke my heart. It had nothing to do with her, but I involved her, anyway. I hurt her when I walked out. Maybe even more because she had accepted me without question.

"I missed you," she cried, squeezing me.

Nick's hand rested on my shoulder, confirmation that he was still here, supporting me as he promised.

"I missed you too. I'm sorry I left without saying goodbye."

As she cried, I wrapped my arms around her, crushing her against my chest. How could I have walked away from her? What if I had to walk away again?

"I forgive you, but don't leave me again." She sniffed and wiped her eyes clear of her tears.

I couldn't promise her that.

When I looked up, my mother was in the doorway. Fatigue etched her face. Tears streamed down her cheeks as she reached for me and pulled me into a hug. Her shoulders shook with each sob, tugging on my heart, telling me how horrible I was for leaving. She spoke in Japanese as she welcomed me home over and over.

When my mother finally released me, she walked over to Nick and wrapped her arms around his waist, holding him tight. "Thank you for loving my son."

He crushed her in his famous tight hug and said, "Thank you for raising someone so easy to love."

When Mom released Nick, she touched my arm and ushered me into the house. "Come inside," Mom said. "Your father got a call a few minutes ago, but he will make it quick."

My heart pounded as Mom led us into the house, to the

living room, where she ushered Nick and me beside each other on the sofa, facing a display of family pictures. I looked around. I hadn't been away long, but it seemed like a stranger's home. Something seemed different, and I couldn't put my finger on it.

Nick bumped my leg with his knee and nodded at the photos on the wall. At first, I thought nothing of it until the order seemed out of place, and my eyes landed on a rainbow of colors at the center of the photo wall. The pictures I had left on my father's desk the day I left were framed in a collage at the center of the wall, surrounded by family photos. In the center of the picture collage was my favorite image of them all: Nick and I smiling at the camera with red glow-paint dripping from our hair and shoulders. People danced behind us, waving glow sticks and Pride flags. I couldn't believe what I was looking at. Nick and I were flaunting our pride for everyone who came into our home to see.

"Do you like it?" Tami asked. She flashed a wide smile at me, holding her hands behind her back as she leaned toward me, waiting for my reaction.

"You did this?" I asked, walking up to the wall.

"It took a few days to convince them to put them up. But once I had Mom on my side, Dad caved."

I couldn't believe it. All the pictures were in the collage except one. "Where's the last picture?"

"In my office," Dad said, suddenly beside me. "Do you want to see?" He looked like he hadn't been sleeping well; dark bags and bloodshot eyes marred his stern face. As he walked away, he turned to Nick, who was still sitting on the sofa. "You too, young man."

We trailed behind him, and I grew increasingly nervous the

closer we came to his office. The door was wide open, the desk light was already on, and he now had two chairs in front of his desk instead of one.

"Please sit." He motioned to the chairs and sat at his desk, facing us. He picked up a new picture frame and rubbed his thumb over the front before he handed it to me. My throat tightened as I took in what I was seeing in the picture. The missing image. Nick and I kissing under the enormous pride flag. This was the moment that my dad kept closest to him?

My father cleared his throat and looked at me. "Before you left that day, you said this was the happiest day of your life. I spent a few days looking over each photo you left me, then I looked at older pictures of you. Until this picture, I had never seen you filled with such joy." He sniffed as he lifted his glasses and wiped his eye with his knuckle.

"Why did you choose this one to keep in here?"

"Whoever caught this moment must've had perfect timing. I can feel the love between you in this picture. This one made me see what you were trying to tell me." He wiped his eyes again. "Thank you both for teaching me a harsh lesson. I didn't realize it before, that the things I did and said hurt you, Taka." He let a moment pass before he continued. "I don't fully understand it yet. My upbringing has made it difficult for me to adjust to your relationship. Many people my age were raised to think your kind of relationship is wrong. I understand this is something I must work through." He stood and walked around the desk, stopping in front of me. "Though it will be a big change for me, you are my son and I love you."

My chest tightened as I looked at him. It felt genuine, like he honestly was trying to change. For me. Because he loved me.

"Thank you," I said, standing and pulling him into a hug. It was the first time I had hugged my father since I was a child. He cried, resting his chin on my shoulder, his arms shaking as he squeezed me tight.

"I'm sorry, son." His breath hitched as he inhaled. "Please come home. We won't be perfect, but we will learn together."

I wasn't sure if I should, but as I held my father and cried with him, I wondered why I would fight it. They were accepting me. They wanted me back, even if it meant I wouldn't be the son they always wanted.

"I'll come home."

He grabbed the back of my head, pulling me into another tight squeeze before stepping back. He wiped his tears behind his glasses with a shaky smile, then shifted his gaze to Nick. "Nick, I haven't met you yet. Tsuyoshi Akiyama, please call me Yoshi." He reached out, offering his hand for Nick to shake. "Thank you for supporting my son when I didn't." He released Nick's hand, then tugged him into a hug.

The tears flowed as I watched my father hug my boyfriend, and I couldn't believe my eyes. Relief swelled in my heart, overshadowing the fear trying to creep back in.

Dad patted Nick on the shoulder, then took the picture frame from me, placing it back in the spot on the desk he had cleared for it. "Your mother should have dinner ready." He checked the position of the picture one last time before leaving his office, expecting Nick and me to be behind him.

Nick grabbed my hand as I watched my father walk along the hallway, a pep in his step for the first time in years.

"Did that really happen?" I whispered.

"It did." Nick grabbed my head and pulled me close,

pressing his lips to my temple. "I'm so happy for you. Also, I'm starved."

Hand in hand, we walked toward the kitchen, where my family was busy setting the table. They looked up at us as we entered the kitchen and smiled warmly. Tami rushed over, squeezing herself between Nick and me, dragging us to the table. For the first time, I wasn't a stranger among my family. There was warmth as we sat around the table, filling the air with laughter.

I could finally be me.

EPILOGUE

OCTOBER 6, 2014

NICK

Taka and I stood outside his house, waiting for our guests to arrive. Our hands squeezed each other's so tight that it was slightly painful. Our nerves took hold of us, but we were there to ground each other. No one would've imagined that the event was so simple, but it was life-changing; something I had dreamed of and never expected to see in my lifetime.

"I'm so nervous," Taka said as the first car pulled into the driveway.

I looked into his eyes, hope blooming but shadowed by fear.

"It will be good. I know it," I said.

Sky and Will walked up to us with huge grins on their faces.

"You ready?" Sky asked as he embraced us both together.

"Because I've been waiting my whole life for this."

"We're ready," we said together. My heart leaped, and my chest brimmed with anxiety.

I smacked Sky's ass as he walked into the house. "Behave when you introduce yourself to Taka's family. Be a good boy."

Sky laughed and sauntered through the doorway. "I'm always a good boy."

Will choked on his laugh, then followed Sky inside. At the threshold of the door, he turned back to us with a worried smile. "Good luck to us all today."

The rest of our friends arrived in a similar fashion. River and her girlfriend, Sarah. Zack, Alex, and Kiran came together. Then the last to arrive was Rylee. It was my first time meeting her, and I was more nervous than I let on.

Rylee sashayed toward us with a bright smile that overtook her adorable face. "It's lovely to finally meet the famous Nicholas." She bit her lip as she appraised my appearance.

"Taka, what have you told her?" I demanded.

Taka shied away with a smile as he escaped into the house, releasing a quiet laugh.

Rylee leaned in close to me. "Only everything, honey."

I grinned as Rylee shot Taka a wink, and her smile morphed into a smirk.

TAKA

"Taka!" Nick ran into the house. "We need to talk about boundaries. Right now!"

I looked at him innocently, then nudged Rylee for her indiscretion.

Sky breezed past us, interrupting the chase that would've ensued. A champagne bottle was in one hand, and glasses were in the other. "I'm ready to celebrate in style," he said.

As I was about to scold him for grabbing it early, a shadow loomed in the open doorframe of the front door. Casey stood there, looking unsure beside a radiant Izzie.

"You made it," I said.

Nick didn't like that I was working to be friends with Casey again, and we had been talking about everything for a couple of weeks. I could empathize with him, but I couldn't find it in myself to hate Casey, because it ultimately gave me everything I had been missing.

In a way, I was grateful.

He shoved his hands in his front pockets and glanced around at the chaotic group filling my house. "Thanks for inviting me."

"Come in," I said, waving him and Izzie into the house.

River ran up to Izzie and tugged her into the living room, where everyone was congregating.

Casey followed, greeting everyone shyly. It would take time to get back the friendship we once had, but we would get there again.

My parents were setting out food on the kitchen table, and Will was helping them wrap up the last of whatever was on the stove. The house was warm and brimming with life and excitement.

"Tami, where's the remote?" Nick asked as he searched over the sofas and armchairs.

"What time does it start?" Kiran asked.

I glanced at the clock. My heart picked up its pace, racing and thundering in my chest.

"Five minutes," Nick said, his voice wavering as he stared at the black screen mounted on the wall.

Everyone joined in the hunt for the remote, turning over cushions and pillows as we raced to beat the time.

Finally, Zack jumped up with something close to a squeal. "Got it! What channel?" he asked, hitting the power button.

Tami grabbed the remote and punched the numbers in. The news channel lit up the screen, and the room fell silent as we each raced to sit, training our eyes on the screen.

"How many minutes?" River asked as she clung to Sarah and Izzie's hands.

"One minute," I replied, my breath light, afraid my lungs would give up on me.

The champagne popped open, jarring us from the screen.

"What?" Sky smirked as he shrugged and poured himself a glass. "We're gonna drink it either way."

No one dared to laugh. No one dared to breathe as we glued ourselves to the newscaster.

"And now we have news coming from the Supreme Court, following their decision, refusing to hear the appeal. This means that same-sex marriage is now recognized in the Commonwealth. As a result, Virginia will begin issuing marriage licenses to same-gender couples immediately."

The living room broke into screaming, drowning out whatever else the news anchor was saying. I couldn't believe my ears. It had to be a trick of the mind. A lie. Someone misreported.

"Champagne to fuel our victory anyone?" Sky held the bottle aloft, then wandered the room, handing glasses to everyone.

NICK

I turned to Taka, taking him into my arms, unsure what to do. Marriage had never been something to consider in our situation, but as I looked into his eyes, all I wanted was to have him in my arms like this forever.

"I know we haven't been together for long, Taka, and in the short time we've known each other, we've been through a lot of ups and downs. But even with all of that, there is one thing I know: I love you, and I want to spend my life with you."

"Nick, are you proposing to me?"

To anyone, it would have seemed sudden. Hell, to me, it was sudden. But when I thought about what our lives would look like ten years from now—twenty years, fifty years—I wanted to spend them together, surrounded by friends and family.

"I am," I said, my heart hammering as I waited for an answer.

"Then my answer is yes," Taka said.

NICK & TAKA

The kiss that came from that moment was filled with so much love that our chests tightened like our hearts would explode. We weren't sure what our future had in store, but we hoped that no matter what came our way, we would be together.

Because our love is enough.

Our love is real.

AFTERWORD

I'm about to be very vulnerable here, so if you've made it this far, thank you for reading *The Gravity of Us*. It took me a long time to figure out the words to express in this afterword. I questioned and doubted myself every moment of this project. I'm sure I'll doubt myself once it's published as well. But ultimately, it is my favorite story I've ever written so far; it's now a part of me, and I will forever cherish it. *The Gravity of Us* made it out of drafts that I never expected to see the light of day. It captured my heart in its grip and wouldn't let go.

If you're a reader who is new to me, welcome. I feel like I'm still a baby author, and something I have said in the past is, "I will be happy if even one person takes something from my writing." This is true for *The Gravity of Us*. I will be happy if one person tells me this book means something to them and that it helped them in some way. I write because I love to tell stories. I write because I have things to say; this is the only way I know people might hear me. I'm not perfect. I know I'm flawed; I'm my own worst critic. If there is any criticism to be had about me or my writing, I promise I've said it all and worse to myself.

Nick and Taka appeared in my head one day, and they had a story to tell. I know that may sound crazy to non-writers, to think that these characters in my mind have their own will and talk to me. They tell me their story, and I feel their emotions as if they were my own. I cried writing parts of *The Gravity of Us*. My heart broke with them. I laughed with them, and I was angry alongside them. Taka and Nick will forever have a place in my heart.

This novel is for anyone who is questioning why they don't fit in, why they like who they like, why they feel like an outcast, even as they are surrounded by people they love. It is for anyone who doesn't feel seen, hidden under a mask. It is for anyone who feels they are not enough and are afraid of losing everything if they reveal their true self. It is for anyone who feels different and fears that no matter what they do, they'll never be accepted.

I want to talk to a group of you I hope resonates with this story, so bear with me here. I'm blessed to have a couple of friends who know the authentic me, and I'm grateful to have a partner who is my best friend, but even so, I feel so alone. It feels like I'm always the one to reach out to my friends or family. If I never reached out first, would they ever think of me? It doesn't feel like it. Most relationships I have feel surface level. I know others can relate to the type of loneliness I'm talking about; the kind of loneliness I gave to Taka, where you're surrounded by people but have never felt more invisible. Invisible enough that if you were gone tomorrow, maybe, if you're lucky, a couple people would care. Those of you who know what I'm talking about, I'm writing for you. If you've never experienced this type of emptiness, I pray you never do.

Please know you are enough. You are loved. If no one else says it to you today, know that I love you.

Writing this story was an emotional roller coaster I wasn't prepared for. I nearly gave up multiple times, but I'm glad I pushed through. It was a journey of self-discovery for me. Writing this in tandem with therapy sessions, I discovered I'm non-binary. I'm still in that "self-discovery" stage, and seeing the world through Taka and Nick's eyes has opened up a new level of realization for me. Before writing this book, I always pushed those thoughts and feelings deep down inside of me where no one would ever see. I used to think, "I'm bisexual," and left it at that for most of my life, but as my dive into myself progressed, I realized gender doesn't matter at all, and sometimes the thoughts I had were so confusing that I wasn't sure how to talk to anyone about them. I pretended the thoughts were normal and to think nothing of them. I would tell myself, "Everyone thinks that sometimes," or "Don't be weird. People will think you're a freak." I'm coming out in this afterword because in my day-to-day life, I'm AFAB (Assigned Female at Birth), and I do not deviate from that presentation. I've only talked to my therapist about these feelings, but here I am, laying it all out on the table where anyone can see. I felt it was the right place for this confession, in this afterword, following a story of self-acceptance and love. So, thank you for coming on this journey with me.

I have one last topic I want to touch on because I understand there is a lot of controversy around authors writing outside of their lived experiences. Taka is Japanese and I am white, American, and AFAB. Writing about someone else's experience may offend people, but I truly hope you can tell that I hold so much respect and love for Taka and Nick. I do not claim to know enough about any culture outside of my own, and I hope I entered the space of telling Taka's story respectfully. No amount of research or interviews could put me in any position to claim I know enough. I'm in an interracial relationship, so I enjoy reading diversely, and I love to write about diverse relationships wherever I can. I hope no one is offended by anything I've written. I understand intent does not equate to impact, so if I have offended anyone, know that I am genuinely and deeply sorry. I will not make excuses or attempt to explain away. Feedback is something I take seriously and file away into my "lessons learned." While I've worked extremely hard to break down my privileged biases, I know that I am flawed, will make mistakes, and will always have room to learn and grow.

Thank you for sticking to the end. I appreciate each and every one of you. May your soul burn bright, always.

ACKNOWLEDGMENTS

Lorna, my fantastic editor, thank you. You helped me improve not only this story but myself as an author.

Jess, Rachel, and everyone at Amplify Publishing, thank you for believing in *The Gravity of Us*. Thank you for your hard work at each point in this project. I appreciate you all.

J, thank you for being my life partner and putting up with me. We've been together so long and grown as people. You take all of my whims in stride, and I appreciate you more than you could know. You are my rock. I love you.

Geri, thank you for every moment of support and encouragement. For being my sounding board and friend. For supporting Taka and Nick from day one, loving them as much, if not more, than I do. For the "unfs" and cursing me as you cried. For the laughter and joy. For sharing in my unhinged behaviors and indulging me. I love you dearly. Thank you.

Tom, I can hear you laughing right now as you tell Geri you will not read this. I don't expect you to, but I appreciate your support and encouragement anyway. You are a wonderful friend. I love you.

Kelly, while we read the chapter which will not be named together, my asking you to read this was probably a lot to ask. You're like the big brother I never had. Please know you bring so much to my life, knowing you're always there to talk to. Thank you for all the kind words and for cheering me on. Thank you for being a dear friend. I love you.

Marvin, your snippy remarks, your freaking out when Geri and I get to talking, the times Kelly joins in the fray, our bickering like a family and sharing our hobbies. I live for these moments with you. I asked you to read this early into my writing of it, though it is not your usual genre, and I appreciate the support you've shown me. I love you, and thank you for being you.

Geri, Tom, Kelly, and Marvin, I never anticipated you would become this massive part of my life. A safe place for me to exist and be myself. You are my best friends, and I consider you my family. Thank you for finding me.

To my found family in the storm, you are all wonderful. All these years that we've been together, even if across the country, we are a family. I love you all. Thank you for believing in and supporting me.

DW, you've listened to my ramblings, cried with me, and followed me along this journey. Encouraged me. Helped me break down my barriers. Create new boundaries. Explore myself and what that means. Urged me to do whatever I set my mind to because I am enough. Thank you. I hope you know how much you've changed my life.

Dan, thank you for your words of encouragement and unwavering support. I know you're reading this, and you may think of me differently again, but that's okay because I don't think I left you angry this time. I'm truly grateful to have met you.

Britt, this is likely far outside your wheelhouse. Thank you for sharing my excitement and cheering me on. Hopefully, you find this story interesting and inspiring. You and I have been through a lot together, and I'm so happy I met you. You and I clicked from day one, and even though life takes hold of us and time flies by, I think of you every day. I miss you, love you, and appreciate you more than you could ever know.

P and K, thank you for your love and encouragement while listening to me talk crazy nonsense. Listening to me spew the disaster of my mind fueled by ADHD, coffee, and exhaustion. Thank you both for supporting me in all the ways you know how while I keep my life together with Band-Aids and tape. I love you.

To all of my beta readers, thank you. Your feedback was integral to this story. I appreciate all of you.

ABOUT THE AUTHOR

Jamie Avery King is an author of paranormal, fantasy, contemporary, and LGBTQ+ romance. They live in the Washington, DC, area and grew up loving everything fiction. Jamie's passion for fantasy worlds and tales of finding love has been channeled into their love of storytelling. When they aren't writing and dreaming up new worlds, they play video games, read, or hang out with their dogs and partner.

JAMIEAVERYKING.COM

@jamieaveryking @jamieking_author